W9-COM-335

Yasmeen Haddad

Loves

Joanasi Maqaittik

CAROLYN MARIE SOUAID

Yasmeen Haddad

Loves

Joanasi Maqaittik

A NOVEL

Baraka
Books

MONTRÉAL

ISBN 978-1-77186-124-3 pbk; 978-1-77186-125-0 epub; 978-1-77186-126-7 pdf; 978-1-77186-127-4 mobi/pocket

Cover photo by Pierre Dunnigan
Book Design and Cover by Folio infographie
Editing by Elise Moser and Robin Philpot
Proofreading by Brownwyn Averett

Legal Deposit, 4th quarter 2017

Bibliothèque et Archives nationales du Québec
Library and Archives Canada
Published by Baraka Books of Montreal
6977, rue Lacroix
Montréal, Québec H4E 2V4
Telephone: 514 808-8504
info@barakabooks.com

Printed and bound in Quebec

Trade Distribution & Returns
Canada and the United States
Independent Publishers Group
1-800-888-4741 (IPG1);
orders@ipgbook.com

We acknowledge the support from the Société de développement des entreprises culturelles (SODEC) and the Government of Quebec tax credit for book publishing administered by SODEC.

Société de développement des entreprises culturelles
Québec

Funded by the Government of Canada
Financé par le gouvernement du Canada
Canada

In loving memory of
Doreen Shaker Cheeseman

YASMEEN MOVES THROUGH THE CITY TRYING TO FORGET. The sidewalk is wet and slick, window displays of skeletons and zombies with eyes spun back in their sockets—a veritable Festival of the Dead—calling to her. The Halloween moon is conspicuously absent. She crosses a dark intersection bordering on a derelict park she normally avoids. Except for a crepe-thin layer of snow on everything, the grass is brown and worn and the trees are bare. At one time, before the pigeons and the homeless moved in, it was a sanctuary of mown grass and manicured hedges, a landmark named for its centrepiece bronze of a famous explorer, John Cabot, scanning the horizon with a map in one hand and the other shading his eyes.

As though answering a dare, Yasmeen saunters toward the park. She notices some motion at the base of the statue, a shabby man looking small and unstately before the monument's grandeur. Something in his appearance makes him vaguely familiar, his lopsided Montreal Canadiens tuque, his unsteadiness, the brown paper bag in his lap.

"*Qanuippiit?*" she calls out. A sharp wind blows the hair backwards off her face as she approaches him.

The surprise in his face leaps out at her, the fact she can speak his language. She feels the burn of his eyes as he drinks out of the brown bag, sizing her up. She is wrong; she's never seen this man before.

"Where did you learn to speak Inuktitut?"

"I was up north for a while."

He takes another slug and looks down at the space beside him. He glances in her general direction, then down again at the same space. She hesitates but can't find a reason not to join him. The marble steps are cold.

They sit together in silence, observing the ebb and flow of the city. Once upon a time, she would have stoked the conversation. She would have asked what community he was from, why he was here, when he was returning to the North, she would have bombarded him with an earful of questions. She would have hardly waited for his answer before moving on to the next. She doesn't do that anymore, she's learned to let things happen in their own time.

"You look like a smart girl," he finally says. He horks up a mouthful of mucus and spits it across the darkness. "Maybe a teacher."

She nods, impressed by his guess.

"Lots of girls go up north to be a teacher. And to be in love with an Inuk." He smiles. "I had a *Qallunaaq* teacher once. She was smart, she left before she found a man." He drinks a little more, sniggers and passes her his bottle.

Yasmeen shakes her head no.

They return to their comfortable silence. The snow picks up, needles them with icy pellets. He pulls the hat down over his ears. A fat, wet flake falls onto her lashes and melts down her cheeks. She sits there quietly. The fact that she can go on this way, indefinitely, with a thousand things to say and no real urge to say them, amazes her. And doesn't.

After a while he stands and stretches, wobbly on his feet. He scratches his head and furrows his brow, trying very hard to remember something. He looks wistfully into the distance. "Tell me everything you know about winter," he says.

RAIN

ONE

"Are you insane?" barked Yasmeen's mother. Samiyah Haddad had tried everything to convince her daughter that setting off for the middle of nowhere was a bad idea. But time was running out. "It'll be like living in an icebox, and the polar bears will get you if you don't starve to death first." It wasn't a battle, it was a war, and things were slipping out of her control. "I can't win for losing," she harrumphed. "Whatever happened to law school?"

Yasmeen rolled her eyes. "That was your idea."

Samiyah was hunched over a frying pan, mangling the vegetables with her testy stirring. "For heaven's sake," she groaned, blasting the fan, waving away the billowing steam. She pursed her lips over a wooden spoon, slurping to taste. "Needs something." She tossed Yasmeen the last yellow onion from the net, the papery shells flying everywhere, and handed her a paring knife.

Yasmeen sliced through the deep layers. Her eyes filled with the sharp sting.

Samiyah pointed. "Get another from the fridge, cold ones are easier to work with." She sighed and shifted her weight to the other foot. Her eyes narrowed. "They don't cause you tears and heartache like your children do." All week she'd complained of insomnia, up at four every morning, pacing the kitchen with a cup of hot milk. At breakfast she mentioned how she

13

was having a rough time sleeping, maybe her diverticulitis was acting up again.

"What's a year, anyway?" Yasmeen shouted over the roaring fan. "In the scheme of things." She rolled a newspaper and fanned the steam out the window.

Years ago, her best friend Morgan coached her on how to deal with parental disapproval, how to downplay certain things or say whatever her mother wanted to hear and then just turn around and do as she pleased. Over time she'd gotten good at it, the little white lies, the staying out later and later. She learned how to keep her "real" life separate and hidden from the family. She got so good that even Morgan, with all her one-night stands and crazy shenanigans, was impressed. Then Yasmeen's father died and Samiyah went berserk with her parenting, as though if she didn't, her kids would turn out all wrong and then the world would judge her as a terrible mother. She uttered her dire warnings, wagging an index finger. Good men didn't marry girls who slept around. It was all about honour. Who would marry her if she had a soiled reputation?

Exasperated, Yasmeen began looking for opportunities to cut loose without causing her mother to have a conniption—a job overseas, something lucrative and respectable. But she knew that one way or the other, her mother would read it as a betrayal. As though Yasmeen were somehow turning her back on family. Family was sacred to her mother, untouchable. It was everything. The outside world came second. You didn't break with family. You didn't tarnish the family name. You kept family skeletons in the closet where they belonged. You took the good with the bad. You stood by one another, the way her mother had stood by her father, even when things were at their worst. To cap it all off you put a smile on for the world, especially if you were a woman.

But it was a different world now. Her parents' immigrant past was just that. It was past. Yasmeen knew if she didn't take off while she had the chance, her mother would slowly work on her until her dreams evaporated altogether. And then heaven help her. How would she break free? Yasmeen's greatest fear was falling into lockstep with the rest of the world, people living lives of bored indifference, sleepwalking through decades until they woke up unable to remember where all the time had gone. If she wanted a real life she had to ditch the safety net, her suburb of clean sidewalks and immaculate lawns and Sunday suppers with appropriate suitors; she had to go away, far away, further even than the flickering beacon across the river, city of nine-to-fivers and trendy dance clubs. She had to pick up and leave and not look back.

"It's only a year."

"I was already married at your age."

Yasmeen cringed. "Sometimes you have to take a less direct route."

"What's that supposed to mean?"

"It means what it means, I guess."

Samiyah dropped the pyramid of onions into the oil, stirring quickly as it sizzled in the pan, dense steam rising again. It was typical of how she behaved when things weren't going her way, a brusqueness colouring her actions. She laid it on thick—haughty disappointment, showy displays of disapproval. Samiyah had a highly developed technique for insinuating guilt, sharp talons in her silences, clenched jaw, narrowed eyes glinting with disdain.

She pushed past Yasmeen to get a bell pepper from the fridge. "Tell me, what sane person leaves a city with all its comforts and opportunities to go all the way up to … where the hell is this place again? The jobs here aren't good enough?"

"I'm only twenty-three."

"You keep reminding me."

Yasmeen wiped her hands on the back of her jeans and switched off the deafening fan. She took an awkward step toward her mother, lowering her voice an octave. "Look, I don't want to get tied down so soon. I'm still young."

"What are you trying to imply? That my life was a waste?"

It was her typical reaction, Samiyah twisting everything to sound like Yasmeen was trying to punish her. Or ridicule her. But it wasn't so. No way was she trying to do that, bring up the past, all the stuff with her father. Her mother was the one causing all the fuss. Yasmeen just wanted her life to be *her* life. She wanted freedom, plain and simple. She tried to remember the clever, snappy things Morgan told her to say to get her mother off her back. *The guilt truck stops here. Terminus. Everyone off!*

Yasmeen had no intention of going through life dragging her ethnicity behind like an old steamer trunk. She wasn't about to become a clone of her mother, a controlled woman afraid of her own shadow. She refused to have her comings and goings scrutinized under the microscope, she wouldn't be probed and interrogated and she certainly didn't want to feel like a criminal for having emotions and feelings.

But that was the rub. For all her big talk, Yasmeen wasn't so great at voicing opposition. Especially when it involved her mother. It had taken a while, but she developed a strategy, and with that, a thicker skin. The couple of times she had tried it, just blurting out what was on her mind while she imagined, that very instant, someone appearing in the headlights of an oncoming car, it worked. Something about following an action through to the end, to impact, to the knuckle-white screams and the smash of metal and glass, gave her courage. Just say the words, she thought to herself. Say them straight out.

"I'm not ready for a husband and children."

After it flew out of her mouth, Yasmeen couldn't be sure if she'd actually said it or only thought she had. Or if, instead, she'd given in to emotion and had a hissy fit, stamping her feet and shouting *I'm never getting married, so just forget it. Dad would have been on my side.* The whole tirade without an ounce of sugar coating.

A nimbus of smoke hung over them. Samiyah yanked a bulb from a plait of garlic and loosened a handful of cloves. She worked in silence, shucking their skins, while Yasmeen dawdled at the sink, scrubbing the onion smell from her hands. She felt a smidgen of guilt but mainly she felt a lightness of being. She snapped off a sheet of paper towel, drying each finger slowly and deliberately as her mother's mallet pounded the chopping board repeatedly, again and again, until the last of the garlic was smashed.

Yasmeen peeked at her watch. There were still friends to see, last-minute items to pick up at the drugstore, vitamins, razor blades, foot scrub, birth control pills. "Well, I'm off," she said.

Her mother spun around, thin-lipped. "And to boot, you spend your last night at home gallivanting around town …"

"Mum. For cripes' sake."

Everyone at the party was operating on adrenalin and nerves. Including Yasmeen. For months their assigned villages had been coloured pushpins on a giant wall map of Northern Quebec, an area bordered by Hudson Bay to the west and Hudson Strait and Ungava Bay to the north. An area the size of Venezuela, all of it covered in permafrost.

Yasmeen had always dreamt of travelling to exotic places. When she was a child her father bought her a box of glow-in-the-dark stars. He stuck them on her bedroom ceiling so that at night when he tucked her in they could look up at them and pretend they were camping out under the twinkling sky. He told her his own bedtime stories about the astronauts preparing to land on the moon and the great explorers who had sailed centuries ago, looking for the New World, gold and silk and the Northwest Passage. He promised that if she went to school and put her mind to it she could become anything she wanted to be, somebody important, even an astronaut. Shoot for the moon, he told her. A man's reach should exceed his grasp or what's a heaven for?

It got her thinking about life outside their peaceful suburb. Summer afternoons she dragged Morgan out with her, five kilometres to the highway that bordered the St. Lawrence River that the natives of Hochelaga canoed and Jacques Cartier explored. The two of them barely twelve, the light catching in the spokes of their CCM bicycles. Breaking their parents' rules just to get a look at the pigeon-grey skyline of Montreal. Standing in the scruffy weeds, socks down around their ankles, they poked their noses through the chain-link fence and invented juicy stories about living in a place where you wore high heels and a purse over your shoulder and were constantly on the go. Back then, she never dreamed she'd want anything more. It didn't occur to her that the exciting city wouldn't satisfy her, that one day she'd get on a plane to fly almost fifteen hundred kilometres north, to the Arctic.

The farewell party was happening at Sayard's place, an airy, high-ceilinged walk-up in a part of Little Italy where rents were dirt cheap, a typical student apartment sparsely furnished with odds and ends from yard sales and thrift shops. A B-52s song was drifting from the stereo and people were laughing and swigging beer as though it were any normal night. Sayard floated around the room, popping into and out of conversations as she cleared away the leftovers.

Leaning against the wall Yasmeen observed their merriment, eager for the night to be over. She could have easily left town a week ago. She would have been happy. A week ago everything was ready, her bags packed, the flight booked and confirmed, all the loose ends—medical appointments and banking—tied up.

Sayard rattled toward her with an armful of dirty dishes, her honey-brown hair tossing from side to side. "Help me with this, wouldya?" She gestured for Yasmeen to relieve her of some of the pile and they entered the kitchen sideways through a swinging door, heaping everything in the sink. Sayard heaved a sigh of relief. "Thought I'd drop the whole shitload," she said. They both laughed nervously.

Yasmeen popped the cap off another beer. "You psyched?"

"Haven't even packed yet."

"Seriously? I think I was ready when I was six," said Yasmeen. She tore a strip of pita and wiped the bottom of the *hummus* bowl with it.

"Nervous?"

"Me? Are you kidding?" Yasmeen laughed, stuffing the bread into her mouth. "My mother's being pissy about my leaving, though."

"Mothers, meh."

"She just doesn't get it."

Sayard pulled a platter of fruit and cheese from the fridge. "What do you want her to get? She's from another generation."

"I want her to get that it's not only about the job. It's about everything." She watched Sayard snip the grapes into smaller clusters and arrange them attractively around the dish.

They heard a champagne cork bounce off the living room ceiling and hit the wall.

"Time to celebrate," said Sayard, hurrying.

"Let's do it."

Yasmeen carried the platter out while Sayard ferried the cocktail napkins and a tower of plastic wine glasses. By the time they got there, Finn was already walking around with the chilled green bottle and a dishtowel draped over his arm, saying "Chin-chin, sustenance for rickety plane rides." Finn was the jokester of their gang, a lanky Nordic guy, not her type physically but whose black humour she couldn't get enough of.

She watched him approach Claire who scowled and announced, batting her eyes, that she was driving, thank you very much. It didn't surprise Yasmeen. The two were always locking horns over one thing or another. Yasmeen had developed an instant dislike for her when Finn asked at an early information session whether the houses up north were equipped with real bathrooms and she'd snapped, "*T'es-tu sérieux, bonhomme*? It's 1983, not 1938." Claire spoke a brash Shediac French and looked more like a wrestler than a teacher, in Yasmeen's opinion.

The music got switched off and everyone began to gather around Professor Caldwell who kept clearing his throat as though he had a breadcrumb stuck in it. Used to seeing him in a suit and tie every day, Yasmeen quite liked him in casual clothes, trousers and loafers and a cable-knit cardigan with patched leather elbows. They matched his gentle blue eyes and receding hairline.

He began his speech. They were to stop calling him professor. "From now on it's Frank," he said, wearing the moment on his face. He looked long and hard at each of them as though they were on the cusp of a profound change in their lives. Yasmeen was convinced he was feeling nostalgic about his own evaporated youth. He raised his cup to them, eyes dewy. "To the seven of you." His smile broadened, emphasizing the age lines around his eyes. "You've all worked hard for this opportunity."

"And a toast to you, Frank," said Finn. "A huge thanks for getting us this far." Claire grimaced.

"Don't thank me until you all come home safe and sound." Frank chuckled at his awkward attempt to be funny.

They broke off into nervous giggles, clinking cups across the circle.

He rolled down the projection screen and invited everyone to find a seat. "And now for my final lecture," he said. Claire rushed to his side to plug in the slide projector. The lights dimmed.

Yasmeen nestled into Finn's lap and they hugged one another like strangers who bond after a terrible tragedy. It made her think about serendipity, the luck and circumstance of being born and turning up in certain people's lives.

Frank pulled a spiral pad of handwritten notes from his back pocket. He jiggled open a pair of reading glasses and adjusted them on his nose. He had the serious, no-nonsense look of Polonius lecturing his son on the proper way to conduct himself in the world.

"Twin Otters are not the planes you're accustomed to," he said, advancing to the first slide. "For one thing, they're really small and the wind bounces them around a lot. Try to remain calm if it's a shaky flight. Remember, there are no johns aboard, so plan accordingly. Bring along a kit of toiletries and a good supply of trail mix in case your bags don't arrive with you. Also, a good sleeping bag in the event the plane has to make an emergency landing and you're forced to spend the night outdoors. You can't count on the weather, even at this time of year." While he paused to clear his throat, Finn cracked a joke about sleeping with a herd of caribou to keep warm. Everyone laughed except Claire.

"*Imbécile,*" she muttered.

Frank pressed on. "Finally, and this is critical. No matter how well you adapt, no matter what strides you think you've made, you will always be a Qallunaaq to them. Don't try to be more Eskimo than the Eskimos."

His use of "Eskimo," the old name given to them, a pejorative by modern standards, startled Yasmeen. It sounded hollow in her ears now that Inuit had become the more acceptable word and serious efforts were underway to reinstate Inuktitut place names in the North.

UNCORRECTED GALLEYS

Perhaps she was reading too much into it. Perhaps she was being a little too earnest, as Morgan often criticized. Before she knew it, Frank changed the subject. He covered some technical protocols related to administration and record keeping, but she wasn't paying much attention. She watched his face in the glow of the slide projector.

He looked drained, as though preparing and passing on these final notes had emptied him. He tucked the pad in his back pocket and signalled for someone to switch on the lights. "I think we should call it a night. Some of you have planes to catch. And for the rest of you, it won't be long now. Only a couple more days."

As the party broke up, he slipped a personal note to each of them. To be read later, he said. They thanked Sayard and clomped down the corkscrew staircase, issuing their teary good-byes on the sidewalk before fanning out in different directions. Yasmeen hugged Finn and Finn hugged back. He kissed her on the cheek and left. The street was quiet again.

Yasmeen looked up at the tremulous gnats in the halo of a streetlamp. She would have preferred rain or heavy wind or a hailstorm, something dramatic to mark her departure, but it was a perfect night. One or two stars were visible. Still buzzing from the champagne, she decided to skip the long bus-and-metro ride and splurge on a cab. Why not treat myself, she thought, on my last night in town.

Climbing into the cab she was hit with a waft of cologne and smoke that reminded her of the Skala, her favourite souvlaki joint on Park Avenue where she and her friends sometimes went after a movie. The place was usually packed with loud Greek men wreathed in cigarette smoke and reeking of a similar bad cologne.

The driver wore a gaudy gold ring on each pinkie and seemed to be inspecting her with his dark eyes. She caught a slice of his bushy brows through the rear-view mirror. Her mother's warning echoed through her. You never know. Better safe than sorry. Yasmeen checked the information on the cabbie ID. She'd figured right about the nationality. Costas Papadakos. The guy looked like he was itching to talk.

"Please, is okay I smoke?"

She wanted to say no but the cigarette was already between his lips and he was pressing the lighter on the dashboard.

"You live far. Is good you take taxi. Not safe for nice young girl. I take you fast home …" He sped up, then braked suddenly. "*Malaka pousti!* Sorry. Detour. Many detour. Montreal is always detour. French doesn't know how to build good roads. In my country, we build roads many centuries ago and still good … Here, complain, complain but never do nothing. All they know is drink beer and play hockey. They want to have own country but can't even fix roads. My country give the world civilization, democracy, philosophy and even baklava. French, they give sep-aratists, hot dog and poutine."

Yasmeen remained silent. She didn't want to encourage him. She didn't want to get sidetracked into a whole debate about Quebec politics. Any other night she would have. She would have challenged him. She would have said, in a diplomatic sort of way, if he thought Quebec was so bad, why didn't he go back to his wonderful country and drive donkey carts? It bugged her, immigrants who came here, made a good living and then trashed it every chance they got. It had been a great night up until now. Why was she letting him spoil it? She closed her eyes to shut him out.

As far as great nights went, sex with Harrison ranked right up there. It was her first time. Even though technically they never made it past third base, Yasmeen always counted it as sex. It was the rain that stopped them. If it hadn't rained, they would have gone all the way, she was pretty sure of that. Harrison was her first cousin on her father's side. And her favourite. One time when he was visiting, her parents arranged a sleepover for them in the backyard. That's how everything started. The adults didn't twig to it maybe not being the brightest idea, she being thirteen and he, sixteen.

"I like your pillowy mouth," he used to tell Yasmeen whenever they saw each other at family events—weddings and funerals, mainly. He liked to touch it and she liked it when he did even though she pretended she didn't. Her crush deepened into something more the year he grew his hair out and started wearing long, loose shirts and striped bell-bottoms, the summer he brought her his scratched up copy of *Dark Side of the Moon*.

Harrison's fingers felt for the elastic waist of her pyjama bottoms and eased them down. It flustered her but she didn't stop him. The night was so quiet she could hear the neighbours in their houses, laughing, playing piano, running the water for their evening baths. The heat issuing from his hand felt like the full sun on her pale, winter skin. She looked away from him, beads of sweat collecting along her hairline and in her elbow creases and behind her knees. She closed her eyes and dug her nails into his wrist as a part of him touched a part of her. Her innermost regions tingled. She hated it. She loved it. It was like crossing over into something larger than herself, larger than Harrison too, like entering a cordoned-off place she shouldn't be, so good and so bad she couldn't decide which it was. Floating in its pleasant torpor, she snuck a look at him. He smiled.

They were vaguely aware of an acid-white flicker in the sky, but they weren't about to stop what they were doing. Surely it would pass over, she thought, surely it wouldn't … but it did.

First came a crack of ear-splitting piano thunder. They bolted upright. Then the sheeting rain washed down.

Yasmeen fumbled for her pyjama bottoms. She yanked them up and bunched the sleeping bag under her arm, racing barefoot up the porch steps through the screen door, slamming it behind her. She smelled a dank whiff of herself like the mushroom vapours of earth. She prayed her parents wouldn't smell it on her too. The door hinges squeaked as Harrison let himself in behind her.

The house bloomed with light. Her mother appeared on the upstairs landing with a handful of fresh towels. Moments later, her father emerged bleary-eyed from the bedroom in a bathrobe and brown knee socks.

Harrison shook the rain from his hair while Yasmeen dropped her sleeping bag on the living room carpet. Her bangs clung to her forehead and something was rumbling through her like a herd of buffaloes migrating to lower ground. She ran to the bathroom to assess the damage. She was pretty sure of what she'd find in the crotch of her bottoms. But it was a brownish smear, not the vivid red she expected. Its stain had crept across both sides of the seam, soaking into the floral pattern of the pyjama where Harrison's finger had entered.

In the harsh bathroom light, everything looked different. Her face was glowing the way it did when she spiked a fever, only it was a robust glow. She had anticipated this day, ever since health class when the school nurse distributed the small green booklets with diagrams and flow charts of a woman's secret passages, long dark hallways that released golden eggs. When your bloods come, she explained to the girls, you've officially crossed the threshold into womanhood.

The following day Yasmeen told Morgan everything but swore she would kill her if she breathed a word to anyone. Morgan's mother had a big mouth, always on the phone blabbing to a neighbour about somebody else's business if she wasn't shriek-ing at the girls to quit prancing across her flowerbeds, pretend-ing to be Lipizzaners. Cut that out, you're almost teenagers! You're embarrassing yourselves—and me along with it! Yasmeen's mother never had a good word to say about Morgan's mother. "It's a shame that woman feels so compelled to keep up with the Joneses," she'd scoff. Despite their mothers, Yasmeen and Morgan remained inseparable.

The car thumped. Yasmeen's eyes shot open. The cab driver cursed again.

"Sorry. Hole in road. They make holes too, for to take more money from my taxes to do nothing." He pronounced nothing "nutting."

She stared vacantly into the night as he detoured through Old Montreal, past the bedraggled port, the flashing Five Roses sign that was as much of a landmark as the thirty-foot steel cross on the nipple of Mount Royal. He accelerated through Mill Street's derelict stretch of mesh fences and concrete silos, rattled across the rusty Victoria Bridge into the tranquil, tree-lined sub-urb of Ste-Marie-de-Constance. He lurched to a stop in front of her house. She tipped him a little less than the customary 15 percent and said good night in French.

"You live in nice place. Maybe I buy house here for my chil-dren. Good night, lady. I wait until you are safe in house."

"Don't worry about it," she said.

"Is no problem."

She waved him off. Outside the door as she fumbled for her keys she felt Frank's note tucked into her pocket. She read it in the dim glow of the porch light, four words hastily scrawled: Search for the beauty. She couldn't imagine a more enticing message.

Her mother was still up when she walked through the door. The lights were off except for the flickering blue pulse of the TV, and Samiyah was sitting round-backed in her usual spot on the couch, dozy head slumped forward. In her quilted bathrobe and fuzzy slippers, a crocheted blanket folded over her knees, she reminded Yasmeen of a caterpillar in its cocoon casing.

Yasmeen tapped her on the shoulder. "Go to bed, Mum."

Samiyah jerked awake, disoriented, rheumy eyes darting everywhere.

"I'm home now, go to bed."

Samiyah nodded, shoving away the afghan. She stood up, wobbly on her feet, and pecked her daughter on the forehead. Yasmeen went to help her, but she insisted, shuffling toward the staircase, that she was fine on her own. She turned and said, "The kids are asleep." By kids she meant Yasmeen's nineteen-year-old brother, Tarek, and her sixteen-year-old sister, Rose.

Yasmeen switched off the TV. She made the rounds the way her father used to, checking that all the doors were locked, detouring into the kitchen to tighten the drippy faucet that he had never had time to fix while he was alive.

Late as it was, Yasmeen couldn't think of sleeping. She wanted to pick up the phone to call Morgan, fill her ears with all her excitement about going, but it was long past midnight. Morgan was probably asleep. She decided instead she would write her a long letter after she settled in up north.

A blush of moonlight slipped through her bedroom window, just enough to see by. She stood at the commode, examining herself in the mirror. It seemed impossible not to take inventory of her defects—her medium wiry frame, less-than-average height. She had never considered them defects until now. In one of her lectures on why she shouldn't go, her mother warned her she had neither the build nor stamina to survive the kind of cold up there, the kind that kills in an instant. The longer she stared at herself, the more she saw her mother's mocking reflection glaring back at her.

The bright headlights of a passing car swept across the ceiling, illumining the glow-in-the-dark stars she had always refused to let her mother take down. They had stayed through every bedroom makeover. She missed her father. He, at least, had recognized her spark, and from an early age. He was the one who took time with her at night, holding her small hand by the open window while she waved and said good night to Mister Moon. He would have been proud to see her go.

She reached for the down-filled coat on her bed with its tunnel hood, its price still dangling from the sleeve. For extreme sub-zero temperatures, the clerk had said. She snipped off the tags and wriggled into it, inhaling its virgin newness. Her heart did a double flip. It cartwheeled and stag-leapt and sprinted to the ends of the earth and back. It released its big bouquet of balloons to the sky. She imagined Neil Armstrong's butterflies as he prepared to plant his small foot on the cratered moon, his giant step for mankind. She pictured his pure, unfettered joy.

TWO

Breakfast was repeating on her. Her mother was of course to blame, refusing to let her fly on an empty stomach. Up a whole hour before Yasmeen's alarm went off, she laid out a hearty banquet: a medley of citrus, porridge made with steel-cut oats, bacon and eggs, toast smeared with honey. "It's got to stick to your ribs, God knows when you'll eat again." She shoved a spoon of cod-liver oil into Yasmeen's mouth as though she were still a child. Yasmeen swallowed it obediently. She ate everything on her plate.

Now it was all a churning, undefined mass in her belly. Pure sludge. Through the small window, a dizzying avalanche of cloud and sea advanced and receded. She could hardly tell whether they were flying right side up or upside down. For all she knew, the sky was the raging sea and they were heading straight for it. She imagined the icy water closing around her, pulling her down.

Don't look, she thought. Close your eyes.

She had had the exact opposite reaction earlier in the flight as she watched the dwindling network of roads, the stalwart trees dwarfing into shrub and sedge before disappearing altogether into a scrolling plain of rock and sea. Piece of cake, she had thought. I can handle this.

Now as the plane was in full descent and her stomach was flip-flopping, all she could smell were the nauseating releases of her co-passengers in the snug plane, coffee breath and sulphurous farts, intermittent whiffs of dirty socks and armpit odour. She cupped her palms over her nose. No matter what, she wouldn't be caught dead ralphing into the vomit bag.

"Breathe," came a voice from the window seat beside her.

She glanced over at the man with whom she had barely exchanged ten words since takeoff. He was focused on the book in his lap.

"Air pockets. Not to worry."

He had the manner of an army drill sergeant, curt, disciplined, but he also had the look: short hair, dark trim moustache. Even his boots had a military sheen. She adjusted her theory when she noticed the striped golf shirt under his windbreaker.

He turned the book face down, stretched and yawned and checked his watch like someone who'd done the trip a thousand times. It was a Rolex, though she doubted its authenticity. What would someone who could afford a Rolex be doing in the North? She leaned back into the headrest and closed her eyes.

"You needn't worry," the man repeated for emphasis. "We're flying with some of the most experienced pilots in the world."

"So they say." She opened her eyes.

"Just keep swallowing." He turned and extended his hand. "I'm Elliot, by the way."

"Yasmeen."

"Teacher?"

She nodded.

"Same here. Second year and ready to roll."

She shifted anxiously, never having flown in anything so small in her life. Even though Frank had reviewed the specs with them, seating for nineteen passengers only, it still came as a shock, flying in it for real. She couldn't imagine how cramped it would be with an overload of cargo or a patient on a stretcher with a slow-dripping IV. For its size it had an impressive name, the De Havilland Canada DHC-6 Twin Otter. But it was really just a small plane, a compact white carrier with red, orange and yellow striped markings.

All Yasmeen could think about was stretching her legs, shaking out the cramps. Trying to get the blood circulating again. She could have used a glass of water or the light touch of ginger ale to settle her stomach. But there was no meal service on these planes. There were no flight attendants. It was just the passengers and the cockpit with a ratty curtain between them.

The curtain was pushed open. Yasmeen could see straight through to the pilot (white) and co-pilot (Inuit) shifting levers and flicking buttons and switches on the illuminated control panel. The view through the panoramic window was a murky cocktail and she wondered how they could see where they were going.

Something thudded against the floor of the plane. It was like driving in a car and accidentally running over something, either a cat or the branch of a tree. Engrossed in his book, Elliot didn't even bat an eye. Inuit passengers across the aisle either snoozed or stared out the window, unfazed, as though they were riding a city bus at rush hour. As though their shuttle service up and down the coast had always existed, as much a part of their lives as dogsleds and kayaks.

Elliot offered her a stick of gum from his shirt pocket. "Helps the ears." He smiled and tugged his lobe like he was talking to a child.

"Sure. Thanks." She closed her eyes again, trying to envision her feet firmly planted on solid ground. Her mouth flooded with the sweet, starry burst of gum. She thought of the floured pink kind of her youth, how hard her jaws and teeth had to work to soften it enough to chew. She and Morgan had once collected over a hundred Bazooka Joe comic strips to send away for sea monkeys and a pair of X-ray glasses.

Elliot bumped her arm as he snapped the book shut with a portentous whistle, followed by a drawn-out *soooo* …

"So?" She repeated absently, not bothering to open her eyes.

"So it's looking like it might be a lemming year," he said.

"Lemming?" It sounded vaguely familiar. "Oh, you mean those brown mousy things. I've heard of them. Don't they commit mass suicide, or something?"

"Yes, but no. I mean, that's actually a myth."

"Oh. Interesting."

He continued without taking note of her reaction. "Every four years or so the population goes through the roof, so a bunch of them pack up and move on. Great swarms travel over huge landmasses to the sea and then plunge off cliffs to their death by drowning. But researchers … now what would they be called?" He paused for dramatic effect. "Lemmographers? Lemmologists? Anyway, whoever they are, they claim that it's not suicide, it's just an accident of nature. It's the way it is."

It wasn't the most stimulating topic. Yasmeen didn't know why people always felt compelled to make small talk with a perfect stranger on a plane or train or bus. What was the point when they would probably never see each other again? Now she had all this business stuck in her mind, rodents falling off the face of the earth, a solid wave of flailing, doomed creatures. She opened her eyes.

"Yasmeen, Yasmeen, that's what kind of name?"

Here it comes, she thought. Now he was going to tell her how much he loved *Lawrence of Arabia*, how nothing beat seeing it on the big screen. She was used to it. "It's Persian for Jasmine," she said, trying to be agreeable. "But I'm not Persian, I'm Arab. Syrian, actually."

"That's what I thought," he said.

She waited for him to bring up the movie. He didn't. There was nothing out of his mouth about Peter O'Toole or the extraordinary desert scenes.

Instead, his eyes grew wide. "I know some Syrians in Montreal, maybe you know them?"

"I doubt it."

Yasmeen's mother had a habit of blurting things out during a lull at a party. She liked the attention. It didn't matter that whatever she said might embarrass her daughter, who was usually present in the room wearing some fancy dress she'd been made to wear. It didn't matter that she always told the same old story, that everyone had heard it a thousand times already.

"I still can't get over how much you looked like an Eskimo baby when you were born."

Yasmeen would shrug and stare at the floor.

"You have to admit it." And then, as though her word weren't proof enough, Samiyah would pull the colossal family album from the credenza and flip to the hospital photo taken just minutes after the delivery, the ugliest record of Yasmeen that existed in the world. In it, she had a black comb of hair and dark, squinty eyes set too far apart.

When she was in elementary school, Yasmeen checked out pictures of Eskimos in the encyclopedia her father had picked up for a song—he liked picking things up for "a song"—and tried to imagine what it would have been like rubbing noses in an igloo as cold as a refrigerator. As it happened, her third-grade teacher, Mrs. Fishwick, had a thing for the Eskimos. She read aloud their myths and legends to the class in their spare time before recess. She stuck little coloured flags on a large wall map of Canada to show the isolated, faraway places where they lived.

33

One Friday, Mrs. Fishwick spooled a black and white film into a projector and warned them with her taut lips that if the bell rang before they were through, they would stay in for lunch to finish watching. The movie followed a tribe of nomadic, pre-historic-looking people in furs and caribou skins through a typical day. It showed how they chopped, filed and shaved whatever they found to make the tools and weapons they needed to survive. It showed them in their crowded igloos gumming down blubbery spears of walrus and smiling with their horrible teeth. Their mouths reminded Yasmeen of the neglected piano by the boiler room in the school basement, a wretched keyboard of stained and chipped ivories. The film jerked and jumped and had long spidery hairs wiggling through it.

Soon after that Mrs. Fishwick arrived with a heavy coffee-table book from the local library and placed it in their special display case at the back of the classroom. Only students who finished their math stencils first were permitted to sit on the shag carpet and flip through its glossy pages. Yasmeen, the teacher's pet, could often be found there.

After Mrs. Fishwick corrected her work with a red pen and pasted the sticker of a bright butterfly on her page, Yasmeen would trot back to her desk to tidy up her books, flinging her hair behind her importantly before making her way to the Reading Corner. She took great pleasure in walking past the idiot kid, Brian, the one the French teacher called Brain because of a misspelling on the attendance list that went uncorrected. Yasmeen lifted her chin in a superior sort of way and stuck her tongue out at him. Brian snivelled his complaint.

"For heaven sakes, you again?" Mrs. Fishwick loathed tattletales.

Yasmeen glanced sheepishly at Morgan as the teacher led him by the ear and out the door, where she continued to make a federal case of his whining in a voice that bounced off the walls and echoed down the hallway all the way to the principal's office. Yasmeen smirked into her hand.

She relished her little pranks far more than the serious business of sitting down with the book, although once the chaos died down she took pleasure in leafing through, examining the pictures. Her favourite was an antique photograph of an Alaskan village, a cluster of seaside dwellings perched on a cliff of patchy vegetation. No matter how many times she stared at it, she couldn't get over how people could live in such a rugged, perilous place and survive. It was everything her parents' solid brick house, with its cozy furnishings and gleaming appliances, was not.

They descended through a veil of fog, the plane fishtailing, rain hammering at the fuselage. Fingers interlaced in her lap, Yasmeen stared unblinkingly ahead, the hypnotic effect of the sped-up windshield wipers taking her mind off the nausea. The dense atmospheric soup was beginning to thin out. Through strands of cloud she could make out the driving spray of Hudson Bay and a haphazard cluster of modest dwellings at the mouth of an estuary. The middle of nowhere, her mother had said.

The plane took another air pocket.

Yasmeen wondered about her personal items, the ones she had neatly arranged in her knapsack, twist-tied Baggies of almonds, Peruvian wool socks with leather heels, snow goggles, Scrabble tiles in a purple Crown Royal bag, the brass compass that had belonged to her grandfather, the 35-mm camera her father had given her on her eighteenth birthday, snagged at a fire sale. She supposed that everything was every which way by now.

The surf in her ears intensified as the little lozenge of a plane tilted and levelled out again. She felt the wheels release. They bumped down onto the airstrip and sped along with a force that propelled her head backwards against the headrest. She swallowed as though a golf ball were stuck in her throat.

Count to ten, she reminded herself. Breathe. She closed her eyes.

When the plane finally ground to a halt, Elliot nudged her, his mouth flapping.

"What?" she shouted. She leaned in closer.

His reedy voice trickled through her ear canals. "As I said, no need to get your knickers in a knot. See? We made it, all in one piece."

The engine shut down. She was relieved; the tension whistled out of her, *pffft* like a balloon deflating. Though her chewing gum had lost its flavour, Yasmeen chomped on it maniacally, trying to clear the passageways of her ears. A sudden pop produced the highway sound of whooshing tires on a rain-slick road. The world flooded back with crystal clarity; voices, coat zippers, seat belts releasing with a shutter-like click.

Headset horseshoed around his neck, the pilot spun around and grinned, his voice clear as gunshot. "Welcome to Saqijuvik, population 346. *Bienvenue à tous.*"

The co-pilot climbed out of the cockpit to lift the exit door. A grey midday light welcomed them. Immediately the aisle filled with passengers rushing to deplane, Inuit women toting babies on their back, fidgety children, another pair of teachers—one, a stout, bubbly girl with short, strawberry hair; the other, older and more matronly, wearing a trench coat buttoned to her chin. As the line inched forward, a seasonal worker in a plaid flannel vest and steel-toe boots doled out his unopened snacks, single servings of peanuts and Dad's cookies, to other people's cranky toddlers. He pulled his ears and made silly faces at them, waiting for their expressions to brighten. A wave of excitement rippled through Yasmeen, the reality of having arrived and the realization of the important role that she was about to play. There was no gloating on her part. From the very start she made sure her intentions were pure, a far cry from previous generations of whites who came north to effect change but who had brought dysentery, smallpox and tuberculosis instead, decimating entire populations.

Yasmeen joined the long line headed for the exit. Through the tiny windows of the plane she took stock of life on the ground, wet, disorganized, a whirlwind of activity, as though the Barnum & Bailey caravan had just blown into town. Villagers were gathered around the plane in rubber boots and slickers, their welcoming faces glazed with rain—boys with baseball caps drawn over their eyes, girls wearing too much lipstick, construction workers, old ladies with twisted spines and hardly a tooth in their heads, kids with runny noses scurrying everywhere. A thousand things flashed through her mind at once. She was struck by how many of them were diaper age or younger. The true people of the earth, she mused.

She felt Elliot nipping her heels from behind. "Move along, move along, let's get the show on the road," he insisted. She threw her knapsack over her shoulder and hastened down the steps to solid ground.

Mangy, mat-haired dogs flew past her, pushing their noses into the offloaded cargo—cardboard boxes stamped Kraft and Pepsi, jumbo-sized cases of Pampers and toilet paper, Gerbers, Royale. Most of the year's bulk goods, she knew, had arrived earlier in the season on a large ocean-going vessel called the Sealift, non-perishables and heavy machinery, boats, Skidoos, electrical appliances, mechanical equipment. It boggled her mind to think of all it took to run a place, especially a remote, fly-in village without any access to roads, all the planning and foresight required to ensure they were well stocked for the year.

Yasmeen noticed the pilot checking the time on his watch as the co-pilot prepared to board a line of departing passengers eager to escape the rain. Elliot was already chatting with one, a guy wearing a black leather jacket and gloves with the fingers cut off. "Yasmeen Haddad, meet Joanasi Maqaittik, one of the big celebs around here," he said. "Best radio host in town." Elliot clapped him on the shoulder. "This guy really knows his music."

Joanasi shrugged. He hardly looked at Yasmeen.

"Where're you headed?" said Elliot, slapping the rain out of his hair.

"Kuujjuaq. I have a radio course."

"How long you gone for?"

"Maybe two or three days, or one week. *Aatsuuk,* I don't know."

"Radio. Cool," said Yasmeen. She noticed his boots were unlaced, the way people in the seventies used to wear their Kodiaks. She wondered whether it was a fashion thing with him as well.

Elliot shot the breeze with Joanasi, catching up on village news, dropping names she didn't know. Yasmeen stood there, trying to look interested.

She was relieved when she spotted her luggage about to be tossed from the plane, a couple of duct-taped boxes and her brother's old hockey bag. It gave her an excuse to bow out of the conversation. "Well, I guess I'll see you around sometime."

Joanasi looked curiously at her.

She pointed toward the plane. "I really gotta go, my stuff is here now … It was really nice meeting you. Joanasi, right?"

He didn't answer. It *was* Joanasi, wasn't it? She was pretty sure.

He chucked his cigarette and shook hands with Elliot. As an afterthought he reached for Yasmeen's. He had a firm grip, but not bone-crushing. "See you," he said.

"Yeah, okay then, see you." An airline employee lobbed her bag onto the mounting heap of crates and containers on the muddy ground. She made a beeline for it, hair flapping like a

RAIN

horse's tail, and dragged it, along with her boxes, to the sidelines where there was a little less confusion.

A woman caught her eye, someone with a polka-dot kerchief folded in a triangle over her hair and knotted at the chin, the way 1950s housewives wore them. She was snaking excitedly through the crowd, waving her arms at Yasmeen. A stocky man with thick forearms and a poor complexion lagged behind her, smoke trailing from his nostrils. He flicked his cigarette butt.

The woman's hand shot out to shake Yasmeen's. "Qanuippiit ... I mean, how are you?" she said, her face sheened in the mist that was making everything feel moist.

"*Qa-nu-ingi-tunga.*" Yasmeen was glad she'd made the effort to learn some of their simple greetings. She didn't want to arrive sounding like an ignorant tourist. She wanted to make a good first impression, demonstrate that she had the character to live in such a cold place.

"*Kinauvit?*"

"Pardon?"

"She wants to know your name," said the man. His helmet of hair and the sprouts of wiry stubble on his chin glistened from the rain. He had a warm but official demeanour. Yasmeen recognized the school board emblem stitched to the pocket of his windbreaker. She clasped his hand with inflated enthusiasm, avoiding direct eye contact as Frank had instructed. They all smiled at each other.

"You must be the centre director," she said. "I'm Yasmeen."

"*Yasmee-ngai,*" said the woman, sounding out the syllables of her name like a child learning a new vocabulary word.

"*Yasmee-ngai,*" she repeated, embarrassed when she remembered the correct response was just *aah.*

The woman giggled.

"I'm Paulussie, the school commissioner," said the man. "And this here nosy woman is my wife, Sarah."

Sarah elbowed him playfully in the ribs. There was a familiarity about the way they kibitzed, a hint of something that reminded Yasmeen of her own parents in the good old days, the way her mother always criticized her father's driving, his foot too heavy on the brakes, his own complaints that with Samiyah around he could never get a word in edgewise.

Paulussie continued: "I'll be filling in for Sarah's brother this year, the real centre director. He's down south for a medical issue … I guess you could call me a jack of all trades."

"Jack of all trades and master of none," mocked Sarah.

The plane was finally loaded up, the door snapped tight. A brawny wind from the propellers lifted the hair and coat tails of everyone still standing around.

Paulussie tossed Yasmeen's luggage into a scarred pickup truck with a spider-leg crack across the windshield that looked like it had been there since the year one. He gestured for her and the other teachers to pile in. Elliot was still milling about shaking hands with people when Paulussie caught him by surprise with a friendly sucker punch. They began sparring like old-time boxers. Sarah giggled and told them to quit horsing around, she wanted to get out of the rain. Elliot saluted and hopped onto the back of the truck with the luggage. The rest squeezed into the back seat as Paulussie revved the motor.

Yasmeen sat on a spot of ripped upholstery patched with crisscrossed pieces of duct tape. She made small talk before officially introducing herself to the others, Sam (the heavy girl) and Iris (the matron). Slowly the truck shifted forward over the terrible ruts and puddles of the dirt road, rubbery wipers wheezing back and forth, swishing the rain away. A pine-cone air freshener jiggled from the rear-view mirror, too subtle for the robust mix of diesel and cigarette smoke permeating the truck.

They drove up alongside a child squelching through the mud with his head down and his coat flapping open. Sarah stuck her head out the window and called out to him in Inuktitut. When the kid refused to look up, she dismissed him with a wave of her hand and rolled up the window. Yasmeen guessed he was probably one of theirs. And yet, instead of disciplining him like her own mother would have done, they left him alone. It impressed her.

Paulussie navigated the road carefully, expertly, shocks absent, every part of the truck squeaking, grooved tires sinking into the muck as they passed a nondescript cemetery and a dump of scrap metal and broken Skidoo parts on the outskirts of town. He slowed to acknowledge a decrepit pickup approaching them from the opposite direction. It had a punched-out headlight and a loud exhaust pipe. Tooting the horn, he scooched over, cracked his window and shouted something to the other driver, whose bronzed arm was dangling over the door, a half-smoked cigarette between his thumb and forefinger. He was wearing a yellow hard hat. The guy smiled and nodded at them.

"That's Tommy," Paulussie announced to everyone and no one in particular. "You'll meet him."

They bounced past a giant satellite dish, a scatter of rusty oil drums and ramshackle sheds in varying stages of decomposition. There were no street names or sidewalks or civic numbers. The village seemed haphazard and improvised, as though lumber and nails had been parachuted from a plane and wherever they landed, something got built. As far as she could tell, Saqijuvik was just a treeless expanse of flimsy wooden houses curled around a grey stretch of water. Nothing had a basement, everything stood on footers because of the permafrost.

"Look, there's my church!" Sarah shouted. She pointed to a building of yellow corrugated metal. A sign above the door read "Jesus Saves—Pentecostal Church." Across the road, facing it, was an older, dome-shaped structure that resembled an igloo. "That other one, that's the Anglican Church," she added.

The waning drone of the distant plane caught Yasmeen's attention. She stared out the window, following its solitary white trail until it dissolved into nothing. Her heart sped up. She thought of how far away she was, how isolated and cut off from the rest of the world. She thought of her father, two years gone, and how he would have shouted *Yahoo, Yasmeen! Hold onto your hat!*

"You're stuck here now," Paulussie shouted over his shoulder. He laughed and winked at Sarah, who returned his smile. "Everybody okay back there?"

Sam nodded.

Paulussie dug around in his pocket until he pulled out a crumpled pack of Export As and a lighter. Knees bracing the steering wheel, he poked a cigarette into his mouth.

Sarah shooed him with her hand. "You smoke too much, old man."

"Izzat so?" He spun around with an impish grin, enjoying the extra attention. He lit the cigarette and took back the wheel with both hands. Sarah sighed in defeat. They vaulted past another few shacks and abandoned warehouses, the radio station, the municipal office, a lopsided building he called the Pool Hall, and the pell-mell grounds of a rambling construction site. The skeletal structure at the center looked like the titanic ribcage of a blue whale.

"Check out the new school," said Iris, with what sounded like cautious enthusiasm. Her lips hardly parted when she spoke. Though she'd been in the North three years, it was her first in Saqijuvik and her first as principal of a school.

"If all goes well, it should be done by December," said Paulussie. "And then we're gonna have a big shindig."

Sarah gave his shoulder a tender squeeze.

Yasmeen tensed up. A feeling of panic came over her. She felt fraudulent. Had she merely deluded herself, thinking she could teach these children what they needed to know for life in the North? They, after all, were the ones living here. It was *their* home. They knew every inch of the place. What did she know by comparison, a girl from the city with her books and theories? She remembered some of Frank's lectures about what her role was, what she could do to enlighten them. The modern world was at their doorstep. At best, she could make it navigable. That she could do.

"In the meantime," said Paulussie, butting his cigarette into the ashtray, "you'll use the old portables as your classrooms." Although it was meant as an apology, Yasmeen was glad to hear that for at least a couple of months she'd get a taste of the old system. Not a single, centralized school operating on a schedule of bells but a makeshift space embracing a looser concept of time. Closer to the Inuit way.

Paulussie took a wide turn and stamped on the brake. "First stop," he called. "Yasmeen."

Her heart surged. She marvelled at the view. A house. There.

A small clapboard bungalow a dozen steps from the rocky beach.

A house with a hunter-green door.

Hers.

Yasmeen barely waited for Paulussie to shift into park. She hopped out and ran through the rain for a closer look while Elliot and Paulussie ferried her things into the house. The paint on the front door was peeling off, but it didn't matter to her in the least. The point was the house. Her own tiny piece of the North. All she wanted was for the rest of her life to start. Here, in this place, nearly two thousand kilometres from everyone and everything she knew. She wanted it to start right now.

THREE

Her mother would have had a field day with Mr. Clean.

The house had the shut-in smell of dust and stillness like the summer cottages her father used to rent for them in Maine, where no one could touch anything or use the toilet until Samiyah ran around with bleach and disinfectant. The walls were naked except for a calendar opened to the month of June with a picture of a gleaming Harley-Davidson, the days crossed off in red. She found a glass and twisted open the kitchen faucet but only rusty water gurgled out of the tap. She let it run while she made the rounds, taking inventory.

Bisque broadloom carpet, worn in patches;

Black rotary-dial telephone with flaccid, floor-length cord;

Standard-issue maple furnishings: couch, loveseat, bed, dresser, table and chairs, several with cigarette burns;

Avocado-coloured kitchen appliances and grease-coated backsplash;

Mismatched utensils, cookware banged and chipped with age, whistling kettle, coffee maker with glass carafe and cracked filter basket, spice jars smudged with fingerprints.

She saved the bathroom for last, the cruddy bathtub and the infamous nineteen-litre honey bucket installation that Frank had almost had an orgasm describing, essentially a metal gar-

44

bage can with a replaceable plastic liner and the accessories to go with it: a year's supply of industrial garbage bags, one full canister of chemical deodorizer. The next best thing to a water-borne sewage system. Finn had nicknamed it the "makeshift shitter."

She hauled her bag and her cardboard boxes into the middle of the living room and moved the couch so that it faced out onto the storm-tossed estuary. She flopped into it and watched the slanted rain, the slapping green waves capped in foam.

One morning, when Yasmeen was six, the semitones of her parents' voices woke her. It was dark in her room, like it was still night. Curious, she pulled on her bunny-ear slippers and tiptoed down the stairs. The front door was wide open and her father's brown valise, the one he took on summer vacations, was standing upright by it. A taxi was waiting in their driveway with its roof light on and the windshield wipers going. She noticed her mother leaning against the wall rubbing her temples the way she always did when she had a headache. Her father was by the door lifting the collar of his trench coat. Before he walked out into the rain he turned to Yasmeen as though he'd just remembered something important. Winking, he pulled a quarter out of her ear and handed it to her, saying, "I'll be back soon, *Habibti*." She didn't see him for a whole month after that.

After his funeral two years ago, Yasmeen recalled that rainy morning in detail, how he left without an umbrella, shooting down their walkway without looking back. She remembered the months and years after he returned from that mysterious trip, how every day after work, for the rest of his life, before her mother even had supper on the table, he opened the liquor cabinet and poured himself a straight shot of Scotch. Sometimes he poured a second or third, or turned in early, taking the glass with him to bed. It didn't seem out of the ordinary. Like most fathers he worked hard. Like most he had a drink after work. Then he got sick and it was too late by then to pack his bag and send him back to the place that made him well the first time.

The day of the funeral, they all drove together in a limousine that smelled of sickly sweet ladies' perfume, up the grave-dotted mountain—she and her mother and her sister and brother, without a word—until Samiyah rolled down the window to let some air into the car and blurted: *I had three children to think about, did I need another?* Yasmeen knew it was just her grief talking. The relatives sent funeral wreaths dyed unnatural colours, turquoise and lime green, horrible shades. One was in the shape of a clock with its hands stopped at the time of his death. Everyone huddled together as a family by the pyramid of loosened earth while the priest sprinkled holy water and praised her father's "great journey into the undiluted light, returning him to the beginning, to the lake of pure calm." Yasmeen never knew her father to be a great swimmer. She didn't understand what the priest meant by it. She couldn't tell if it was real or if she'd imagined it, but in a quiet lull she heard her father's booming voice in her ear. Don't be sad, Habibti, he was saying. Forget the lake, I'm headed for the stars. It put a smile on her face.

Elliot expounded on his theory at dinner. Most whites who come north, he argued, have something big to work out, something in their past or present that isn't sitting right. They aren't normal by southern standards. They're wanderers, dreamers, deviants, misfits. They're social outcasts or borderline depressives seeking refuge from the emotional turmoil of their lives.

He spoke disdainfully, excluding himself and the other teachers from his categorized pathologies. According to him, none of them fit the profile of the marginal type, someone "a little off," as he put it, underscoring his words with air quotes. Yasmeen was skeptical. She wondered how he knew this with such certainty. He'd only just met her. And what did he know of Iris and Sam, the other new teachers?

Yasmeen was cocooning in her new place when Sarah's supper invitation came. She hadn't unpacked a single thing. The storm had subsided. The shrill ring of the telephone startled her. Who even knew she was in town? Tonight? Oh, sure. Sarah instructed her to bring nothing but herself, she'd see to the rest.

Now night was peering in through the dining room window, a radiant sky swept clean by the rain. Absent was the dim, sulphury afterglow of the city. Yasmeen couldn't recall the last time she'd seen so many stars.

Sarah made her grand entrance with a steaming bowl of caribou stew. She blushed as everyone around the table applauded. Hair scooped into a high ponytail, she looked almost too young to be the mother of two. Yasmeen jumped up to offer a hand, but Sarah gestured for her to sit, she had everything under control. She disappeared again into the kitchen and returned with a medley of soup bones marbled in fat. She set it down in front of Paulussie and took her place across from him, fanning herself with a napkin. She poured everyone a glass of water from a plastic pitcher, which had a peeling decal of Mickey and Minnie Mouse, and lifted hers in a toast. "Well, then, welcome to Saqijuvik, everybody. The new guys and the old."

Yasmeen's eyes drifted upward to the poster taped on the wall behind Sarah, an electric orange sunrise with the words Jesus is Coming Back scrawled across it. It suited the décor of the house, every surface cluttered with trinkets and mementos from various trips down south: assorted plastic figurines, religious icons made in China, fake gold crucifixes, ashtrays of all shapes and sizes, silver-plated spoons engraved with city names.

"A bottle of wine would have been nice tonight," said Paulussie, slurping the marrow from a bone.

Sarah glared. "You're not so nice when you drink."

A chilly silence fell over the room as everyone retreated into their private rituals of eating—chewing, swallowing, drinking, stirring, salting and peppering food. For a long while no one spoke. Yasmeen glanced across the table at Jacqueline, the village nurse, whom Sarah had also invited. When they were introduced at the door, Jacqueline said "*Enchantée*," and kissed Yasmeen once on each cheek the way French girls do. She wore a long loose top over leotards and gold-toed sandals that seemed more appropriate for the city. Jacqueline was practically a local, having lived and worked in the village for four years already. She arrived at Sarah's arm in arm with her six-foot-tall Inuit boyfriend, Tommy, the one they had passed earlier in the truck.

"It's good to be back," said Elliot, rotating the ice cubes in his water.

Paulussie murmured something in Inuktitut to Tommy. Tommy lifted his eyebrows in reply. Sam, the heavy-set girl with the strawberry hair, thanked Sarah for inviting them, which set off a crossfire of thank-yous from everyone at the table.

The conversation resumed. For hours they talked over the tinkling glassware and clattering cutlery, through the din and thickening haze of cigarette smoke, companionably, as though they'd known each other for years. Based on her few hours in the village, Yasmeen could already tell that she'd enjoy her life in the Far North, where the distances between people evaporated.

"I have a nice bottle of red, but it's back at the house," said Iris with a regret that sounded insincere.

Yasmeen swallowed her mouthful. "I might have one too, at the bottom of a box somewhere. I'm not quite done unpacking."

"I thought this was a dry community," said Sam.

"Yeah, no booze allowed. At least that's what they told me at the interview," said Yasmeen.

"That rule's for us, not for you guys," said Paulussie.

"That doesn't seem fair."

"Maybe not to you. Actually, we made that decision together as a community. We thought it was best for us."

"Best?"

"Some of the other villages have social clubs."

"What, you mean like a bar?"

"Yep. Saturday afternoons you can line up there to get a drink or buy a six-pack."

"There's one like that in Fort Chimo," said Iris.

"Kuujjuaq." Tommy glared as he corrected her. "Fort Chimo is *your* word."

Iris blushed. "I stand corrected."

"Not to change the subject, but I, for one, just love the fact that I can look up and actually see stars."

"Speaking of which, I can't wait to see the northern lights."

"Oh, my god, yes. I've heard they're stunning."

"You can't even imagine."

Elliot wiped up the last of his stew with a crust of bread and held it by his mouth. "I once read somewhere that the reason why natives can't hold their liquor is because their genetic constitution isn't programmed for it. They don't have the something or other it takes to break it down. Apparently, in another few generations it might not even be a problem anymore." He popped the morsel of bread into his mouth.

"Elliot!" Jacqueline's face was redder than a tomato.

"What?? What did I say?"

"Yeah, maybe we should just change the subject."

"Don't Elliot me, I'm just repeating what I read."

"You *Qallunaat*, you really love your books, don't you? Well, here I am, me, a real live Inuk, and I just want to say once and for all— "

"That's enough, Tommy, *ça suffit*. I mean it. "

"Yeah, cut it out, Tommy. They just arrived, give them a break."

"And you. *T'es vraiment con!* Why do you even bring it up?"

"What did I do?"

"You and your stupid theories. *Gros tata.* "

Tommy reached over and pecked Jacqueline on the forehead. "*Aukaa*. You know I'm only kidding."

She pouted and rolled her eyes. "It's hard to tell sometimes."

Elliot shot Jacqueline a playful look. "Don't be so serious."

"Put it this way, white people would rather read than have sex. Inuit people would rather have sex than read."

"Paulussie!"

"I don't see the connection."

"Talking about missing the connection, my mother thinks I'm actually going to be living in an igloo up here."

"And that surprises you? Just listen to the news. Americans still think that regular Canadians live in igloos."

Tommy stiffened. "What do you mean regular Canadians?"

"Sorry, I didn't mean ... you know what I mean."

"*Gros tata.* "

"Okay, let's just say once and for all, for the record, we're all of us, in this room, every one of us, regular, equal Canadians. Is everybody happy now?"

"*Wô, minute là! Tu me niaises? Moi, je me considère Québécoise.*"

"Let's not go there either, Jackie. Not tonight."

"*Câline*, and here I thought we were going to have an argument! You know how much I love tripping you up."

"Hold your horses, *mam'selle*! Who won the last one? I believe it was me, *n'est-ce-pas?*"

"You're a legend in your own mind, *mon ami*."

Sarah reached for the empty plates and piled them in front of her. "I'd like to hear from the new people for a change. Yasmeen, your name, it's so beautiful."

"My mother wanted to call me Noor, the Arabic word for light."

"That's pretty, too … "

"But my dad didn't go for it, so they finally agreed on Yasmeen after the flower, Jasmine. My mother's an avid gardener …"

"Hey, me too."

"And then there's my mother's name, Samiyah."

Elliot tipped back his chair. "Once I was in a cemetery in a hick town called … shit, I can't remember, where *was* that place? Anyway, I was wandering through and I saw a tombstone with the name Murch Skillies on it, and I says to myself, 'Who goes through life with a name like Murch Skillies?' and I scratched my head and thought about it and I figured he had to have been either one of two things, the dapper captain of the Love Boat or some burly fisherman with a shaved head and a tattoo on his neck." He paused for a breath. "Being in a backwater town, I went with my second theory."

"Elliot, you know I love you, but can we please let Yasmeen finish?"

"Finish what?"

"She was trying to tell us about her mother."

"Samiyah—that almost sounds like *my* name, Samantha. I guess by now you know that everyone calls me Sam for short."

"It means Exalted One in Arabic. But enough about me, Sarah, what about you? Someone mentioned you're the priest at the Pentecostal church."

"Let's not get her going on that."

"Pastor, not priest. Priests are Catholic."

"I wouldn't mind checking out your service sometime."

"Of course, anytime. You're more than welcome. All of you."
She beamed across the table at Paulussie.

"Where in hell are the toothpicks?"

"Right in front of you, you silly man," she said. "It's a good thing you have your head attached."

"Okay, enough, you two lovebirds," said Elliot. "When's our next hunting trip, Paulussie?"

"You tell me, Boss."

"You don't strike me as the hunterly type," Yasmeen interjected.

Elliot pointed to a miniature gold pin fastened to the collar of his golf shirt. "Note the hunting horn," he boasted, raising his chin up. "For about ten years, until I started working up here, yours truly was an official member of the Hunt Club. How do you like them apples? Or should I say 'snowballs'?"

"Haw, haw."

"Go ahead and make fun, but Paulussie and I had a couple of great days last year, remember, buddy? Remember that killer bear?"

"Yep, I sure do." He tapped a cigarette from his pack.

"My rifle's the one thing I took with me after the divorce. Besides my socks, I mean. And my Calvin Klein briefs."

"Too much information, *mon beau Adonis.*"

Elliot continued. "I got another one for you."

"Spare us."

"What's a synonym for vegetarian?"

"I give up."

"Bad hunter."

"Very funny."

"Actually, it is."

"What about the weekend after next?"

"What about it?"

"Labour Day. I was just thinking it would be fun to take all the new teachers—and you old timers—on a camping trip. Before school starts. What do you think?"

"Sounds like a plan."

"I'm in."

"Me too."

"What about you, Iris? Can the school principal afford to take a break from her busy schedule?"

"I think I can manage a day." She blew her nose discreetly into her napkin, folded it and stuffed it in her sleeve.

"Tommy? We'll need a second boat. That means you."

"Aatsuuk, maybe. Whoever brings the bottle of gin gets to go with me."

"TOMMY! *Taima!*"

"Kidding."

Before tea was served they ironed out the details of the trip, the time, whose boats, who'd bring what supplies. One by one they weighed in on the idea of roughing it with just a tent and a few provisions. Yasmeen could hardly wait.

"You're going to fall in love with this place," said Jacqueline.

"Hear, hear." Elliot lifted his glass as though it were a crystal wine goblet. He tilted it back and forth in the light, sniffed the rim and laid it back down on the table before veering off on a tangent about a cruise he and his ex-wife once took. "It's hard to imagine any other kind of life," he chortled, "after strudel and cappuccino on the banks of the Danube."

Yasmeen had always been a light sleeper. The slightest disturbances woke her—a fly trapped between two window panes, a humming refrigerator, a subtle shift in the barometer. But here, the minute she hit the pillow, Yasmeen descended into the dark vapours of sleep. She floated and had strange dreams that she remembered afterward.

One dream was about crocuses that wouldn't stop growing. They sprouted up out of the soil until they became giant snow-capped mountains that surrounded her like a wall. Then the peaks melted and everything slid down into the ground, clicking into place like a lock-slot over a steel bolt. She had other dreams, too, like the one about a primitive tribe that believed animals and people shared the same souls. They had no language, they just went quietly from place to place. Time was fluid. They travelled by the light of the stars. It was more of a dream she watched from the sidelines, but somehow their joy flowed into her, crossing the hemispheres of her brain, rippling through her scalp, down her neck and spine into every follicle of hair, every vein and ligament, every limb and finger and toe, every dormant cell along the way.

There was also a surreal dream that was just a casual conversation between her and the radio guy Elliot had introduced her to, Joanasi or whatever his name was. They were on the airstrip in the pouring rain and everything they were saying was code for something else, which they both understood, as though they were on the exact same wavelength. He questioned her on her musical tastes, whether she liked rock 'n roll or not.

That's a no-brainer, of course I do.

Stairway to Heaven?

Who doesn't?

Freddie Mercury?

Do you really have to ask?

Air Supply?

Now you're pushing it.

Just testing.

She stared at her feet. Seconds before she woke up he said a very sweet thing. It took her by surprise.

You smell like snow.

FOUR

Their sharp-nosed canoes moved in tandem, slitting the water like shark fins. Yasmeen and Iris rode with Paulussie and his two boys, Jimmy and Silasie, and Elliot, who looked a class above everyone else in his Tilley hat and designer sunglasses. Tommy followed in the other boat with Jacqueline and Sam and a moraine of supplies—tents, sleeping bags, fishing nets, food and a spouted canister of gasoline.

The land was pristine, a violet-blue relief that seemed to scroll on forever. Yasmeen closed her eyes, lulled by the gliding rhythm of the boat.

By the time they reached their destination, a narrow apron of land spotted with boulders and uneven patches of low-grow- ing vegetation, the clouds had come unmoored and dusk had softened the forms of plain and sea.

"The best blueberries in the area are found right here," said Paulussie, dragging the canoe in with Elliot's help. He glanced around with affection and explained how four decades earlier, in the exact same place, his mother had squatted over the damp lichen to give birth to him. It astonished Yasmeen that such a small thing, such a small big thing as the land, could give a man such deep joy.

When the tents were spiked, Yasmeen and the other women wandered around with the children to collect whatever moss

55

and roots and driftwood they could find for kindling. The air had begun to cool. Tommy sat on a bald rock in the distance, flicking the firefly embers of his cigarette.

After a couple of false starts, Paulussie got a decent fire going. He told the children to keep feeding it until it woofed into a steady flame. When he was satisfied, he lit a cigarette and levered himself into a comfortable position on the ground, legs splayed apart, an arm resting over his thick stomach.

Elliot wiggled in next to Yasmeen. He tipped his hat up and inspected the sky. "Holy moly," he said. "Doesn't it just boggle the mind that there are so many living creatures on this planet? I mean, experts figure there could be anywhere from three to a hundred million species and barely a million of those have even been catalogued."

Yasmeen stared into the orange flame. The intense heat on her cheeks made her feel sleepy.

Elliot pressed on. "Scientists say that at the present rate, it could take over a thousand years to classify the rest! Can you even begin to fathom that? Can you? It means that some species will become extinct before anyone even knew they existed!"

Jacqueline lifted her arms into the air, snapping her fingers. "So, *carpe diem*. It took me nearly twenty years to come to terms with the idea that we only go around once." The fire hissed and crackled.

Something about Jacqueline's bohemian manner appealed to Yasmeen. She had a casual sense of abandon that shouted I'm here, take me or leave me as I am. Her movements were fluid and sensual and communicated a bewitching message to men in general and Tommy in particular. The two seemed to have a physical and psychic connection, an ability to detect the other's low-frequency signals and vibrations the way certain animals did. And then there was the key tattooed onto her ankle, which Yasmeen took as a symbol of their love. She wondered whether Tommy had one too.

⬚

Years back, Yasmeen saw a play in Toronto in which the main character, played by someone with a Jeremy Irons sort of accent, was obsessed with the Chinese poet, Li Po. The actor, whoever he was, was superb. Incredibly convincing in the role.

Yasmeen thought a long time about where her tattoo would go. She tried out a few different places on her body, drawing a small x with her pen, until she finally settled on her right hip just below her belly button. There, she could safely wear a bikini without her mother noticing it. Going through the whole rigmarole to have it done was rather like going for an abortion in a seedy part of town, but with far less at stake. She went alone so no one could talk her out of it. Morgan reprimanded her when she found out.

"What the fuck, you tattooed *lipo* on your body?"

"It's not *lipo,* you nimrod, oh my god." Yasmeen rolled her eyes. "Can't you see the upper case letters and the space between Li and Po?"

"What then?"

"You think I had liposuction? And that I decided to walk around advertising it? Well, I didn't. Obviously."

"I know that, what do you take me for?"

After that, Li Po, not the poet but the tattoo of his name, became Yasmeen's barometer for men. It was how she gauged who was and wasn't worth her time. If the guy was hot but a little rusty on his poetry, she went easier on him. If he tried to bluff his way through or impress her with some bloated, academic-sounding jargon but didn't have a royal clue whatsoever, her bullshit detector kicked in and she immediately dumped him. In any case, Li Po was really for her. The tattoo. It wasn't for some random guy to approve or not approve.

❋

Elliot nudged Yasmeen in the ribs. "What's the most memorable thing you've ever experienced? I mean, something that really knocked your socks off."

She couldn't think of much. She hadn't done Europe like her friends with trust funds. She hadn't seen the Taj Mahal or Stonehenge or the Great Wall of China, except in magazines or in other people's travel albums. Lake Louise was the best she could come up with on the spur of the moment.

"Good one," he said as though she were a student who required encouragement. "All that turquoise water. Just fabulous."

"I must have taken about a billion pictures from every possible angle, but I could never quite capture the true colour, you know?"

"I'm just happy to be here," interrupted Sam, with the awe of an infant discovering her hands for the first time. "It's so incredible, all of it."

Paulussie bellowed out to Tommy, still perched on his rock. "*Kaapaa*! Bring the beans and some bannock. We need to eat."

Tommy lifted his baseball cap and rubbed his forehead with the back of his wrist. He thought for a minute, then put the cap back on his head. Chucking his half-smoked cigarette sideways, he ducked inside the tent, emerging, moments later, with a wiry black fishing net draped over his arm.

Elliot's eyes lit up. "Now you're talking, buddy!" He rubbed his hands vigorously together.

Jimmy and Silasie ran to catch up with Tommy, nipping at his feet like restless pups. "*Iqalutsiuriarumavunga*! I want to fish, too," they squealed, chasing him down to the shoreline. Elliot and Paulussie jumped into their rubber boots and caught up to them.

Yasmeen watched from the campfire as the men waded knee-deep into the water, casting the net wide. She'd never seen people honestly earn their food before, actually go out and hunt for their dinner. City people had their favourite haunts, supermarkets and bakeries and butcher shops. There were *poissonneries* and farmers' markets. If it wasn't around the corner, it was only a bus ride away. All you had to do was decide, and there was much to choose from behind the glass display counters: artisanal cheeses, cool French pastry, Chorizo, sausages, and a hundred varieties of mushroom; long sweet peppers and wrinkled black olives floating in brine. There were imported vinegars and bottles of first-pressed oil, there were chocolate truffles and exotic coffees and bagels and crusty loaves of bread hot out of the oven. You just had to load it into your grocery cart. The only hunting people did in the city was for a parking spot or for the cash in their wallets.

She hugged her knees into her chest and shuddered as a dark stiff breeze skipped across the hollow of her spine. A spark from the fire popped and flew into the dusky air like a star going nova.

Voices shot up from the water as the men splashed around the net, the darkened silhouettes pulling and tugging the slippery weight of what was flapping and flailing inside. The children leapt out of the water, shouting *Iris, get a bucket, get a bucket!* and soon everyone, including Yasmeen, was gathered at water's edge watching the spectacle. Cigarette screwed into the corner of his mouth, Paulussie knelt with his knife and slit the giant fish from head to tail in one fluid motion. They carried their excitement back to the blazing bonfire, sharing the fresh raw catch around the circle. Yasmeen watched Tommy slurp back his waggling morsel.

"*Mamaqtuq*," he said, rolling it around in his mouth. "Very tasty."

Yasmeen lunged for a piece and passed the plate along. Iris shook her head politely, pulling a clean handkerchief from her

Voices shot up from the water as the men splashed around

pocket. She spread it out on a small flat rock and laid down the handful of blueberries she had collected while they searched for kindling. One by one she nibbled them down.

Tommy belched as he stuffed more fish into his mouth. He gorged on it with great pleasure, the way Yasmeen enjoyed a good prime rib with Yorkshire pudding. She closed her eyes and pushed beyond her squeamishness, biting into the cold squishy sliver in her hand. It slipped effortlessly down her throat. She was surprised at how fresh it tasted. Like the ocean. The burping and farting of Paulussie and the children, their thanks for what the great earth had provided for them, seemed a natural part of the occasion.

A honking convoy of geese startled her. She gazed up at their ragged formation, arcing into the sky's darkening vortex, as though she had never seen a bird before or the undisturbed eloquence of nature, everything rolling along as it should, as it was meant to be. In perfect time. She felt a stirring at the base of her spine as though a cobra that had been tightly curled there all her life were finally uncoiling. The voices around the fire had evaporated and her shoulder blades released, and an immense pleasure took root and bloomed inside of her. She thought about the people who had once made do with a piece of flint and a simple harpoon, people whose spirit required nothing more than a raw scrap from the earth or sea, simple and unembellished.

"Earth to Yasmeen ... Hey you, dreamer over there ... Yasmeen!"

"Huh? What??"

"I said, are you in for marshmallows?" Elliot was peeling a melty, blistered one from the blackened tip of his skewer. He offered it to her. She shook her head.

"I'll take it," said Sam.

"You know, the one thing missing here," he said, "is a decent ski slope." He deliberately brushed Yasmeen's shoulder to hand Sam the marshmallow.

It seemed a stupid thing to say, a comment that didn't apply here. Yasmeen caught Iris sneaking a look at Paulussie who was picking fish out of his teeth and searching his pocket for cigarettes. Her face was frozen into its usual half-smile. Probably, Yasmeen mused, she thought exactly the same thing about what Elliot had said. Saqijuvik wasn't a winter resort where after a full day on the hill you headed to the knotty-pine lodge for a cup of hot chocolate. It was a primal place where people didn't manipulate nature for their own benefit but, rather, lived in harmony with it. Yasmeen felt a cold drop of rain on her hand.

Tommy said, "Okay, enough waiting." He pulled a bottle from his jacket, uncapped it and passed it to Paulussie.

Paulussie beamed. "That's my man." He curled his stubby fingers around the bottle and took a slug. He swallowed down a second and third gulp before handing it off to Elliot.

"Thanks, old buddy. You too, Tommy." Elliot toasted them with the lip of the bottle.

Paulussie wiped his mouth with his coat sleeve. His eyes gleamed as he stared into the fire. "An Inuk becomes a man when he kills his first polar bear. I became a man when I was thirteen years old."

Except for the rasping wind everything was quiet. No one blinked or moved or uttered a word, their faces radiant in the blaze of the fire.

"Father was very proud of me. He said, 'To have killed the Great One from the land at such a young age. Now you are a hunter like me and your grandfather and your great-grandfather.' Everyone was so happy, and we sang and danced and ate that bear until we were all tired and fell asleep."

In the distance, a faint streak of lightning flickered. A strong wind blew the flame sideways, flattening it out before it shot upright again. Eerie shadows floated across their faces.

"There's some mountains closer to the other coast," Paulussie continued. "They call that place Tuurngait. It means 'spirits.'"

"Oh, I think I read about that," interrupted Sam.

Yasmeen glowered at her.

"Probably in *National Geographic*. If memory serves me right, the good spirits heal sickness and help the hunters have a good hunt." She looked to Paulussie for confirmation, but he was still wedged in a past memory. She paused a moment and carried on. "I heard they use special rituals to fight against the evil spirits and that the evil spirits can sometimes even possess humans." She glanced around the circle, pleased with her contribution.

Paulussie waved impatiently for the bottle. "It was around there that I saw the bear," he said. "Even though there weren't supposed to be any at that time." The rain was hopping down in splotches.

"What about us, we don't get any?" Jacqueline grumbled. She switched to her sultry voice and stuck out her chest. "C'mon, boys. Pass."

"It's going to pour any minute," said Elliot. "Maybe it's time to move this inside."

Iris stood up and brushed the dirt off her jeans. "Good idea."

The children tagged each other and ran for the tent, yelping and bounding like wolverines, their cries piercing the darkness. The others scrambled around gathering up the blankets and dishes, trying to beat the sky before it opened up, but it was already too late. Rain was washing through Yasmeen's hair and eyelashes, draining down her collar and neck. She buried her head under an arm and made a run for it, drenched pant legs clinging to her skin.

In the girls' tent, Sam and Iris rolled out their sleeping bags while Yasmeen towelled off, fingering the water out of her ears. Through the mouth of the tent she saw that Paulussie hadn't moved at all. He was still outside in the veiling downpour, a solitary serene figure by the doused campfire, knees hugged into his chest. The weather seemed inconsequential to him, a minor inconvenience, just part of the routine. He sat perfectly still in the hammering rain, the empty bottle lying beside him.

Yasmeen lowered the tent flap. She peeled off her damp clothes and zipped herself into bed. It was so lushly dark she couldn't tell whether her eyes were open or closed. When her pupils adjusted she noticed Jacqueline wasn't in her sleeping bag. She wondered whether she was off doing it in the boys' tent with Tommy, the way she imagined it was in the old days when they humped each other in the igloo regardless of who was around.

She thought of the day they passed Tommy in the truck just after their arrival, the little stirring in her he had caused unwittingly, even before she saw his face. She recalled his tanned arm dangling casually over the side of the pickup, fingers curled around a half-smoked cigarette. Her knees weakened just thinking about it.

Hands had always been a thing with her. She felt they said something about the person they belonged to. That day in the truck—she'd noticed Tommy's weren't the fair, manicured hands of some of the men she had dated back home. They were the sort that built things out of nothing and were nicked and scarred and rough to the touch. They were the hands in her erotic dreams she never spoke of, not even to Morgan, her best friend, who, now that she was in graduate school doing her master's in women's studies, would have accused Yasmeen of having a retrograde gene.

Yasmeen had a soft spot for big, square work hands, gritty, earth-smelling hands, hands that could shove a woman without intending to. She wondered what Tommy's felt like on Jacqueline's body, whether they were rough or gentle and how they teased or terrified her. She imagined his hot intimate breath, his fingers twirling her hair. She thought of them stroking her thighs as her bosom swelled.

63

When Yasmeen opened her eyes it was morning. The air in the enclosed tent was cold and scaly, and rain was streaming down the canvas walls. Jacqueline was still missing.

She glanced over at Iris, snoring lightly, tortoise shell glasses folded by her head. Even asleep, her short, dull hair remained neatly parted and combed to the side. She had a bland, pota-to-coloured face with raisin lips that tapered to a point and barely moved when she spoke, and a furry birthmark by her ear in the shape of a leaf. There was a profound sadness about her, the sadness of a woman midway through life and alone, with no idea how she got there. Yasmeen pictured her with a cup of Red Rose tea and lemon, knitting Christmas scarves for a multitude of nieces and nephews who never sent out thank-you cards.

The tent pitched from side to side. She was suddenly aware of a kerfuffle outside, a scuffle of feet, a spate of voices. The surging wind carried their sounds erratically on its back, levels fluctuating.

"Knock knock, anyone home?" Elliot's head appeared under the open tent flap. He ducked inside, rain-soaked. "Holy crap, it's brutal out there. We might have to build an ark."

Iris bolted upright, fully clothed from the night before. "What's going on?" She breathed on her glasses and wiped them with a corner of her shirt before putting them on.

"Looks like the storm's getting worse," Yasmeen said.

Elliot shrugged off his coat and shook the water from his hair. Some of the spray landed on Yasmeen. "So? Can I enter your humble abode?"

She waved him in with forced enthusiasm.

He sat at the foot of Yasmeen's sleeping bag, unconcerned with his lack of boundaries. "I'm guessing we're stuck here 'til things let up."

Aware of the voices, Sam began shifting around in her sleeping bag. She rolled over, dishevelled, and fingered the gunk from her eyes. Her pyjamas, an oversized plaid shirt, was pretty much what she wore every day regardless of the occasion. "Man, oh man," she croaked. She sat up and slouched forward, adjusting her bra cups. "So what's on the menu this morning?" She licked her fingers and smoothed down her slept-in hair. No matter what she did to tweak her appearance, she always had the look of a medieval barmaid.

"There's still the leftover fish from yesterday." Elliot winked.

"Oh, yum. Didn't we bring any eggs?"

There were no eggs and the fish was long gone but they had the makings of a decent breakfast, a loaf of white bread, peanut butter, a dozen plastic packets of store-bought jam and a communal thermos of tea. The whole gang was crowded into the girls' tent. Paulussie's boys were horsing around, punching each other, knocking things over. Jacqueline was there too, looking perfectly refreshed, like she'd just had the sleep of her life. Yasmeen peered at Tommy and decided that yes, they had probably done it last night. Paulussie reviewed the game plan to sit tight. They weren't going anywhere, not with the weather so vile.

After breakfast, Yasmeen and Iris loaded the dirty plates and cups from the previous night into the bucket they had used for the fish, and dashed outside to rinse them. Yasmeen was desperate to pee. With the rain so unforgiving she didn't care that there wasn't a tree or scrim of tall grass to hide behind. Squatting a few feet from the tent she released her muscles and let out a swift jet of ammonia-smelling urine. It steamed on contact with the muddy ground. She dabbed herself with a clump of moss and dropped it over her piddle. She couldn't remember a time she had emptied so completely.

Elliot and Sam were amusing the children with rock-paper-scissors when she returned. After a while, Tommy and Paulussie got bored and left. Yasmeen lay on top of her sleeping bag, staring up at the sloped ceiling, watching the rain slither down. It was a spacious tent, well built, functional. It served its occupants well: no one was getting dripped on, no one appeared to be adversely affected by the inclement weather. She made up a song about the day, trying to make everything rhyme with rain. When she tired of that she invented finger games to play. She felt a twinge of arthritis in her joints, or maybe not, maybe it was just a hyper-awareness of the complexity of her hands, their push against inertia. Things she had never noticed before. She wove a braid in her hair, wound it up into a bun and shook it loose again. She had no interest in what time it was. Unlike Jacqueline and Sam who needed outside stimulation, constantly running between the two tents, Yasmeen enjoyed the simplicity of doing nothing.

Elliot tried to be the life of the party. He rattled off some random facts about himself, like how dark chocolate made him sneeze and how because his body lacked certain trace minerals he had to add twenty drops of a special liquid to his morning glass of water in order not to get dehydrated. Information that drew zero empathy from his audience. He launched into a series of knock-knock jokes but by then no one was paying attention anymore.

Paulussie's kids sprawled out on the floor and prepared to play the mouth-pull game, each with a finger hooked between his opponent's cheek and teeth. One shouted go, and they instantly began pulling and stretching each other's mouths until their faces went purple. Iris cupped her hands over her ears, trying to deflect the noise. She reached into her bag and produced a packable yellow rain poncho, which she swiftly unfolded. In a flash her head was through, and she was pulling the oversized cape, with its sharp creases, down over her body. She lifted the flap of the tent and disappeared into the rain.

"Shut the heck up, you two, or I'll beat you myself!" Elliot bellowed over the ruckus. He waved a deck of cards at Yasmeen. "How about a game of Crazy Eights?"

"I suppose," she said. "But I'm bloody freezing." The accrued dampness in the tent made her desperate to pee again. Unable to face the rain, she hopped into her sleeping bag, praying its warmth would lessen the need.

"We could also do what these people do to keep warm," he offered.

"Very funny," she said.

Jimmy was ear-down on the floor, his brother's finger still jammed in his mouth. Silasie was laughing so hard the corded veins in his neck stood out. Jimmy, stamping his heels into the ground, begged his mercy.

"Cut it out, boys!" shouted Elliot. "I mean it! Come play cards with us."

The boys shrugged and rolled off the floor, their shirts cock-eyed, their bare brown stomachs exposed. Jimmy was rubbing his jaw trying to bring sensation back, laughing and whimpering at the same time. Silasie picked a booger out of his nose, rolled it into a ball and flung it at the tent wall. It made a "tick" when it hit. He mumbled something to his brother and the two of them ran outside, forgetting to put on their coats, or not bothering to. Like it was only rain.

When only the two of them were left, Elliot unzipped Yasmeen's sleeping bag and climbed in beside her. He didn't really ask, he just did it, and she didn't say not to. Staring at the narrow bridge of his nose she noticed his lashes were long and dark, like a woman's. When she mentioned it, casually, he said you wouldn't know it but these eyes have gone through the mill. He explained how he'd had an operation when he was three to uncross them and how five years of wearing Coke-bottle lenses restored his vision to a perfect 20/20. Nothing gets past these babies anymore, if you get what I mean.

He drew a Kit Kat bar from his pocket, broke off half and offered it to her. Instead of saying no thanks she told him, "Just so you know, this doesn't change anything."

The first guy she ever slept with was Nathan, an English major who dreamed of moving to New York City and becoming a writer like his idol, Frank O'Hara. When they started dating, Nathan confessed that what he loved most was the honeymoon phase of a relationship, the exciting, erotic period of discovery. He loved the idea of love, loved falling in love, loved the idea of desire, craved it, lusted after it, he just plain loved women. Yasmeen loved that he had chosen her. He said, "Call me N from now on." He passed the Li Po test with flying colours.

Her Middle Eastern heritage was what he loved best about her, said it was intriguing and exotic even though she herself didn't think so. Yasmeen fell for his undiluted passion. She daydreamed about a future with him, the two of them living in a more meaningful realm than the average couple with a car and a credit card. She promised to take any old job just to support him, *his* career was what mattered. Before him, she never thought of giving up her life for a guy. But this was different. He was an artist. If they made a go of it, it wouldn't be an ordinary life.

He was moody but charming. He didn't make the big effort her mother expected of men, properly courting her with flowers, paying her half of the restaurant bill, but when he had pocket money he bought her second-hand books from The Word, his favourite shop, and incessantly repeated that he would buy her the moon if he could.

Being with him was like standing at the precipice. All she wanted to do was jump. She was never sure if he would catch her, but that was part of the excitement. The first time they went to bed he took it slow. After he came she lay with him contentedly, the bed sheets tangled between her legs. He had taken her to electrifying orgasm. In the morning he fluffed her pillow and brought her his folder of poems to read. "Tell me what you honestly think," he said. She didn't imagine they would disappoint her.

They did. Imitative and derivative, his metaphors lacked wings. She thought of lying to protect his ego but decided instead to be forthright, thinking he would recognize just how much he needed her, how much his inspiration would be fuelled by her. It seemed like a good idea. She blurted it out. "O'Hara's poems sound like he's writing on the fly, like . . . like meditations in an emergency," she said. "Yours sound, well, forced. You need to find your own voice." Already she felt her calling—as his indispensable muse strumming her lyre over him. Feeding him his art. She settled into the role.

They continued having sex but nothing ever came close to the first time. He spent his days at the typewriter pecking at the keys and crumpling up paper. She took it as progress. The first time he couldn't get it up, she reassured him that it was because he was too focused on his work, that if he loosened up things would pick up again. She said it didn't matter anyway, it was only sex, their relationship was more solid than that. He mumbled and pushed her away.

The distance between them grew. Discouraged but determined, she stoked his ego, coming on to him voraciously, rocking her hips back and forth even though it felt like sandpaper between them. Once, he swelled momentarily but deflated before he could get any satisfaction. She told him she adored him but he turned away from her, toward the window, and complained that her rhythm was off.

Every night he had an excuse for going out. Whenever she asked if she should wait up he'd say, "Suit yourself, it's your decision." The dream of having something binding and sacred between them, marriage or otherwise, was pretty much over even before Mary showed up in their lives. Who knew where he found her—under what rock? One afternoon, Yasmeen let herself into his place and found the woman lying naked on their bed, his 35-mm camera perched on a tripod and aimed between her legs.

"It's not what it looks like," said Nathan.

It was like waking up from a catnap with a sudden jerk.

"I'm trying out ideas for the cover of my book."

Mary rolled up and pulled the quilt around her shoulders. She sat on the edge of the bed, one leg crossed over the other, glossy toenails like red Smarties. She lit a cigarette and blew the smoke in Yasmeen's direction.

Yasmeen exercised enormous self-restraint, though some of her anger leaked out anyway. "You're such a fucking cliché," she said, rifling though her purse for his stupid key. Barely holding it together. The room smelled like cunt. She aimed for the woman but ended up cracking N's expensive camera lens.

When Yasmeen woke, she was alone in the tent. The last thing she remembered was playing a hand of cards with Elliot. His fake Rolex was beside her on the floor. She wormed out of the sleeping bag and pulled on her boots.

The rain was cutting sideways, whipping the river into man-sized waves. Her boots made squelching noises as she dashed for the boys' tent. When she arrived Jacqueline and the teachers were sitting passively on one side as Tommy and the boys rooted through the cooler, stuffing anything they could find into their mouths. The place was helter-skelter, things just dropped or left in a sticky gob wherever—plastic cups of half-drunk apple juice, empty jam packets, bread slices with half-moon bites taken out of them. Tommy had a jaw full of food and was laughing at nothing in particular. Paulussie was on his knees working to untangle the fishing net. A finger of ash hung from his cigarette.

"We should go out and turn over the boats," he told Tommy. His waggling lips caused the ash to fall. He brushed it away with a quick swat. "Come here, my big man," he called out to his eldest child.

Who knew what time it was or what was in store for them. Who knew how many millimetres of rain had fallen, or the numbers on the barometer, or the exact velocity of the wind outside. Who knew what Paulussie and Tommy knew about getting them out of there and back to safety.

Elliot made space for Yasmeen to sit. "Right about now my honey bucket seems like the height of luxury," he whispered into her ear.

Ordinarily she would have agreed, but what was so great about her broken shower nozzle or the half-hearted water pressure in her taps? Plus it was Elliot saying it. She didn't want to encourage him.

"I think we should start rationing," he said. "Who knows how long we'll be stuck out here in the M.O.N."

"M.O.N?" she said.

"Middle of nowhere."

His words made her smile. She wondered if her mother was channelling her thoughts through Elliot. "Could be we're somehow related."

He gave her a funny look, like what the hell was she trying to say?

"Never mind. What's Paulussie's feeling?"

71

"He says what they all say. Aatsuuk, I don't know. Maybe. When you're hard-pressed for answers around here, you'll find that nobody ever knows anything."

In spite of Elliot's cynicism, Yasmeen trusted Paulussie's instincts for self-preservation. His gentle, fatherly ways appealed to her, how soft yet firm he was with his children, how he knew intuitively when to loosen his grip on them and when to pull back—though mainly he left them to figure things out for themselves. She thought of her own father, how he gave her wings and taught her how to enjoy the finer moments of life, whenever he had the chance. He loved blowing a bundle at Christmas to buy his kids the latest big-ticket electronic gadget, something that came in a box the size of a refrigerator. Something that would be the envy of every other family on the block. She remembered tearing off the paper and ribbons while he sat back, dew-eyed, holding the camera in his hand.

"Just look at them," said Elliot, flabbergasted. "If we don't hide some of this food and a couple of rolls of toilet paper, they'll go through it in no time."

"This is your honest assessment of them? And you keep coming back? Why? I mean, if there's nothing to …"

"My dear, I have only one motto here. It's simple. It's practical. Better safe than sorry. It's worked for me this long."

The day stretched into two and then three. Supplies had dwindled but the men fought off the rain and the gaping maw of the river to put food in everyone's mouths. The thrashing waters teemed with speckled trout. Meanwhile, the women sprinted out in shifts, using their shirts as slings to carry back fresh, cold blueberries. Yasmeen could see how the old imperative, survival, drove them. People were wet and tired of each other, but no one went hungry.

Sometimes when it was really coming down and they were trapped in the tents, Yasmeen would lower the flap that covered their plastic transparent window just to watch the grey, blinding, suffocating veils of water. It made her think of a sandstorm. She loved the idea that although the weather was conspiring against them, they were fighting back and winning, in spite of the wind. Its brute force. Their nylon tents were holding up.

Their little nylon tents.

On the fourth day the sun returned with a vengeance—as though nothing at all had happened. For the first time in days Yasmeen could see the sky, delphinium-blue against the razor-sharp horizon. A droning plane crossed it in a long, straight line until it disappeared behind a fleecy cloud.

They joked and sang as they packed up the campsite. Paulussie and Tommy, assisted by the boys but mainly by Elliot, prepared the boats. The women folded the tents and loaded up the supplies. The water was still rough but not treacherous, and the tide had turned in their favour.

Elliot whistled the theme from *Gilligan's Island* as everyone hopped into the boats. The crews waved to each other light-heartedly. Tommy leapt off his canoe and gave it a big push away from the land. Paulussie shoved theirs too, wading through the water to catch up to them. He climbed back on with a dolphin-tail splash, his solid mass rocking the boat. Elliot started up the motor and stepped away to let Paulussie navigate.

Paulussie kept a close eye on the changing surface of the water. Yasmeen knew from her reading that he wasn't just winging it, he was carefully calculating the force of the waves as they hit the hull and splashed over the side, collecting in a pool at the bottom of the boat. Elliot took instruction from Paulussie like a trooper, advising them when to shift their weight from one side

73

to the other. They travelled this way until twilight set in with its dramatic show of sky, a feathery pink-and-black expanse.

As the village floated into view Yasmeen could see that the moon had cut a bright swath along the water, like a road leading them home. She surveyed the scalloped shoreline with its boxy structures, its cluster of dwellings including hers with the flaking green door, a handful of twinkling porch lights.

Paulussie cut the motor. Yasmeen searched for Tommy's canoe but couldn't see it anywhere. She eyed Elliot but he shrugged uncertainly. Paulussie pointed to a constellation of rocks poking out of the water, hemming them in. He ordered everyone off and onto one of them, large and flat enough to stand on. The water flashed its foamy underside.

Elliot climbed off first, steadying himself against the thrust of the bay before reaching his hand out to Yasmeen. "Concentrate on your feet, not the water."

"I can do it myself," she said pulling her hand away. The boys blew past her, barking like seals.

Clutching her coat collar with both hands, Iris lost her balance on the gummy surface. Elliot shot his arm out just in time to save her from falling. She blushed and said thank you.

When everyone was safe Elliot went to help Paulussie pivot the boat and free it from the obstructing rocks. The kids fooled around, tagging and pushing each other, unaware of the gravity of the situation, or else fully aware but unfazed, having dealt with it numerous times before and gone home to a good night's sleep, the way Yasmeen did after a healthy day in the country. Paulussie was remarkable. He wrestled the boat out and got them all back on board without a single casualty.

The village drifted toward them like a sleepy whale. Tommy's canoe was already docked by the time Paulussie arrived with Yasmeen's crew. Elliot made himself useful, hauling the supplies off, helping the men flip the boats over. A crowd had gathered onshore to wave them in, leathery faces with eyes like beacons. Everybody was shaking hands with everybody. Yasmeen was beginning to understand it was customary to do this when people returned from somewhere. She noticed the radio guy, Joanasi, meandering toward her with his hand extended. "So, you made it home," he said, not as a question but as a simple matter of fact.

FIVE

Yasmeen discovered the pleasures of having the radio on all day, its reassuring presence. It happened by accident, the day after they returned from camp. She was dusting and tossing around ideas for the first day of school, and though all the talk was in Inuktitut and she couldn't make out a word, she recognized its soothing effect on her. It was the timbre of the voice, a particular vibration that struck a chord in her and gave her the sensation of being in the close company of a friend. It was like sharing an intimate space. There were no motormouth traffic girls, no manic sports reporters racing though hockey scores. This radio was so low-key that sometimes there was no talking at all, the dead air just hanging there for however long it went on, until a stammer or a spluttering cough broke the silence.

Something curious caught her ear, the way the announcer took a long time to exhale after he inhaled, like he was holding onto a thought that he didn't ever want to let go. It sounded like the voice of someone who enjoyed letting the velvet cigarette smoke linger in his lungs before releasing it. She was almost certain it was Joanasi's.

Just as she was deciding that yes, it was probably him announcing Friday's upcoming Bingo Night, one of those lemmings Elliot had mentioned on the plane darted past her, right in her own house. She chased it into the kitchen, following the patter of feet. It had a tapered snout and a short tail like the one Frank had shown in his slides, and was barely the size of a human hand. Her mind went into the dizzying logistics of how to corner it. She wasn't sure what she would do after she did. One thing at a time, she thought. She grabbed the broom and swung it haphazardly. The pesky thing scurried past her into the living room.

Yasmeen held the broom the way her father's favourite movie star, Errol Flynn, held his dueling sword. She advanced on the rodent, part of her recognizing how ridiculous she looked, but she didn't know how else to rout it out and she couldn't let it run around indefinitely.

Her ears perked up when she heard that Mick Jagger was up next. She didn't catch what song, but it wasn't so important. What was important was this, now. Figuring out a strategy. She tried to imagine what Joanasi, a radio personality but probably also a hunter, would do in *her* place, facing the same shifty creature. Would he skewer it between the eyes? Behead it with the full length of the broomstick? For sure, afterwards, he'd have the wherewithal to do what was necessary—sweep it along the floor to the front door and then outside, but not like it was nothing. He'd have respect for it. He'd leave it like a gift in a special place where a bigger animal would go looking for food. He wouldn't feel the least bit guilty about it, knowing he was doing what was necessary to keep the cycle of life going. This could all be a load of crap, though. A romantic notion fed by *The Nature of Things*. She shook her head.

"Come out, you little shit." Her body stiffened, waiting for the lemming to resurface. She waited and waited. There was no sign of him anywhere. She thought of how bats could squeeze through holes the size of a quarter, settling permanently in a building's insulation. Did lemmings have the same expertise?

77

She wasn't keen on the idea of her intruder becoming a permanent resident in her pipes or walls, skittering up and down and around. Keeping her awake nights.

A lemming year, Elliot had said.

She waited it out while the afternoon light softened, casting a pinky glow on the walls. She breathed the way a yoga instructor once taught her to do, deeply, from her diaphragm. It put her solidly in the moment, allowing her to focus on the battleground, which wasn't a battleground at all but a benign arrangement of furniture and belongings. In her tranquil state she spotted him on the other side of the room, beady eyes gleaming beneath a sock that had strayed from her laundry basket. They were looking straight at her.

She wondered what he was communicating in the language of his gaze. Perhaps that he was only a lemming, with no ulterior motives except the primary one, survival. It seemed like that's what he was telling her. That he wasn't a dangerous polar bear that would maul her with a swipe of his paw. That he wasn't planning to rear up on hindquarters, or bare his teeth at her. No, he was defenseless. He had nothing on her. Nothing compared to her warm house, her drawer full of sharpened knives. She could wolf him down in two bites if she really wanted to.

The more she thought about it, the more she relaxed. She felt waves of guilt, first for wielding the broom like a weapon; second for all the times she and Morgan had strapped firecrackers to the backs of toads for no reason at all except to revel in the confetti of their exploded body parts.

The lemming's eyes were still trained on her. Give me the heave ho, they were saying, but please spare my life. For a fraction of a second she thought of wrapping him in shiny paper like a fancy Christmas gift, sticking on a bow and presenting him to Elliot, the lemming expert. One of the bumper crop, she could write in curlicue calligraphy inside the card. Funny as it was, it was stupid and cruel. She would never do it. This lemming had the right, like everything and everyone, to live his ephemeral life and die of natural causes, out on the land among his own.

Yasmeen tiptoed over, careful not to scare him. Cautiously she lifted the sock off. He looked up at her almost apologetically when she told him to go on now, take a powder, disappear. He blinked. He blinked again. "Go have a life or something," she repeated. Lightly tapping him with the back of the broom she shooed him along the rug. When she got to the door she opened it wide and watched him scurry toward the incoming light.

SIX

The portable that had been assigned as her interim classroom wasn't like anything she'd ever seen on her teaching practicums down south. In addition to desks and chalkboard, this one had a small kitchen at the back with a fridge and stove and a counter stocked with bowls and oversized canisters of instant soup mix.

She began by giving the place a good airing out. She jogged the corners of the windows and lifted those that weren't stuck or painted shut. With a set of Magic Markers she drew a welcome sign for the door. She hadn't planned what she would write, she just let instinct guide her. She knew that whatever appeared on the page would be right. And it was. Yasmeen's Arctic All-Stars. It had a nice ring to it. It made everyone sound like a winner. She made yellow name cards for the half-dozen students on her mimeographed list and then practised pronouncing their exotic-sounding names. Names she had never heard before. She hoped that on the first day she'd be able to say them all without mangling them. *Ulayu. Audlaluk. Qalingo.* She jotted them down on index cards for future reference in case she ever had kids of her own, which was highly unlikely but still in the realm of possibility.

She counted herself lucky not to have a class of thirty-five like her colleagues who had landed jobs at the big comprehensive schools in Montreal. The things she could do with only six! The creativity she could tap into! She wanted to roll up her sleeves and get started as soon as possible.

She wrote the date on the chalkboard in her best handwriting and moved the desks into a semi-circle. On each chair she left three sharpened pencils, a pen, an eraser, a binder with lined paper, and a soup bowl—everything a student needed for a first day of high school.

It was because of Morgan's father, an off-the-cuff remark he had made, that Yasmeen decided to become a teacher. It was the way he said it, the forlorn look on his face. Mr. McEwen had a shitty desk job, as Morgan kept reminding her, and he always came home hyper-depressed even though it paid a bundle. "Who knows, maybe he's boinking his secretary," Morgan suggested. As though she needed some excitement in her life. Yasmeen once overheard her parents say that the reason Morgan's father had gone out and bought himself a red, fully loaded Pontiac Trans Am was because he was having a midlife crisis. She always thought if Morgan really wanted family drama, why not take some of hers; there was certainly enough of it to go around.

The girls had dyed their hair black that summer. They wore it long and parted down the middle and wore liquid eyeliner and matching black chokers with a silver buckle in the centre, all that black accentuating their paleness, which was the point. It was a stinking hot day. They were in their string bikinis, pigging out on Morgan's mother's famous pickle-in-the-middle sandwiches. Even when it was sweltering they were never allowed to lounge around in their swimsuits at Yasmeen's. There was no prancing about half-naked in *her* house.

Mr. McEwen had taken a sick day. He was sitting across the kitchen table from them in a velour bathrobe, pretending to read the obituaries while they babbled on about their dream careers, high-paying jobs with benefits that included travelling around with bands like The Cure and The Velvet Underground. Wouldn't it be awesome, they kept repeating. Morgan's dad cleared his throat and lowered his newspaper so that Yasmeen could see only his eyes and the bridge of his nose. She noticed a real sadness in the way he looked at her. It was like Morgan wasn't even in the room with them. He stared for a long time. "Teaching is a much nobler pursuit," he said, and returned to his obituaries.

His gaze remained. It left its print in the air the way a sparkler emblazons the darkness in its wake. The idea didn't seem at all strange to Yasmeen, as though it had always been sitting quietly inside of her, biding its time, waiting for something to release it.

The fire-red button on the telephone, the emergency button, was flashing.

"Lock up the portable and meet me at your place," whispered Iris.

"What's going on?"

"Hurry, I'll explain when I see you." She hung up.

Yasmeen threw her plan book into her bag and collected the rest of her things. It was dusk and the wind had picked up. Rushing to beat Iris to her place she stumbled but managed to stay upright, her big rubber boots kicking up a spray of rocks in her path.

She leaned into the handrail to catch her breath. "What's up?"

"Close the door," said Iris, lining up her boots like dutiful warriors. She crossed into the living room and twisted the blinds shut. "Better yet, lock it."

"Can't." Yasmeen hung her jacket and bag on one of the hooks of her coat rack, a painted two-by-four nailed to the wall of her entrance. "The lock's been busted since I arrived."

Iris clapped a hand over her mouth. She sank into the couch, little red splotches creeping up her neck. She unzipped her coat and sat it beside her.

"I've put an order in to Maintenance but they said it might be weeks. Anyway, who locks their doors here? Everyone just walks in. I kind of like that about the place." Yasmeen was more preoccupied with the dirt and debris pelting the window. She wondered if winter was about to arrive early. "So, what's all the fuss? Is there a lemming crisis or something? Been there, done that."

"It's not a joke." Iris fiddled with the collar of her shirt. "I've seen this sort of thing in other villages."

She was trying to sound diplomatic but Yasmeen saw through it. "Okay, so what?"

"Bootlegging. There's contraband booze in town." She said it didn't matter how it got there or who brought it up north, the point was it didn't bode well for them.

"Us?"

"The whites," said Iris, rising to peek through the slats of the blind. She lowered her voice as though someone might be listening. "Apparently, our friend Tommy's gone off the deep end."

The deep end. What did that amount to, Yasmeen wondered? It sounded like hyperbole, like someone trying to stir up excitement in a one-horse town. "Where's Jacqueline in all this? Can't she calm him down?"

"I can't answer that."

"If it's true, if he's really plastered, I'm sure she can deal with it, they've been together four years, for Pete's sake."

"Elliot called me just before I called you—in case you think I'm exaggerating. Apparently, Tommy made an appearance over there. Going on and on, of course, about the usual."

"The usual?"

"Never mind. We'll need to barricade the door however we can," she said, pushing up her shirtsleeves. "If Elliot's hunch is right he'll be making the rounds, so we're better off sticking together. There's safety in numbers. Now, come and help me."

"Aren't we going a little overboard?" asked Yasmeen.

"Trust me. You can never be too careful at times like this. I've seen too many booze-related incidents, and not pretty ones." Though Yasmeen was skeptical, her own mother's mistrust of drunks and Iris's earnestness tipped the balance on the side of caution. And while her father was never violent or abusive when he drank, he sometimes looked like he could be pushed over the edge.

They hauled her bookcase, with all the heavy books in it, across the floor, leaving behind a pair of dried-up turds. A parting gift from her little friend, Yasmeen supposed. She pinched them into a tissue and tossed them into the honey bucket while Iris scanned the room for extra fortification. They dragged over the couch and armchair and coffee table. They piled the four kitchen chairs on top of the couch. It made Yasmeen think of a bad horror movie, where the heroine goes nuts barricading herself in the house, trying to fend off a bug-eyed, three-headed alien. When they were done they collapsed on the floor in exhaustion. Red as a tulip, Iris attempted a joke about a Catholic, a businessman, and an atheist waiting in line at the pearly gates. She got most of it wrong but laughed casually, almost light-heartedly. It seemed completely out of character. Yasmeen chuckled and went to put the kettle on.

Blam. Something hit the house. It sent a shock wave through Yasmeen. The teacups slipped from her hands and shattered on the floor. When she dashed back into the living room she found Iris with all the blood drained out of her face, slowly backing away from the mammoth fist that had burst through the door, wrenching it off its hinges. Their blockade was destroyed, furniture strewn about the room. Tommy was glaring through bloodshot eyes. He was clutching a 26-ouncer, a dark stain spread over the crotch of his jeans.

He tried to climb over the wreckage but his foot caught on the leg of a chair and he tripped and fell backwards onto his tailbone. He flew into a rage. "Fuck you, you fucking bitches!"

He rolled onto all fours and wobbled upright. The floor quaked under the solid weight of him. He kicked the chair and staggered toward the kitchen with his bottle. He banged into the refrigerator, eyeballed it and waggled a finger. "Watch it or I'll kick your sorry white ass all the way to Salluit!"

Suddenly the idea of addressing the fridge as though it were human seemed hilarious to him. He laughed and burped concurrently. When the joke got old, he set aside the bottle to massage his injured fist. He licked the blood off his knuckles.

Yasmeen hoped he'd forget his motives for showing up and go home and sleep it off. They could chalk it up to a bad night and let bygones be bygones.

Iris dropped her shoulders and relaxed. She looked at Tommy. "How about some tea?" she said. "And maybe a game of cards."

Tommy's eyebrow arched up. "Don't you fuck with my little brother, do you hear me?" He took a swipe at Iris but missed and fell on the floor again. "You called the cops, you little fucker, didn't you?"

Yasmeen looked at Iris but saw that she was just as puzzled as she was. Iris regained her composure and gently repeated the offer of tea. "Sit down and relax a little," she said.

Tommy's eyes narrowed to slits. He vaulted upright and pushed his face into hers. "Shut the fuck up, you ugly fuck."

Yasmeen thought for sure Iris was quivering inside. She wondered how she was keeping it together. She, herself, was on the edge of fear but not terrified. More jumpy than afraid. At the same time she felt a kind of disbelief, a lag between her and the situation, as if the scene involved another set of people and she was just watching it all from a cloud. It didn't seem possible that they wouldn't live to tell the story.

Tommy inched backwards until he was butted up against the wall with nowhere to go. "You come here, you take our land, you call the police on us." He snivelled up a river of snot and tears. "I'm going home now to get my gun and I'm coming back for both you …"

His face changed abruptly, brightening like the sky after a terrible storm. "Ohhh, look who's here? My very best buddy, Joanasi. Qanuippit?"

Qanuingngi, the voice answered back from the opening where Yasmeen's door used to be.

Yasmeen wondered what Joanasi was doing there with a rifle on his back, as though he had just returned from hunting. Was he stopping by because he heard the ruckus inside?

Tommy rose tentatively but fell backwards again, muttering in garbled Inuktitut. He levered himself up a second time, shaky on his feet. "I'm going now," he said. "I'm going now with my good friend, Joanasi." His chest inflated as though he were invincible. He drew in a cavernous breath and kicked his boot high into the air, ramming it down on the broken door. "I'm going, and I'm getting my gun. And I'm coming back for you." He tapped Joanasi on the shoulder as he staggered past him down the steps, coat half-on, half-off.

Joanasi volleyed Yasmeen a look that seemed to say both *sorry* and *I never judge my friends*. What else could he do? She nodded with understanding. She thought ahead to what would happen afterwards, putting herself in Tommy's shoes. She reversed their roles and tried to see it from his point of view. Probably she'd flop into bed and get a good night's sleep and consider everything again in the sober light of day. She'd remember they were

86

friends above all, even though others of the same race had once exploited her. She would lower her head to keep the peace, crawl back without really crawling, contrite but not too contrite. And most likely she'd be forgiven because in his heart of hearts he would understand that *she* really was the victim here.

Later that night, as a precautionary measure, Paulussie went door-to-door collecting the teachers for a sleepover at his house. Yasmeen was pretty sure the storm had blown over and that Paulussie was just trying to appease them. He drew the blinds and invited everyone to find a spot on the floor. In no time, the living room looked like a reprise of their camping trip, a muddle of sleeping bags and toiletries and folksy crocheted quilts. People were tiptoeing and whispering, trying to avoid waking the children and alarming them. Jacqueline was at Tommy's mother's place waiting for things to calm down.

By the time everyone was settled it was nearly two in the morning. Sam brushed her teeth and announced she was hitting the sack; all this excitement was too much for one night. She threw her T-shirt over the lamp to dim the light. Iris got into her sleeping bag with all her clothes on. She tossed this way and that, sighed in frustration, unzipped her sleeping bag and went to get some papers to look over. Voices wafted from the kitchen. Yasmeen's ears perked up.

"You should have seen him," said Elliot. "He completely flipped his gourd."

"Hm," said Sarah.

"I mean, he was worse than I've ever seen him."

Paulussie sighed.

"I actually thought he might kill me."

"The kids." whispered Sarah. "Lower your voice."

It was clear to Yasmeen that they thought Elliot was over-re-acting. Probably he resembled Morgan in his constant need for a crisis, something to remind him that he existed. And Tommy, was he so wrong to lash out? Was it even about right or wrong? There was no denying that the missionaries had had ulterior motives and that the government had forced the Inuit into unfair land deals. Frank had recommended all kinds of reading material on claim agreements, housing, and healthcare in the North and Yasmeen promised herself before leaving Montreal that she'd be different. That she would *make a difference.* She had no interest in integrating her students into a world that exploited them and subtly chipped away at their culture. She intended to keep that promise.

On her way home from the Co-op two days later, Yasmeen spotted something blowing against the provisional door that Paulussie had rigged up for her, a rough piece of plywood on hinges barred with a padlock. She squinted. From a distance it looked like Kleenex. By the time she reached it she saw that it was actually a corner scrap of loose-leaf thumbtacked to the door. She put down her grocery bag and tore it off. Scribbled in blotchy ballpoint, it was smudged where the writer's hand had accidentally rubbed across the ink. "Sorry about the other day. i will fix your door soon," it said. "Lets be friends again, Tommy."

Yasmeen smiled. She made a proud fist and raised it trium-phantly into the air. Yessss! What did I tell you? Though no one was within earshot she sensed a presence, her father close by, cheering her victory.

September 21, 1983
Dear Morgan,

I once read that the Inuit word for white men (*Qallunaat*) means "men (I take that to mean women, too!) with thick eyebrows." I also heard it means "men with large stomachs." Do you think there's a message in it? Am I (and my large, bushy-eyed colleagues) just up here looking to fill an insatiable emptiness—greedy for food, greedy for life, greedy for love even? And if so, why so greedy for a universe of ice, where nothing grows?

Frank told us that the word tundra literally means "nothing." Did you know the tundra (nothing) covers about a fifth of the Earth's surface?

There are only two seasons here. The first is darkness, eternal night, when the drowsing sun barely lifts its head. The other season arrives in a burst, like the blink of an eye. Just enough time for wild flowers and berries to flourish quickly and die just as suddenly (I read that somewhere). I suppose they would call it summer—this warm jet of air, these short-lived weeks of open water and renewal. Next June, when night disappears almost entirely, the village will empty out. White teachers, including me, will go south again. They will board up the school. Against this bald silhouette of earth, families will paddle off in their boats toward the remembered smell of sea and char.

Dear old friend. Please forgive my little poetic foray. It's been a weird couple of days. Hope things are good with you and that your parents aren't driving you insane. Oops, I forgot. My mother's the nut job.

Big hug,
Yasmeen

PS. Apparently, jasmine is most potent after dark when it opens its tiny petals and releases its fragrance into the cool night air. There's a garden buff here named Sam who knows all this stuff. How could I have gone my entire life not knowing this?

SEVEN

The custom of dropping in at all hours, unannounced, quickly grew on Yasmeen. The visitors were mainly curious strangers who had glimpsed her around town, and kids, some she taught and some she didn't. The children arrived in packs. They stayed for ten minutes or an hour, unzipping but never removing their coats. They helped themselves to her board games and colouring books. They lounged on her couch watching whatever was playing on Saqijuvik's one channel, CBC North, with its news reports from Cornerbrook. They drew hearts and stuck them on her fridge. They spoke into their hands, in whispers, occasionally bursting into laughter over a trifle. They trained their eyes on her, watching as she ate dinner or did laundry or baked a pan of brownies. She enjoyed having them around.

One night Elisapie stopped by for a visit. She opened her coat and flashed her new Boy George T-shirt. The brightest of Yasmeen's students, she worked hard in spite of her issues. Elliot had gladly provided the backstory—that she'd gotten pregnant the year before when she was only thirteen and given the baby to her grandmother to raise so she could continue her education.

For half an hour she sat politely on the couch watching TV while Yasmeen corrected spelling tests and drank from an oversized coffee mug that had belonged to her father. Yasmeen observed her discreetly. Like many girls in the village, she wore shiny lip-gloss and a light dusting of blue eye shadow. Eventually the girl wandered over to where Yasmeen had her papers spread out. She dropped down cross-legged onto the floor and said, "You have no kids?" like it was a question.

Yasmeen continued correcting without looking up.

"You're twenty and you got no kids?"

It felt like a weird conversation to be having with her student, like a boundary had been crossed. "Twenty-three, to be exact," she said. As an afterthought she added, "Maybe one day, but not yet. I'd like to do some travelling first." When she looked up, she saw Elisapie's puzzled expression that seemed to say, what planet do you come from, anyway?

On Monday, after a beautiful weekend of Indian summer, Yasmeen walked into a class of students gliding backwards in stocking feet. They were competing to determine who could do the best imitation of Michael Jackson's moonwalk. They'd seen it on *Good Rockin' Tonight*. Yasmeen wondered how the pop star would react to the irony of a satellite dish beaming his popular walk into a place almost as remote as the moon.

Yasmeen clapped her hands. "Okay everyone, back to your seats."

Elisapie asked if they were doing the Community Heroes unit today.

"That's the plan," said Yasmeen. "It's Qalingo's turn to present a special guest. I wonder who it will be." She slung her camera around Salatee's neck and said, "You'll be our photographer for today. Don't forget to take a lot of pictures."

Salatee glowed.

"Okay, let's everyone take out our Duo Tangs and something to write with." She sent them one by one to the pencil sharpener while she went to prepare the soup for recess. As she was filling the big aluminum pot with water, Qalingo strutted in with his visitor.

Qalingo wore his usual dark glasses into class and an Expos baseball cap, one from his vast assortment of hats. Yasmeen was surprised when she saw his guest, the first community hero she actually knew in person. Previously they had interviewed the mayor, a throat singer, the driver of the sewage truck, and the best soapstone carver in town.

Yasmeen smiled. "You again," she said.

Joanasi shrugged, looking slightly but not altogether uncomfortable being the centre of attention. Yasmeen gave him her chair, asking would he like a glass of water.

"It's okay," he said. She didn't understand if he meant yes or no, so she went to get him one anyway. The students took their seats.

Elisapie gnawed the pink eraser on the end of her pencil. She raised her hand and asked Joanasi what it was like to work at the radio station.

"Fun," he said, glancing at Yasmeen to get a sense of whether he was doing it right.

"The floor's yours," she said. "The kids just want to write about who you really are as a person. Say whatever's on your mind. There are no wrong answers."

He said, "Well, okay then." He slid down in the chair and stretched out his feet. "The radio station is really fun." He pulled his mesh cap down over his eyes and fiddled with the peak. "I get to play all the music I love, as long as we have it. Sometimes we don't have the songs I want to play, though." He laughed. "Too bad."

Elisapie rushed to copy down everything he said. Qalingo just listened, spellbound, forgetting to take notes. He sat with his elbows propped up on the desk and his chin in his palms.

Yasmeen jumped in, modeling the interview process, hoping the students would catch on. "Like what music?" she said. " … for example."

Joanasi straightened in the chair and pushed his cap back up. "Like maybe The Police, the new album, and *Shout at the Devil*. Yeah, that. I wonder how I'm gonna get my hands on it, the mail takes forever here."

Yasmeen nodded and smiled and said she knew The Police but not the other song, who was it by? He eyed her in a way that dragged out the suspense.

"I give up," she said.

"Mötley Crüe," Audlaluk blurted out, tickled that he knew the answer before his own teacher. He had a face like a penny worn from rubbing that always made him look like a wrinkled old man. She gave him the thumbs up and said, "Okay buddy, your question next."

He sat for a long while not saying anything, doodling aimlessly on his paper. His crossed legs swung nervously under his desk, holey socks dragging back and forth across the floor, collecting dust. Yasmeen prodded him but said to take all the time he needed. She reminded him that all questions were good, how else were people expected to learn? Her words encouraged him and soon he half-formulated a question about hunting, about how Joanasi became the best goose hunter in the village.

Yasmeen was glad to learn something she didn't know. It occurred to her that there was much she didn't know about Saqijuvik. Her intention of jotting down all he said, for later reference, evaporated with his captivating story about a bad hunter who decided to leave home because what he really wanted was to be a caribou rather than a man. Joanasi told it masterfully. He explained how the man ended up in a large village run by caribou and how he begged the chief to let him become one of them, though when he finally did he had trouble keeping up with the herd. It took time for him to acquire their skill.

"Don't stop now," said Yasmeen. "Just when it's getting interesting."

Salatee followed his every move with the camera, self-conscious about setting off the noisy shutter. She bent on her knee for a shot, then changed her mind, moving in for a better angle.

Joanasi reached for the glass and drank. Yasmeen was glad she had thought of the water. He licked his lips and leaned forward to look each kid squarely in the eye.

"One day when the man was old he decided he wanted to see his family again. He asked the chief for permission. The chief let him go. The man walked many days. When he saw his village in the distance he was so excited he forgot all about the traps hunters set and got caught in one. Two boys with rifles were waiting for him. Before they could shoot, the caribou that was really a man cried out for mercy. It scared the boys. He told them, 'Don't shoot, just tear off my skin with your knife.' The boys obeyed and were surprised to find a man inside. They were surprised to learn that the man was actually their father who had left them when they were very young."

Yasmeen's new door had gleaming chrome hinges. It was more than she had hoped for. Paulussie had made an executive decision. There was no point trying to fix what was broken beyond repair, he said. He scrapped the old one and ordered a composite door, caribou-brown with a hollow core. It came with an elaborate locking mechanism and a set of keys that were left to her in a small envelope in her teacher's box. Yasmeen thought it strange to be given a lock when nobody in town locked their doors, except in cases of imminent danger. Nobody even knocked. It was unheard of. People just walked in, sat down and behaved as though any neighbour's house was theirs as well. She liked that.

EIGHT

There was one good day for groceries at the Co-op, usually the day after the plane arrived from the South. Wednesday had the best pickings of fresh produce, dairy and frozen foods, although there wasn't a lot of it. Shelves and freezers were stocked late Tuesday afternoon so that by Wednesday morning, the few new fruits and vegetables in town were on colourful display. Yasmeen figured out by the third week that if she wanted a bag of potatoes or a container of yogurt or one of the few sweet peppers that had arrived on the plane, she had to get it on Wednesday, otherwise it would get snapped up and she'd have to wait a whole week again.

Even so, Yasmeen preferred the electric atmosphere of Saturday mornings when the store crowded with villagers chatting over grocery carts, picking up supplies to tide them over until Monday morning, the Co-op being closed on Sundays. It had the feel of a general store with its eclectic mix of clothing, canned goods, guns, hardware, electronics and toys, everything double the price of what people paid down south. Occasionally the store manager, a white man who had lived there for over twenty years, arranged activities for his youngest customers, treasure hunts or relay races with lollipop giveaways. Just about every toddler left the store with his lips dyed a bright candy colour.

One Saturday, Yasmeen discovered the dusty area behind the accounts office, a neglected back room of empty grocery boxes and two army-green metal furnishings, a dented filing cabinet with a Windex spray bottle on top and a lopsided shelving unit jammed with handcrafted mittens, hats and duffel socks and carvings of all shapes and sizes. Each article had a little tag attached to it with an elastic band. The tags had red serial numbers on them and number codes and spaces for handwritten information, all in syllabics except for the name of the artist, which was in English. But there were no prices on them, or at least none that Yasmeen could figure.

She admired a pair of mittens and tried them on. A perfect fit, she took them to the wicket of the accounts office, where people lined up on Thursdays for their weekly cheques, and inquired how much. The woman removed the tag and punched a long calculation on her adding machine.

"Are you Sarah's sister?" Yasmeen asked while she waited.

The woman shot her a peculiar glance and continued keying numbers. She shook her head.

"Sorry, I just thought, it's just that you look an awful lot like Sarah," Yasmeen finally said. "You know, the church pastor."

The clerk tore off the part of the adding machine roll on which she had printed up the cost and showed it to Yasmeen. The ink was faded but readable. Two hundred dollars, it said.

"That's fox fur," the woman explained, as though she needed to justify the price. She ran the back of her hand along the hide.

But Yasmeen had already decided it was fair. Her heart was set on it. "Let's do it," she said and wrote out a cheque.

The woman slid the mitts into a plastic bag that was too big for them. Her expression shifted from serious to playful. "You're right. Sarah is my sister, I was only joking."

"You had me going," said Yasmeen.

"We kid around a lot here, you better get used to it."

On her way to the exit she was stopped by a woman and her toddler. "I could have made you a pair for half the price." She lifted her eyebrows to emphasize the truth of her claim. "Aren't you one of the new teachers?"

Yasmeen nodded. She smiled at the child, who turned his head and hid between his mother's legs. The woman introduced herself as Annie and invited Yasmeen to her place for coffee.

Coffee? She stammered. Yes, absolutely, she would love to. In her excitement, Yasmeen almost dropped her bag with the mitts. She couldn't believe her good fortune. It was her first invitation to a real person's house, besides Sarah. She doubted any of the other teachers had been welcomed so enthusiastically.

They walked together, heading away from the part of town where the teachers and the other whites lived. The boy, Tivi, lagged behind and eventually dropped out of sight altogether. Annie didn't seem to mind; there were plenty of other parents who would see to him if he needed anything.

"Maybe you would like to buy a wall hanging I made," she said, picking up the pace.

Yasmeen smiled and said, "Maybe, possibly, I'll have to take a look at it." She walked briskly alongside her until they reached their destination.

Annie stooped to pick an old butt out of an ashtray on the floor. She lit it, took a quick puff and stubbed it out. Her husband or boyfriend, whatever man was in the kitchen, turned around and mumbled something to her in Inuktitut.

"This is my new friend, Yasmeen," she told him. He barked a monotone hello, switched on the TV and went to flake out on the mattress in their living room, which was really only an extension of the kitchen. He reached into a hamper overflowing with laundry and pulled out a bed sheet to cover himself.

Annie grabbed the last mug from the cupboard and picked one off the drying rack, squinting inside to verify that it was clean. She spooned some instant coffee into them, put the kettle on and went to fetch the white plastic bag that was sitting in a muddle of boots by the door.

Yasmeen sat at the table with her coat over her shoulders. A rerun of *Three's Company* was on. The man was already asleep, the sheet all tangled up in his legs.

"This is it," said Annie, unrolling her wall hanging, a modest embroidery of a mother with a child on her back, standing by an igloo. Overhead was a yellow sun with long rays that reached down and almost touched them.

Yasmeen fingered it gently. She wanted it, of course, but she had already blown a bundle on the mitts. She hesitated to ask the price. It sounded so mercantile.

The kettle whistled and the man groaned and rolled over on the mattress, pulling the sheet up over his head. Annie poured hot water over the coffee crystals and reached into her pantry for a jumbo container of Coffee Mate. "I usually charge one hundred dollars for these, but for you, since you're my friend now, how about eighty?"

"What if I buy it next week?" Yasmeen hoped she wouldn't be insulted or think she was putting her off.

"How about seventy?"

"Next week for sure," Yasmeen said. She heaped some of the Coffee Mate into her cup and stirred with the same spoon Annie had used.

Annie slurped her coffee. "It's just that, well, um, maybe someone else will buy it before next week. I don't want you to miss out. How about you pay me half now and the rest next week?"

Yasmeen produced a cheque for half the amount.

"This is so great," said Annie. "I'm out of cigarettes." She leapt from her chair and shrugged on her coat. "Oh dear, you haven't finished your coffee." She was apologetic but restless. She

99

insisted that Yasmeen take her time, enjoy, it was no rush, but Yasmeen decided it didn't seem right to make her wait.

Retracing their steps back to the Co-op, Yasmeen voiced a thought. "Is there a sewing circle here I could join?" She said it with such enthusiasm she didn't know what had possessed her. The only time she had ever made anything it had been a disaster, a skirt for Home Economics that she accidentally sewed on the wrong side of the fabric.

Annie's face brightened. "Of course. You can come along next week," she said. "I'll teach you everything I know."

Yasmeen made her way to the designated house, the one that Annie had told her to go to. Each week the sewing ladies met at a different place depending on who felt like hosting. Annie explained they were the same women who got together for Friday Night Bingo. Yasmeen was early. She had left her house well ahead of the appointed time, preferring to wait outside and arrive with Annie. At least it was someone she knew.

The house belonged to a woman named Pasha. It resembled Annie's except it had separate bedrooms, two by the looks of it, and a larger kitchen. Pasha smiled and shrugged her shoulders when Annie introduced them. "She doesn't speak English," Annie warned.

Yasmeen pointed to herself and said "*Yasmeen-uvunga.* I am Yasmeen." Pasha said *aah* and signalled for her to sit. The armchair had a squeaky spring. She looked around, trying to seem casual rather than nosy. She liked the relaxed homey feel, furniture arranged for convenience rather than style. Mainly there was a couch, pilled and coffee-stained, and a pair of mismatched wall units crammed with an assortment of household items in no discernible order—electric can opener, rumpled animal hides, skeins

of wool, jars of baby food, Sears catalogues, Star Wars action figures, videocassettes. Every surface had a knick-knack on it.

By the time everyone trickled in there were about a half-
dozen seated helter-skelter, anywhere they could find a spot to
work. Some sat on the couch embroidering mittens, others were
hunched on the floor cutting thick, white duffel with a pair of
heavy scissors. The woman who had sold her the mitts at the
Co-op, Sarah's sister, arrived with a large roll of nylon under
her arm and was showing it around. Pasha had a paper cut-out
of somebody's foot, a child-sized one that she appeared to be
using as a pattern for *alirtiks*, the tall, warm socks people wore
as inner linings for their sealskin boots. Ever since she had seen
them in photographs, Yasmeen had wanted a pair.

Annie picked a scrap of duffel off the floor and handed
Yasmeen a needle and a length of red yarn. "The best way to
learn is to start at the beginning," she said. She commanded her
to stitch a flower any way she could.

Yasmeen held the wool up to the light and tried to push it
through the eye of the needle but it kept splitting and curling
away. It was impossible to get it through.

"You're lucky," said Annie. "In the old days, we used an ivory
needle and sinew cut from the hind legs of a caribou. All we
had back then was the light from an oil lamp. This is kid stuff."
She giggled.

The other women chit-chatted in Inuktitut as they went
about their business, pausing occasionally to light a cigarette or sip their mug of tea or erupt into a great belly laugh.
Occasionally Annie translated for her, but the evening essentially
took place in a language Yasmeen didn't understand. Grateful
they'd accepted her into their special circle, it didn't bother her
in the least.

When Joanasi walked through the front door, Yasmeen was
still struggling to thread her needle. His sudden appearance took

her by surprise. Pasha looked up from her work and questioned him rather curtly. He stooped down and kissed her head before replying with a lengthy explanation. When he noticed Yasmeen staring at him he pointed at Pasha and silently mouthed, my mother. I live here.

He returned to what he was saying but appeared to open it up to everyone in the room. Annie sat back on her heels, dragging on her cigarette. She answered something back to Joanasi and then another woman cut in, a little more forcefully. Joanasi cranked up the volume on the radio, which had been on low until then.

Yasmeen couldn't catch the gist of what they were saying until Annie piped up and told her it was about Halloween. "We're trying to decide if it's cancelled or not."

"Oh my god, I'm supposed to be somewhere!" she said. "I totally forgot." Yasmeen bounced up off her chair and touched Pasha graciously on the shoulder and said *nakurmiik* and joked with Joanasi that they had to stop meeting like this.

She wiggled into her coat and asked Annie to translate for her that she was sorry, but that she would return next week for sure. She folded her patch of duffel with the needle still sticking out of it, and stuffed it into her pocket.

Sam's was where she was supposed to have been while she was sitting at Pasha's trying to improve her sewing skills. As the union rep, Elliot argued it was important to present a common front on the issue of Halloween. The meeting was a last-minute idea. Sam had offered to host it at her place. Despite her tardiness, Yasmeen was first to arrive.

Unlike Pasha's house, cluttered with stuff but void of greenery, Sam's was a veritable jungle, overrun with leafy plants and African violets and potted cacti with bright blooms in their centres. Ferns in macramé slings hung from hooks in the ceiling, looping philodendron and spider plants with long hairy tendrils. Sam once admitted to Yasmeen she couldn't go anywhere without taking along her favourite things, including her plants. They reminded her of home and kept her grounded. Yasmeen was stunned when she saw what Sam had carted with her from the South, a full trousseau of oddball provisions she felt she would never find in the Arctic: Three pounds of dyed pistachios, Scottish shortbread, individual sachets of Sweet' N Low, Vermont maple syrup, three 40-ouncers of Johnnie Walker Red and two cartons of Players Light (which the Co-op sold but at an exorbitant price). She also brought along her dog, Bailey, for company, a hapless mutt with black-and-brown cow markings and ears that dragged along the floor.

"So what's the story on Halloween?," Yasmeen asked. "Any decision yet?"

"They're talking about it on the FM," she said. "As we speak."

"So turn it on."

"I don't know about you but my Inuktitut is a little—how shall I say?—rusty."

"For fuck's sake. Why would Paulussie go ahead and let us get the kids all worked up about it and then tell us no? Where's the logic in that?"

"It's not him, it's all the evangelical nutcases." She said it knowledgeably, as though it were a fact of life that everyone should know by now. "I'm not talking about the normal ones, if you can call them that, who play by the rules. The ones who just pray and go home and eat dinner with their families. It's the others I'm talking about, the hypocrites."

"Hypocrites?"

"Yeah, as in drinking themselves into oblivion, beating up their wives and then going to church on Sunday to pray their asses off for forgiveness."

Were they talking about the same village? Sam's version of Saqijuvik didn't jibe with Yasmeen's experience of it. It didn't even come close.

"Take your coat off and stay awhile," said Sam.

Yasmeen pulled down her zipper. She stuffed her hat into her pocket, accidentally jabbing her thumb on the needle she had hurriedly stuck into the duffel before leaving Pasha's place.

They heard a stampede up the porch steps. Sam snatched the Johnnie Walker off the table just as the front door flew open and a clutch of rosy children in tuques and coats poked their faces in, smiles of crusty snot under their nostrils.

Sam shooed them back outside. "Not tonight, kids."

"Awww!"

"Vamoose!" she said. "Maybe tomorrow."

They watched them scamper off into the grainy darkness. Sam was about to shut the door when Yasmeen noticed Paulussie headed toward the house with his head down and his hands in his pockets. He was kicking up clouds of dust.

"My woman is crazy sometimes," he grumbled, pushing past them. He unzipped his jacket and installed himself at the table, slapping down his pack of cigarettes.

Sam plucked a clean glass from the dish rack and poured him a shot from the bottle she had hastily hidden away. She slid the glass across the table and said, "I'm taking one of your cigarettes," pilfering two from the pack before he even had the chance to process her request. She stuck one between her lips and tossed him the other.

He let it dangle, unlit, at the corner of his mouth while he dredged up all that he was stewing about. "It's just like last summer when Sarah got it in her head she had to convert all the poor Anglican … heathens." He said "heathens" through clenched teeth. Sam reached across and lit his cigarette before lighting hers. He took a long haul. The tip flared like a tiny brush fire.

"So what happened last summer?" said Yasmeen.

"I thought everyone knew." Paulussie glugged down the whisky and banged the glass on the table, signalling for another. He leaned forward in the chair. "Picture a big bonfire just up on the hill and everyone dropping their stuff in, tape recorders, cassettes, records ... everything that the *devil* gave us," he said. "We had to burn all of it, even the Hank Williams." He shook his head and repeated "crazy woman" under his breath.

Yasmeen turned the radio on, hoping he would fill them in with the missing pieces of the puzzle. She twiddled the knob until she got a clear signal. Paulussie shushed them and leaned back to listen, eyeing the coal of his cigarette. She heard the word Halloween in English, but everything else was in Inuktitut. Callers went on and on with their prolonged explanations, clarifications, justifications, some with a hint of outrage, others maintaining the usual monotone.

Paulussie shook his head and frowned. He squashed his cigarette in the ashtray and lit another. He snapped his jaw and blew a smoke ring across the table. A voice came on that sounded like Sarah's.

Another delegation herded up the steps—Jacqueline, followed by Tommy and Elliot. They dropped their coats on the couch and joined the others around the radio. Bailey yawned and stretched his body out like a sausage. He lumbered over and curled down next to Sam's feet.

"News?" said Elliot, clapping Paulussie on the shoulder.

Paulussie shook his head. "Sarah's warming up for a fight."

"How does it look?"

"I hate to say this, but I think it's going to be cancelled."

"So tomorrow we go to school and rip down all the decorations, is that it?" said Elliot.

"Yep. Probably."

Tommy sat quietly, brushing drywall powder off his knuckles. He caught Yasmeen's eye and looked away with a sliver of remorse.

Sam carried a handful of glasses to the table and filled them up. Tommy's hand shot out for one. Jacqueline said no Scotch for her. She'd have a beer instead, straight from the bottle.

The radio voices faded into the background as Paulussie decided that the moment called for a toast. "If I haven't said it, I'm saying it now. We're happy to have you teachers here." There was no clinking of glasses, everyone just nodded and drank up. Paulussie thinned out what he had and requested another. "Back in my day, we were sent away to school."

Tommy shifted in his chair. Jacqueline blew across the top of her bottle, mimicking a foghorn.

Paulussie's eyes glazed over. "Our parents thought it would be a good thing. Of course, way back then none of them knew much ..." He lifted the glass, almost missing his mouth.

Yasmeen noticed little smudges of dried blood on the table in front of where she was sitting, caused by the needle that had pierced her thumb. She finger-rubbed them off, wondering what Paulussie meant by "none of them knew much." She watched his cigarette burn down to the filter.

Sam shot a beer cap at Elliot. "So, how was *your* day, *Amigo*?"

Elliot waggled his hand: so-so. "Apart from the kids bugging me about this Halloween thing, okay, I guess."

Yasmeen saw that Paulussie was still drifting in and out of his past. It was no wonder that he needed a drink every now and then. To take the edge off. Who wouldn't, given the circumstances? Despite what Sarah implied, Paulussie was pretty good about his consumption. He never got wild. Tipsy, yes, but never out of control. So what if he had a few drinks?

Yasmeen felt more compassion than sadness for him. The truth of what might have happened to him in the residential school only strengthened her resolve. She could see why the parents of some of her students might be ambivalent about education and how their attitude might rub off on their children. She would have to work even harder to earn their trust and get them to a place where they could hold their heads high and live with themselves, with dignity.

Paulussie cranked up the radio. A village elder was making his case, slowly, languidly, oceans of dead air buoying each of his thoughts. Elliot tapped his fingers impatiently. Sam popped into the bedroom for a fresh pack of cigarettes. She jerked out the foil insert and passed them around. Elliot turned his nose up but Yasmeen reached for one, though she rarely smoked. Elliot flashed her a condescending look.

Paulussie was shaking his head, repeating over and over that he couldn't believe his ears. Everyone knew what he meant. He snatched a cigarette from the pack and flipped off the radio, grimacing. "So, that's it," he said, his eyes bloodshot.

There wasn't a drop left in the bottle. When he got up to leave, the chair accidentally fell backwards and clattered on the floor and he almost lost his balance, but not quite. Elliot rushed to help him, steady him on his feet, but Paulussie swatted his hand away and said he was just fine thank you very much, he had to go now, his precious, loving, broad-minded wife was waiting for him at home.

SNOW

NINE

Almost overnight the mercury plummeted. Mammoth drifts of snow leaned sideways against the village houses. Daylight dwindled to a few measly hours, while night was a vast chamber of darkness, marked by the ghostly breath of people out walking and the hollow *skritch skritch* of boots against the hard-packed surface.

Yasmeen knew city snow, the kind that crippled buses and planes and slid off rooftops in vast sheets or blew dangerously from the hoods of speeding cars. She knew snow that sifted down and deposited a soft, white fur on naked branches and telephone wires before turning grey under the tires of salt trucks and sawtooth ploughs. The year she turned twelve, a terrible storm cut the electric power and blew in hundred kilometre-an-hour winds. It dropped forty-seven centimetres of snow in only twenty-four hours. In the city, snow was snow. Sometimes it wreaked havoc.

In Saqijuvik, snow had nuances that gave the language a depth that English didn't have. People had a name for every conceivable kind. Falling snow, wet snow, compact snow. Snow, broken by footsteps. Snow for drinking water. Thin, powdery snow. Airborne snow. Crusty snow hardened by rain. Fresh, soggy snow. Their fifty or more words had visceral beauty.

Yasmeen's toaster popped and the air swelled with the yeasty aroma of a Fairmount bagel, a treat reserved for lazy weekends. A single lamp burned on the kitchen table where Yasmeen sat in flannel pyjamas enjoying a creamy, dark-roast espresso. As she got up to go butter the bagel, she heard a motor rumble outside her door. Curious, she shrugged on her parka and poked her nose into the nippy morning. A black Skidoo was coughing up smoke.

The driver was one of Elliot's students, Adamie, an earnest boy with an infectious smile whom she had once tutored during her spare period. Yasmeen studied the splinter-grey sled hooked to the back of his Skidoo, its load wrapped in an electric-blue tarpaulin.

"Going hunting?" she called out before recognizing the stupidity of her question. Obviously he was, where else would he be going on a Saturday with a packed sled?

His eyebrows lifted. "Wanna come?"

It seemed impossible he was asking *her*, a woman, when Elliot was his teacher and definitely not shy about soliciting hunting invitations wherever he could get them. She wondered whether maybe he had overheard her telling Sam she wanted the experience of going out on the land. Anyway, who cared how he knew. He was asking her and she wanted to go. Every part of her was screaming *yes, yes, seize the day*.

He leaned casually against the Skidoo and pulled a cigarette out from behind his ear. "You got ten minutes." He cupped his hands against the wind to light up.

Half an hour later, under a bare wash of sun, they were crossing sculptural snow dunes, bobbing up and down over crests and valleys, smoke unfurling behind them. Yasmeen held onto his slender waist. She twisted around, watching the village recede until it was a smudge and then a dot and then nothing at all. Above them, the sky duplicated itself over and over like the sprawling plain stretching toward infinity.

Yasmeen clung to him with all her strength. The last time she'd been on a vehicle that didn't have at least two doors and a hood was on a motorcycle ride with a guy she hardly knew, the time she accidentally burned the inside of her ankle on the exhaust pipe. Her mother said it served her right going on a death-ride like that. Yasmeen shrugged and chalked it up to living in the real world, and if that meant getting a few scrapes and bruises along the way, so be it.

Once on a family vacation Yasmeen took her younger brother swimming and almost got them both drowned. The beach that day was irresistible, clear sky, a fresh salty sting to the air. Before long they were beyond the breakers, unable to swim back. It was only afterwards, when they were huddled blue-lipped under a towel, teeth chattering, the Coast Guard people talking gravely with her parents, that Yasmeen understood the full extent of the danger she had put them in. Even so, she felt only the adrenalin of excitement.

The Skidoo dipped. Yasmeen tightened her grip around Adamie. The landscape had flattened into a vast, white, monotonous plain. Yasmeen remembered Frank's explanation of how repetitive stretches that appear featureless to a white person held important clues for the locals, wind leaving its Braille in the snow, a sudden weft of light or change in the rhythm of the land. They were the maps and street signs of the Arctic, guiding travellers to where they had to go, returning them home safely. Other markers punctuated the land now and then, Inukshuks mainly, rocks piled in a particular way to communicate information or act as a point of reference. They signalled food caches, travel routes, hunting grounds and places of worship. Their monolithic stature suffused the barren land with human presence, a reminder to the people that they were not alone.

Yasmeen couldn't quell the rush of being out on the tundra with someone she hardly knew but trusted nonetheless. This was *his* territory and he was solidly in it. His internal compass would steer them in the right direction, away from harm. She accepted the fact she had nothing to offer in this regard, no acumen or handed-down wisdom. Adamie was her guide, the window into his world. He was her armour. No matter the circumstances, instinct would kick in and tell him what to do. Even at seventeen he was miles ahead of the boys in her class, Qalingo and the others, whose knobby knees and ribs still poked through their clothes. She could easily imagine him slitting the full stomach of an animal, those same hands afterwards fondling his woman, slipping them underneath her shirt, up over her breasts, through her collar to her lips and face.

She lost all sense of time.

Unexpectedly, Adamie cut the motor. The wind blew a fine scrim across the landscape. Raw fistfuls of snow pelted her face, each sharp flake like a tiny bonfire on her skin. He removed his mitt and reached down to feel the steam curling off the snow, lightly touching a pair of animal droppings with his bare fingers. He pointed ahead to some white birds, all feather and bone in the wind. "Ptarmigan," he said.

He ran for his rifle. He dropped down onto one knee. From the Skidoo, Yasmeen watched him wheedle his prey into the crosshairs. She forgot about the severe cold. She forgot the paltry sun barely hovering above the horizon. She forgot that they were two specks in a desert of ice. Her heart stopped.

The wind stilled.

Three shots fired into the silence. A slim column of smoke rose and dissipated.

Adamie ploughed through the deep snow to claim his kill. He knelt and dipped a finger into what Yasmeen guessed was their spill of blood. She watched with fascination as he plucked a feather off each bird and planted it in the snow. It felt so sacred and graceful in the pure, protracted silence. When the ritual was done he beamed at Yasmeen.

The dull light looked strangely radiant. Adamie strode into the long, blue arm of her shadow. "Welcome back," she said. He loaded the birds onto the back of the sled and covered them with the tarpaulin. He climbed back on and yanked the pull-cord to power up the engine. The motor was shockingly brusque after the penetrating silence.

"Not too cold?" he shouted over his shoulder.

"A little."

"Hold tight."

The last of the sun dipped below the horizon. She pulled her hood forward, staring into the hazy afterglow.

"The old igloo we passed on the way," he shouted, accelerating. "We'll stop there to eat something."

Cheek pressed against his back she leaned into him, intensely, into the wind, into the snow, into the long cold ride ahead of them, her tension evaporating. Her eyes closed.

When she opened them again, it was completely dark. They were no longer moving. Adamie went to loosen the tarpaulin and gather a few provisions. She tried to move her fingers but the cold had already bitten through her mitts. Her toes were numb.

He advised her to wait while he checked things out, hewing a path from the Skidoo to the igloo. The brittle crunch of snow under his boots grew fainter and fainter until he disappeared inside and she was alone in the absolute silence, cold snaking down her back.

Her imagination rushed to fill the absence. Emaciated, half-starved dogs appeared in her peripheral vision, jaws snapping. They mutated into foraging wolves with an arsenal of teeth. Their eyes were everywhere. Why was Adamie taking his sweet time? How long could it possibly take to investigate such cramped quarters? She sighed with relief when he reappeared at the mouth of the igloo and waved her toward him.

She climbed off the Skidoo and took the same path, sinking her boots into his tracks and following them until she arrived at the tiny opening. She dropped to her knees and felt her way inside.

In the obscurity, he was only a voice. "You okay?"

She felt his breath against her cheek.

He struck a match and they watched the amber flame pour into their sphere of darkness. He removed his hat and shook the wet out of his bangs. She removed hers and copied him. They laughed. She noticed that his teeth were very white.

With one hand he shook out the contents of the rucksack, thermos, votive candle, foil-wrapped bannock. He lit the candle and blew out the match. She imagined she was in a prehistoric cave by the light of the very first fire.

Together they laid down the caribou hide, pinching the corners into the drafty cracks of the igloo.

It occurred to her that if they died that night out in the cold in the middle of nowhere, no one would know it. It wasn't beyond the realm of possibility. They could be mauled by a polar bear or buried alive in a raging blizzard. The Skidoo could break down and they could freeze to death. Anything could happen. She felt her own vulnerability, how inconsequential she was, just a speck in the scheme of things, almost invisible, like the sun, which seemed enormous to humans but was really only one of two billion stars in the Milky Way. After her father told her that, she walked around the house for an entire week with a blanket over her head, pretending she was a dust mote.

Adamie tugged the sleeves of her parka and eased it off as the candle spread its warmth between them. He unlaced her boots and lifted her feet out. She could hardly feel them. He lowered the zip of her snow pants and gently removed them. She couldn't stop shivering despite two other layers of protection, a pair of blue jeans and her long underwear. He kneaded her legs with his hands, rubbing the circulation back. It didn't seem weird at all.

"Qallunaat are like kids when they go out in the snow," he said. He massaged her toes, one by one.

Whenever past boyfriends had tried to touch her feet, she'd squealed and kicked them away. But Adamie's hands felt good on them after the extreme cold. He seemed to know exactly where to touch to bring the blood back.

He moved from a kneeling position to a cross-legged one, facing her. "*Atti,* little woman, give me your hands, they're freezing!" He warmed them with the heat of his own. She felt a pang of disappointment when he let them go.

He unzipped his parka and fished through his pocket for cigarettes. His eyes lit up when he put his hands on them. "It's been a while," he said. He struck a match on the toe of his boot. Leaning into the flame, he lit it and breathed the smoke in deeply.

Yasmeen gestured for a drag.

"Bad for you," he said. "You're a teacher, you should know better."

She could tell he was only half serious. "Come on, just one. To warm me up."

"Okay." He held its moistened tip against her lips with the same fingers he had dipped in the ptarmigan entrails.

She closed her eyes and inhaled deeply, almost forgetting where she was. The smell of ptarmigan didn't bother her. Her only thought was of how people here survived against all odds. They killed animals and then they ate them. She imagined Adamie's ancestor in caribou skins and sealskin boots, wielding his harpoon to feed an entire tribe, using the tricks of light to his advantage. When she opened her eyes, she saw Adamie staring at her. His eyes bore the reflection of a hunter bearing down on a creature, snapping its head back like a twig. Or maybe it was just the combination of excitement and the cigarette making her feel lightheaded.

He unscrewed the thermos and poured some tea into the cap. "Drink," he said. Their fingers collided.

She tried to deflect the awkwardness. "You think I'm funny, right?"

"*Funnyaluk,*" he said. "No more smoking for you." His smile spread like a warm band of sunlight. She took a sip of the tea.

After that he came alive telling her a story his grandfather had told him when he was small, a story about the land, the animals that inhabited it and the hunters who stalked them.

"You're an amazing shot," she said. "An incredible hunter."

"We don't like to brag about what we kill. One day we might not be so lucky."

She listened intently. She wanted to learn everything he had to teach her. For a moment she forgot that he was only seventeen.

"My grandfather told me that the spirits of the dead animals could be listening too, and they could be offended. So we don't show off." He took a long puff on his cigarette.

His coarse hair was especially beautiful. She resisted the urge to reach out and touch his face. Each time the desire came, she slapped it down. It gave her palpitations. She wondered if she was the sort of person who lived exotic adventures just to have a story to tell, or if maybe she was a chameleon who behaved one way around family and friends and another among strangers.

By candlelight he looked like a man. He *was* a man. Already he knew what the land taught and how to survive the elements. A grown woman, what did she know by comparison? Math and history and literature. What good was any of that here in this primal place where all you needed was a strong pair of hands and wherewithal?

"Promise me one thing, Adamie. Promise that even when you finish school and get your diploma you won't forget the old ways."

He looked at her solemnly. She noticed a row of pimples in the indent of his chin.

"You know," she said, "we aren't doing anything wrong."

His lips opened a crack. He blinked and moved toward her. She felt herself working hard to remain calm. His hair smelled of snow and cigarettes. Somewhere in the deepest part of her she wanted him to feel her with his hands. Her instinct was fighting for him. She moved closer, trying not to be obvious about it. His warm breath was blowing across her lips. Any closer and her hair would be in his mouth. She hesitated. She gave in. She pulled back again. She started to say, *You're amazing, this is amazing being out here with you* but realized her talking was getting in the way. She considered letting him kiss her once. Just once, who would it hurt? At the last second, she retreated. She turned her mouth away and gave him her cheek instead. She hugged him with great affection, sweetly, the way it had to be.

She felt feverish when he brought her home. A spidery light sat low on the horizon as the village slept. The only sign of life was a drunk-eyed dog, part wolf, part something else, scrounging around for animal scraps.

Yasmeen climbed off the Skidoo and hugged Adamie with tenderness. He wasn't at all in a hurry to leave. He kissed her hood. She thought of asking him in for breakfast, wanting but not wanting to lead him on. She took her time searching through her pockets for the house key, then feigned remembering that she had left the door unlocked.

Bone-tired, adrenalin still pumping, she watched from the doorway as he putted homeward in the half-light. It felt as though they had been away a long time. She draped her wet parka over the furnace to dry and ran the water for a bath.

She peeled off her clothes. When the tub was filled she submerged herself completely except for her head. She focused on the steam rising from her flaccid breasts and examined the rest of her body, its fleshy contours and bulk, the gurgles it made underwater as her muscles slowly let go and relaxed. She didn't realize she had peed in the bathwater until she smelled its astringent bouquet. It didn't bother her at all. Actually she was impressed with the impulsiveness of her act. She watched each droplet gather at the spout of the faucet before freefalling, breaking the surface tension of the water with an echoey *plick*. She bobbed gently, feeling what it was like to be weightless.

She had a flash of home, how it lay in stark contrast to all she had seen on the ride with Adamie, a world of asphalt and smog where people worked in cubicles drowned in fluorescent lighting, manufactured things that went in a repetitive loop or through a speedy conveyor belt until they were fine-tuned, filtered, carbonated, turbo-cooled, radiated and vacuum-packed for human consumption. Leaving their runoff in the sludge of landfill or any one of a thousand mercury-tainted rivers.

She drained the tub and as she reached for the fluffy towel on the rack, the blood rushed out of her head. Translucent blobs floated past her eyes, a sign that if she didn't sit down immediately, she would pass out. She groped her way to the toilet, sat and waited for the dizziness to pass.

When enough of her strength returned she stood and wiped the foggy mirror with her towel. Light from the bald bathroom fixture made her look overly pale. With her index finger she traced the narrow crevice between her breasts, moving from the bellied curve of one to the other. She probed their moony fullness, noting they were less shapely than when she had first arrived, a consequence, she realized, of not wearing a bra every day. She felt both invigorated and exhausted.

Still shivering despite the bath, she layered on her thickest clothes and wrapped a wool scarf around her neck. She was famished. She switched on the radio and began preparing a meal. She could have devoured an entire caribou, sinews and all, until there was nothing left on the bone. She settled for a bacon omelette and a cup of oolong tea.

The eggs crackled in the hot skillet. She leaned her face over the stove to soak up the heat and began humming to the song on the radio, "You Ain't Seen Nothing Yet," one she didn't particularly like by a band she wasn't overly fond of. Afterwards, Joanasi came on to announce they'd just been listening to Bachman Turner Overdrive. He switched over to the weather forecast, which he always read in English. She could tell by his voice that he was fighting a chest cold.

Waiting for the tea to steep she dipped into her dog-eared book of crossword puzzles, though she was more interested in shovelling the food into her mouth than penciling letters into the empty squares.

After the meal she draped a wool blanket over her shoulders and curled into the armchair. She couldn't settle, the thrill of the outing still whirring through her mind. She pushed away intimate thoughts of Adamie touching her but they haunted her anyway. She kicked off the blanket and changed into different clothes. She waited patiently for ten o'clock and followed a small group of villagers trudging toward the Anglican Church. It was an activity she liked to do on Sundays. She saw how it gave her an advantage with her students who appreciated the efforts she made to integrate. Most times her mind wandered, trying to piece together the convoluted genealogy of the three major families that were the backbone of the community.

As was customary, she left her boots with everyone else's in the entranceway and entered the simple place of worship in her stocking feet. The church was filling up, but she found a spot next to Qalingo and his family. She smiled at them and waited for the service to begin.

Everyone stood and recited a prayer in unison. Yasmeen glanced at Qalingo's mother who was wearing the white papoose-hooded parka that most mothers wore, with bright stitching around the cuffs and a tail-like hem, a beautiful coat called an *amautik*, belted with braided wool. She was rocking from side to side and front to back, trying to soothe her baby. Yasmeen was fascinated by the ingenuity of these coats, the way the enlarged hood allowed an infant to rest against its mother, protected from the elements. She closed her eyes and tried to imagine a child's tiny ear folded in sleep against her back. She wondered what intense pleasure a baby derived from the warmth of its mother's skin, the comforting smell of her hair, the rhythms of her blood.

Yasmeen had great affection for women like Qalingo's mother, whose role seemed so big and so important there were hardly words to express it. The fact that they ensured the continuity of the tribe was reason enough to envy them. They were strong. They had a vital presence and an important mission. Morgan, of course, would have brained her if she knew Yasmeen were even contemplating these thoughts. They'd always agreed that a houseful of children turned women's lives into a shit show. It poisoned their chances at a decent career. Motherhood was slavery. But here, in this place, in the far reaches of the North, Yasmeen couldn't imagine a more fulfilling division of labour, a woman breast-feeding a child while her valiant man hunted for their sustenance.

Just as she was thinking all this she spotted Adamie three pews ahead of her. She did a double take. He had on a brown tweed hat and a dressier parka than the one he had worn the day before. It surprised her that he wasn't home catching up on his sleep. She considered the possibility that he too was still rattled by what had happened between them. She wondered what he was thinking as the minister intoned over the Bible. Were images of Jesus floating through his mind or was he instead remembering their teenage awkwardness around each other? Did he regret her refusal to kiss him? When she craned her neck for a better view she saw that his arm was supporting a greying, arthritic man. The grandfather, she presumed. She remembered Adamie's lips on the cigarette they had shared. She thought of his accuracy with the rifle and how he had taken special care of her in the cold. She remembered the gentle way he untangled his culture for her, the fable he told in the igloo when it was just the two of them, alone, the piece of his heritage that he had shared like a small cutting of his grandfather's hair.

TEN

Everyone from infants to elders turned up to celebrate the opening of the new school. To Paulussie's great surprise, the construction crew put the final touches on in November, three weeks ahead of schedule. The grounds were cleared of broken planks and nails and the protective wire around the site came down. The modern, two-storey structure gleamed like a shiny new chapter in their lives.

A flurry of excitement marked the days leading up to the celebration, women preparing the joyful feast, sewing tassels and fringes on their best embroidered duffel socks, musicians boning up on their country and western, teachers—including Yasmeen—packing supplies into cardboard boxes and oversized containers in preparation for the move. On the day itself, Paulussie sent the kids home at lunch and gave the teachers time off to get ready.

Earlier that morning, Yasmeen took advantage of the fact that all her students had shown up for school, a rare event. She decided to introduce intersecting lines, following up on the previous lesson when they'd gone outside looking for examples of parallel lines and correctly identified the tracks in the snow left by truck tires and sled runners. Had they been properly installed, the hydro poles would have also been parallel, they cleverly remarked.

"That's right," Yasmeen explained. "Parallel lines always remain the same distance from each other. They never ever meet, no matter how far they extend in space."

They dressed and headed for the designated area, an open space behind the portable large enough to run around in. Audlaluk and Qalingo roughhoused in the snow while they waited for Yasmeen to arrive with her clipboard and whistle. Elisapie and Salatee hopped up and down, blowing on their palms to keep warm.

Yasmeen corralled them around her and told them to listen up. "The difference between parallel and intersecting lines is simple. Let's see if you can figure it out yourselves." Since no one volunteered, she picked Audlaluk and Elisapie. Audlaluk grumbled that he didn't want to work with a girl.

"For heaven's sake, Audlaluk," said Yasmeen. She marked two spots in the snow where they were to stand and told them that when she blew her whistle, they were each to run in as straight a line as possible.

"So what did you notice?" she asked when everyone was back inside the portable. The kids were sitting on their desks with their coats still on. She twirled the chalk between her fingers.

"It was cold," Salatee whispered into her hand. She tossed her hair forward, making a curtain over her eyes.

"Okay, true, but besides that," said Yasmeen.

"The lines made an X," said Elisapie, holding out her hands with the index fingers crossed.

Yasmeen clapped enthusiastically. "That's right." She drew a pair of intersecting lines on the board. "These two come together right here." She circled where the lines met. "They have a common point. They *intersect.*"

She explained that most lines in life intersected, that if you extended the two and waited long enough, if you were patient, eventually they would meet.

The gleaming gymnasium was strewn with banners and streamers and shimmery metallic balloons that said Happy Birthday on them, the only kind the Co-op sold. On stage, fiddlers in chequered shirts wailed through microphones and thumped their heels while dolled-up women in flouncy dresses scurried around the room with their Kodak Instamatics. A crowd gathered, banquet-style, along a flattened-out cardboard box set with macaroni casseroles, bannock, frozen rumps of walrus meat, Jell-O and *suvallik*, a sour-sweet concoction of fish eggs and berries. It was the North's traditional table setting: a single piece of cardboard on the floor. When one group finished, another impatient one elbowed in, toothless elders, ladies with babies on their backs, surly teenagers, toddlers with ribbons in their hair. The men took their pocketknives to the blood-red carcass while the women carved out pieces for their children with their crescent-shaped knives. They gnawed and chewed and spat out gristle.

As the feast petered out and the wet scraps were tossed into plastic garbage bags, another haul of instruments collected on stage—accordions, banjos, guitars, black-box amplifiers. A pair of wizened throat singers began a guttural duet of repetitive, hypnotic chanting. They drew it out for as long as they could until they lost the pace and erupted in gales of laughter.

Paulussie pushed his way toward the podium, smiling, blushing, shaking hands with people in the crowd. He wore the new clothes Sarah had bought him, black dress pants and a shirt with a collar that dug into his Adam's apple. On stage he wiped the sweat off his forehead with a hankie that he scrunched into a ball and stuffed into his back pocket. Fidgeting with his necktie, he waited for the applause to die down. He tapped his finger against the microphone and put his mouth up to it and said, "Testing, testing." He unfolded a piece of paper from his pocket and thanked every name on his list, beginning with the mayor and dignitaries who had made the construction of the new school possible. When it was over he sighed with relief. He crumpled up the paper and tossed it into the air and said, "Let the party begin." A harmonica reeled. People paired up to square dance. The neckerchiefed caller lifted his straw hat. He held it over his heart and bowed to the crowd.

Elliot approached Yasmeen wearing a plaid shirt and Wrangler jeans over a pair of cowboy boots with spurs on them. He hooked her arm and tried dragging her into the middle of the floor, but she shoved him off in protest.

"Sorry, partner, I don't dance!" She was still steaming over a tiff they had had earlier that morning in the staffroom when, waiting for the Photostat machine to warm up, he told her that he had some interesting information to share.

"Oh?"

"About your student, Elisapie." He lined his document up on the glass surface. "I found out the story behind her baby."

"Yeah, she gave it away, I know. You already told me."

He pushed the start button and watched the radiated light sweep back and forth. "Seems that the father of the child was her own father." The copier made an unnatural sound before it spat out the page.

"That's horseshit." Yasmeen stood with her hands on her hips, her eyes tapered.

"Apparently not." He lifted the rubber flap and removed his original.

She detected a hint of glee in his voice, the great pleasure he took at having insider knowledge. "I don't believe you."

"Take my word for it. He's in jail down south, but it won't be long before he's back."

"What the Christ? No one would do that to their own kid," she said.

127

"Sweetheart, it happens all the time."

The conversation ended with her walking away from him. And now he was all over her like they were best friends or something.

"Hee-haw, just go with it!" he twanged. Huge rings of sweat were blooming under his armpits. "Think of it as walking to music."

Reluctantly she took his hand and muttered that he reminded her of Jethro Bodine from *The Beverly Hillbillies*.

"I'll take that as a compliment, Elly May."

Compared to the rest they looked like amateurs, Elliot losing the beat and stepping on her feet as the music sped up and the men began passing the women from partner to partner. Yasmeen kept travelling in the wrong direction, clockwise when she was supposed to be going counter-clockwise, do-si-do-ing when she should have been promenading. She felt like a total klutz. Her feet dragged like boulders.

When she found herself eye to eye with Adamie she relaxed a little. His hair was combed and parted to the side and he smelled like a bar of Irish Spring. The last time she had seen him was that Sunday in church after their ride together. She closed her eyes as he took her hand and swept her around. She thought of how he had almost kissed her on the floor of the igloo. She danced fluidly. The instant she opened her eyes she lost the beat and stumbled into his chest.

The flush-faced fiddlers took a quick break to hike up their pants and gulp back cans of soda. Adamie bowed his head at Yasmeen and walked on to the next partner while Joanasi came to stand in his place. He signalled for Yasmeen's hand and moved toward her.

For the rest of the night, they hardly took their eyes off each other. Yasmeen kept finding excuses not to leave quite yet. First she had to take down the decorations, then she had to sweep up and take the garbage bags out. The to-do list kept growing. She had to make the rounds to be sure that no one was hiding in the bathrooms, even though most of the villagers, including Paulussie, had already gone home. Meanwhile Joanasi dismantled the stage, wrapping extension cords around his arm, helping the musicians pack up their instruments. When it was time to lock up he offered to walk her home and she said, "Okay, I won't say no."

A dusting of snow had fallen over the village and a green curtain of electric light rippled across the sky. For no reason— or perhaps because of the northern lights—she broke into the operatic portion of "Bohemian Rhapsody," forgetting most of the words but stumbling through. They both laughed at how bad it sounded. She wished he would put his arm around her but he just kept walking alongside, careful not to touch her. They played 'Fortunately, Unfortunately.'

"Fortunately, it's the weekend," she began.

"Unfortunately, I have to work tomorrow," he continued.

"Fortunately, there might be a storm."

"Unfortunately, I'll be stranded at your place." He grinned and lobbed a snowball at her.

"Meanie!" she shrieked. She removed her hat and swatted him playfully.

By the time they got to her place their eyelashes were coated in ice. Wet snow was sliding off his boots. She shook the crystals of snow from their hats and parkas and laid them to dry over the furnace.

"*Iik kiii,* it's freezing out there," she said.

He followed her into the living room, fiddling with the loose change in his pockets. "You have less stuff than I thought you would."

"I don't need much," she said. "My books, my music. Clothes, of course."

He jiggled the knobs on her boom box and bent the antenna the opposite way. He walked to the bookcase Tommy had savaged and fingered the tattered spines of her books, randomly reading off their titles. "Did you really read all these?"

"Mostly, yeah."

He pulled out her copy of *The Little Prince*. Not the banged up one that had endured all her childhood abuse but the one her father had wrapped up and given her as a high school graduation gift.

"Cute," he said. "A kid's book." He flipped it open to the handwritten inscription on the inside cover. "For my little princess—The end of all our exploring will be to arrive where we started and know the place for the first time." He wrinkled his nose. "Huh?"

"It's T.S. Eliot," she said, "a poet. For years, I thought my dad had written it. Do you want a coffee or something?"

He slapped the book shut and lifted his eyebrows. She insisted she'd be just a minute but he followed her into the kitchen anyway. He slid out a chair and sat. She felt his eyes on her. In her haste to prepare the cups, she accidentally spilled sugar all over the counter. "I hope you don't mind coffee reheated in the microwave," she said, trying not to reveal how flustered she was.

"Fine, no problem, anything hot is good," he said.

She tried to think of other things to talk about while the coffee was getting zapped. "By the way, I forgot to thank you for letting the class interview you," she said. "They super loved it."

"It was fun."

"Yeah. Tonight was fun, too."

"I hope you don't mind my saying this, but you're a better teacher than a dancer," he said. They carried their mugs into the living room and sat facing each other, cross-legged, on the couch. She was relieved that he had finally said something.

"So, which one are you?" he asked. He blew over his coffee to cool it.

"Excuse me?"

"Which of the three M's are you?" He was half joking, half serious.

"Sorry, I don't get what you mean."

He looked away and said, "I don't quite know how to put this." He glanced up again sheepishly. "You know, the three kinds of white people who come to the North."

She shrugged her shoulders. "I still don't get it."

"You really don't know? Well, there's the Mother Teresas, the misfits, and …"

"And?"

"And the motherfuckers." He blushed. "So which are you?"

Yasmeen's eyes flared, though she sensed he was only playing with her. "Wow, what a way to ruin the moment." She set down her coffee cup and whacked him with her book of crosswords.

Joanasi ducked, using his hands to defend himself. "Ouch, ouch! Down, girl!" he hollered while she continued bonking him over the head.

A small part of her wondered whether he actually believed the thing he had said. The rest of her sort of enjoyed the flirting. She brushed casually against him. He bumped back, a little harder. She didn't mind that his fingers were yellow with nicotine.

"Okay, okay, I know you're teasing. But I'll bite," she said. "Who are the motherfuckers?"

"Oh," he said. "I thought you would know that." He pushed a strand of hair out of her face. "The motherfuckers are the construction guys. They make their money, fuck our girls and then they hit the road, Jack." He held her in his dark gaze, straight-faced.

131

It unsettled her. She stared down at her fingernails, wondering how to respond. His expression changed suddenly. "I'm kidding," he reassured her. "I know you're none of those."

"You definitely had me going, there."

"How about some music?"

She was glad for the opportunity to lighten the mood. He flipped quickly through her shoebox of cassettes until he found something that suited the moment. "Yeah, this." He held out his selection for her approval.

"*Let It Be*. Excellent choice."

They listened to the album straight through, slurping their coffee, belting out their favourite lines. They consumed an entire box of Whippets, though it was mostly him. She wondered what would come next, after the record ended, whether they would continue to stall or if he would make his move. It was like being on her first-ever date. At the first bars of "The Long and Winding Road," she laid down her mug and pulled her knees into her chest. "Lennon or McCartney?" she asked, expressionless.

"McCartney."

"You're kidding, right?"

Joanasi tipped the last drop of coffee into his mouth and set the mug down by his feet.

Yasmeen noticed a twitch in his right eye, made worse by his refusal to pursue the discussion. He seemed easily offended. She rushed to fill the silence. "Come on, everyone knows that John was the brains behind the Beatles. I'll take 'Revolution' and 'Across the Universe' over 'Hey Jude' anytime."

He shrugged, non-committal. "Well, maybe. Could be. Who knows." He took her hand into his lap and leaned forward to kiss her hair.

She asked him what he was doing even though she knew darn well what he was up to. She gazed longingly into his eyes. The room was spinning.

"What am I doing?" he said. "You're a smart girl, figure it out."

"It's just that, I didn't think, um, well, I mean I'm ..."

"Shh," he said. He brushed a circle around her mouth with the tip of his tongue.

She could hardly believe what was happening to them, what was happening to her. She cupped her hands on his shoulders and moved toward him. The room disappeared and it was only the two of them and the sound of their breathing.

An hour later—or whenever it was, she had no idea—Yasmeen woke up and found him staring at her. The last thing she remembered was cuddling with him.

"What's wrong?" she said.

"Are you ever gonna take that shirt off?"

She took his hand and guided it underneath, laying his palm on her belly. The roof creaked as though a large animal were pacing back and forth across it. The wind was howling.

"Maybe it's a storm," he said. He moved his hand in slow circles under her shirt.

"Maybe."

"Wanna know something?" he asked.

"I want to know everything."

"When you're out there, in that weather, you have to keep moving. If you stay too long in one place, the snow builds a wall around you. It locks you in. You can't even see your own hand in front of you."

"I guess you'll just have to protect me then," she said.

He licked the fingers of his other hand and pushed her hair behind her ears. He pulled her toward him and smelled her scalp. He breathed across her cheek. She wondered what his hand would feel like on the other parts of her. She imagined him not stopping, not holding back.

She pulled away and fell back on the couch, making a big deal of it. She lifted her arms over her head to help him get her shirt off.

He removed his too, sniffing around her neck and at the sparse growth of her underarms. He eased down her jeans. It almost made her come. Through the window she could see walls of snow blowing horizontally.

He touched the tattoo on her hip and asked what it was. "Who's Lipo?"

"Are you jealous?" She smiled and stretched out like a cat. "You aren't, are you?" When she saw that he might be serious she reached up and touched his nose and said it's nothing you need to worry about, the guy's long dead. She felt the dampness through his jeans as he climbed on top of her and rocked his hips in a fluid motion.

When she woke up the room was flooded with the harsh light of the sun reflected off new white snow. Except for a slight chill in the air, all signs of the blizzard had vanished. Yasmeen peeked over at Joanasi, buck-naked on his side, arm bent with his palm curled up near his face. He was snoring softly. She held her arm up against his to compare their skin, saw how pale she looked compared to him. She covered him with the blanket.

A spidery lattice webbed the windowpane, fine silvery threads catching the sun and intensifying it. She couldn't believe all the loveliness around her. Holy fuck, she felt great. Only the intermittent sounds of men shovelling and clearing the road reminded her that there was indeed a world out there and that everything about it was right.

ELEVEN

The two spent the entire lazy weekend holed up at her place, but now it was time. Joanasi insisted Yasmeen meet his mother.

"I already did. We sew together," she said. "Remember?"

"You know what I mean," he said. The sun was radiant on his face. "I want her to really *know* you."

"Then I guess I'd better put some clothes on." She laughed. He kissed her hard.

As they ploughed through the newly fallen snow, he told her what he remembered about the old days, the winter camps, ice fishing with his uncle. He told her about his father who had died years ago, of lung cancer, and how it suddenly made him the man of the house. Everybody at home relied on him, he said—his mother, his brothers and sister and a grandmother called Minnie.

An aluminum cauldron was bubbling on Pasha's stove, infusing the kitchen with a gamey bouquet. Yasmeen wondered how half a dozen of them slept in this one place, even with the spare mattress in the living room. As if reading her mind, Joanasi explained that his family was on the waiting list for one of the new government houses going up, trimmed in bright Lego colours.

He splashed tea into a pair of mismatched cups and they squeezed in on the couch next to Pasha. The light of the

135

television was flickering in her eyes, but she was more attentive to the sewing in her lap. She squinted through the eyeglasses perched low down on her nose, stabbing a length of embroidery thread through the oblong eye of a needle. Joanasi said something in Inuktitut and she replied, "Aah," pulling her thread through. Yasmeen noted how she did it so easily. Joanasi hooked his arm around Yasmeen's shoulders and transferred his attention to what was playing on TV, a sci-fi adventure movie that someone had left in the video machine. Pasha laughed at all the parts Joanasi laughed at with her lopsided set of yellowy teeth.

Yasmeen joined in though she found the story about a dog named Digby who consumes a bowl of liquid growth formula and becomes a giant sheepdog rather silly. She wished she could converse with Pasha in her language and thought about asking Joanasi to teach her. Her students had taught her how to say *ullaakut* (good morning) and *tuttumik takuvunga* (I see a caribou) but these, she knew, would only get her so far. She tapped Pasha gently on the arm to get her attention and smiled at her from a deep place. "*Iviit kamik uvunga?*" she said.

Pasha stopped what she was doing and looked quizzically at her.

"What are you trying to say?" said Joanasi, trying to conceal a smile.

"Just, nothing, forget it." Yasmeen felt silly and embarrassed. She took a deep breath before continuing. "I thought maybe she could make me some sealskin boots. I'll pay her, of course."

Joanasi translated. When he finished, Pasha looked at Yasmeen and answered in a way that took her a long time. Yasmeen turned to Joanasi for an explanation.

"She said it would be better for you to learn to make them yourself. She said she could help you."

Yasmeen smiled at Pasha, trying to convey her deep gratitude through touch and body language. Pasha nodded and continued with an afterthought, which Joanasi dutifully passed on to Yasmeen. "The next week's sewing circle. It's at Sarah's."

At the commercial break, he took Yasmeen's teacup to the sink and said, "Let's lie down on the bed." She followed him into the bedroom, the one small window of which was boarded up with plywood and covered over with a flowered bed sheet. Joanasi switched on the lamp and threw a pillowcase over it. It gave the room an aquarium glow. She noticed his unmade bed, his crooked dresser with a half-open drawer and underwear sticking out of it. She didn't feel anything in particular about it. It was an adequate room.

For a long time they lay together in silence, the muffled sounds of the household filtering in, the babble of TV, the opening and slamming of the front door, visitors coming and going. She stared at the fluttering pulse of Joanasi's neck.

"Tell me a story from your life," he said.

"No, you first."

He propped himself up on one elbow and gazed into her eyes as he undid her shirt, one button at a time, slowly and with purpose. She could tell he was thinking about his story.

"My father was a good teacher," he said. "When I was seven years old, he brought me out on the land. He asked me what direction the wind was coming from. He said if I could tell him, then he would teach me everything he knew. I was so afraid to disappoint him, so I thought and thought very hard about it, and he told me stop thinking, just feel it. And after I relaxed, I got it right and then he handed me his special knife and said 'Now, Little Man, it is up to you to build our igloo for the night.'"

Joanasi touched the very tip of her nipple with his fingernail. It felt like fire and ice at once. He raked his fingers slowly up and down her breast. She opened her mouth to speak, to ask him how she had been so lucky as to find a man like him, a man not afraid to be a real man. He put his finger to her lips, meaning the time for talk was over.

At supper, Yasmeen devoured everything that was put in front of her. Even Pasha was surprised. Not altogether sure what the food was, she ate it anyway. It tasted rich in oil and fat and she decided that having the waist and hips of a white woman would never be enough for Joanasi. From now on she had to eat well. Hers had to be the body he desired, it had to be of a certain abundance for him to flash that rare, brief smile at her.

Eating on the floor with his family, accepting the meat from Pasha's hand, learning to wield the traditional *ulu*, cutting away the sinew and putting the food between her teeth, was like starting all over again, from zero. It was about learning the tongue, the incisors, the molars. The throat, the stomach. She wanted to unravel the mystery of her body, its infinite capacity; she wanted to understand its language the way he understood his.

Gradually Joanasi moved his clothes into her house, a few items at a time. She cleared a drawer for him and made space in the cupboard and told him to consider it their place from now on. She loved having him in her bed at night.

Life with him ate up much of her time. Leaving in the morning was always a big production, him begging her to stay home so they could have sex all day, Yasmeen tempted but always finding the strength to pull away—usually about ten minutes before the first bell. They struck a compromise. He shortened his hours at the radio station and she stopped hanging out at the coffee machine during her spares. She fulfilled her obligations at school but stopped doing all the extras. She kept her private life private.

Every day at noon Joanasi plugged in his headphones and charged up the turntable in his booth at the radio station, playing songs with hidden meanings, which she listened to religiously as she spooned something raw or hot into her belly for lunch, something he had hunted himself or offered her from the community freezer, slivers of beluga whale or seal or caribou meat. As soon as the four o'clock bell sent the children vaulting home through the snow, she raced back to be with him for the rest of the night. She wrote letters to Morgan trying to articulate her feelings. *Dear you,* one of them said. *Summer or winter, it's a cold place. Almost nothing grows here. It's lonely outside. It's lovely outside. I am a small person on so much land.*

One night before they dropped off to sleep Yasmeen heard what she thought was the arrival of the great caribou herds. She ran to the window. Joanasi got out of bed and stood behind her, arms circled about her waist. "You're very sweet," he said. "But caribou don't come this close to the village. Come back to bed, now."

They settled in again under the covers. She laid her head on his chest. "That story you told the children at school, about the man who changed into a caribou, what did you mean by it?"

He stroked her hair. "My father told it to me when I was a boy. To teach me a lesson."

"Lesson?"

"To be the man you are and not somebody else …" He kissed her on the mouth. "Now, your turn. Tell me about the tattoo of the dead man on your hip."

"It's nothing, really," she said. "Trust me, you're going to be disappointed."

"Tell me, and then I'll tell you if I'm disappointed or not."

"And what do I get if I win the bet?"

"I'll give you a bath that will make you forget every other man you've been with."

"Wow. That's an offer I can't refuse. But don't go telling me it wasn't worth a bet."

"Please," he said. "Don't laugh at me."

"I'm not laughing, really I'm not. I just find your jealousy surprisingly ... sweet. And slightly territorial." She paused, worried that maybe he'd find her territorial comment offensive. When he didn't react, she continued. "Don't get me wrong, though, it's fine with me. It's nice to know that passionate men still exist out there." She liked the idea of a guy who would resort to desperate measures like slicing off a digit or jumping from a bridge if he couldn't have the one person in his life he truly wanted.

Her compliment drew a smile from him.

"Okay, here it is," she began, in a tone that suggested *don't say I didn't warn you.* "Li Po was a Chinese poet who was in love with the moon."

"The moon?"

"Yes, the moon. One night he was walking home dead drunk. As he crossed a bridge, he saw the moon's reflection in the water, and when he jumped in to embrace it, he drowned ..." She paused for dramatic effect. "Oh yeah, one more thing. This all happened in the eighth century. You've got absolutely *nothing* to worry about."

"That's it?" His eyes narrowed. "Why is he on your hip, then?"

"What do you want, I was young. I thought his death was kind of tragic. And romantic."

On the days they got water delivery he spoiled her, filling the tub to excess, bathing her, soaping her ptarmigan-white body with his rough palms. Sometimes he carried her shimmering wet into their bed. "Take me," she would whisper in his ear. "Every way." She wanted nothing forbidden between them. She wanted to disappear inside of him, to slip into him whole and stay there forever. She wanted to be dressed and fed and looked after.

In return he taught her about his culture, warned her about the things outside that could pose a threat to her, a certain kind of snow, the kind you could fall through, snow that was crusty on top but soft inside. He said he would protect her.

Sometimes she closed her eyes and imagined him as her infant child, greedy lips at her engorged breasts. She imagined a whole family of him: she with enough breast for each mouth, all of them drinking from her, their pleasure sending an explosion of desire through her. She thought of Elisapie and wondered how she had had the strength to give up her baby, even if it was true that it was her father's.

Joanasi filled her with a pleasure beyond anything she'd known. Sometimes she lapsed into sleep against his shoulder, then awakened to find him staring at her, the room still awash in the glow of their lovemaking. "Do it to me again," she would whisper.

He hated all the hours that school stole from them but she made him understand that her job was the very thing that had brought her to him in the first place. He nodded and told her she was right, he had no business taking that away from her. To compensate, he monopolized her on the weekends, drawing the shades, locking the door, lounging around in bed with her until supper, as though the outside world didn't exist at all. In good weather he took her out on the land, away from everyone. She barely had time for lesson plans and corrections, and became good at improvising in the classroom. On-the-spot planning, she called it.

One Saturday they left the village before anyone was awake, darkness folding around them. Scarf pulled high over her face, she settled in behind him on the Skidoo, thighs gripping his hips. They sped toward a vein of light in the distance, wind loosening wild drifts of snow on the outskirts of town where a pair of bedded-down huskies slept, noses buried in each other's fur.

She gave herself over to the purity of space, the rasp of the sled runners carving tracks in the snow, the boundless land and sky, nothing for hundreds of kilometres interrupting the horizon. This is what pure freedom feels like, she thought. This is what it means to let go of everything, completely, to think of nothing, to not think, to be all animal, bone, piss, shit, blood, to act only as your body requires, involuntarily.

The world was white. The moment was breath and she was in it, inhaling deeply. Exhaling the silence that begets silence, where everything begins again at the beginning, at the hushed epicenter of everything.

Joanasi found a promising site and ordered her to stay put as he built their temporary home for the night. He tested the hard-packed drift with his probe, then cut the first blocks with his snow knife, methodically building upwards in a continuous spiral. Watching him reminded her of what the Eskimos in Mrs. Fishwick's black and white film did for survival. Those early, skin-clad people didn't have land claims deals and governments building them ultra-insulated houses with kitchens and appliances and parking spaces for snowmobiles—the kind they were all slated to get sooner or later. Those first people made do, and being out on the land with Joanasi was like going back in time. It was a reminder even to him that he was self-sufficient, that his hands could carve and build and feed a village. He had explained all this to her the night of the school opening when they walked back to her place together—his symbiotic relationship with the land, how it made him feel like a whole man, like someone who honours and cares for and nurtures it. "When I am out there, I belong to it and it belongs to me," he had said.

The brief hours of daylight were gone and the wind was picking up again. She watched with admiration as he cut and shaped and fit the blocks perfectly together. He plugged up the cracks with snow to seal out the cold, and waved her inside.

Yasmeen waited as Joanasi shook out the caribou skins and spread them on the ground. He sat her in his lap so that she could see herself reflected in his eyes. There was so much about him to admire: how he embraced life, his refusal to waste energy trying to ward off impermanence and death, things he had no control over. Probably he never even questioned it. Joanasi didn't articulate why he did the things he did, he just did them. He ate and slept and held down a job. He hunted. He saw to it that she was safe, and his.

He held out a morsel of char to her, sideways on the blade of his knife, his tapered eyes watching her lips and tongue reach for it. "*Aippaq*," he said, "I might be in love with you." He lifted the teacup to her lips.

"I love how you do everything for me," she said. "How you take care of me."

"I like how you take care of me too," he answered. He slipped his tongue into her mouth and moaned from a deep place. She told him he could have her any way he wanted. He smiled and said he once heard that, in the old days, if a hunter couldn't find himself a woman for the night he sometimes took an animal. The custom wasn't obscene to her, it was erotic.

Afterwards they laid down together in the vellum darkness, listening to the long-drawn-out breath of the wind. Listening to it blow snow finer than talcum across the plain.

143

She felt him grope her, nudging her out of the brume of sleep because he was ready for her, because he wanted to be inside her and he didn't want to wait. His forearm reached around her waist and pinned her against his solid mass. He swung his leg over her hip, stabilizing her as he forced inside and pushed, grinding his joy into her, his blue-hot breath blowing on her neck. She wept. She remembered the voluminous sky and its river of stars. She remembered Joanasi building the igloo and caulking it against the cold, reassuring her that even if they were naked, it would be warm inside.

He thrust and she winced, feeling he had torn something in the deepest part of her. She bit down on her hand to give her a different pain to think about. It hurt like nothing she could put words to. She was ashamed of herself. She wanted to love it, to not want to cry out, because this was what it meant to belong to the earth and its winter. To be a real woman, so full, so powerless, so utterly bound to the moon's pull.

When he was on the cusp he eased up on her, squirting through her narrow passage, and in that instant she knew she would love him forever. Wavelets of her musky smell filled the igloo. What day was it? She had lost track. How many times had they done it already?

December 1983 (Dates from here on in are meaningless!!)
Dearest Morgan,

Remember a long time ago when we decided no half measures? Well, I met someone. And I'm in it for the duration. He's from here and he's fantastic.

Morgan, it's going so fast and I'm afraid but that's how I know it's right. I like how he makes me feel, weak when I'm with him but also strong, probably the strongest I've ever been. I don't even know how that's possible, but that's how it is. The first time we were really together, I knew.

Has it ever happened to you, to physically ache when you've been away from your lover too long? That's the only way I can explain it. My world now is only fillable by one person. I can't be without him. I need him. My body needs him. I want to be with him for the rest of my life. I want to have his children, as many as we can make together. And the lucky thing for me— he wants me. I mean *really* wants. Leaving here for two weeks at Xmas is going to kill me. Please don't think I'm crazy. This is the sanest I've ever been. I see everything clearly and it's all b-e-a-u-t-i-f-u-l. Money is nothing, love is everything. I understand now what it means to live as the Creator intended us to (and yes, I believe in the Great Creator, as Joanasi has explained him to me!!). You're my best friend, the only one I can tell this to. Be happy for me.

Yours,
Yasmeen

P.S. Re-reading this, I feel that I might be letting you down. I can almost hear you going "what the fuck?" Maybe if I were in your shoes, so far away, I'd think the same thing. Let's talk face to face when I get home. You'll know just by being with me. You'll see it in my eyes.

TWELVE

Yasmeen arrived at Sarah's house and got to work on the duffel socks she had begun with Annie's help. Though she liked Pasha's idea of trying to make her own sealskin boots, it proved to be too difficult a task with its complicated overlay of different skins to make a decorative design. Even the duffel socks demanded a level of skill and artistry she didn't have, but Joanasi convinced her to give it a try. He explained how handmade clothes were more than just functional, they expressed something unique about their maker. He assured her, knowing her as he did, that she would make a beautiful pair. Yasmeen had grown very fond of the sewing circle and all the women who were part of it. She loved learning the techniques of clothing production that had been handed down from generation to generation for over a thousand years. It made her feel more connected to Joanasi.

Sarah popped her head out of the kitchen and announced there was tea and coffee for everyone. A collective aah wafted from the group.

Yasmeen passed one of her alirtiks to Annie for inspection. Annie lifted her eyebrows and showed Yasmeen's workmanship around the circle. The women smiled.

"I think you're getting the hang of it," said Annie as people slowly made their way to the kitchen for coffee and bannock.

Yasmeen sat back on her heels and watched an elder bite the skins she was preparing to sew together. Her old-world method, a method none of the younger women used anymore, fascinated Yasmeen so much she passed on Sarah's last call for coffee. The ladies drifted back into the room.

Annie was preparing to announce something to the group when Paulussie barged in through the front door. He dropped his coat on the floor and kept walking.

Sarah narrowed her eyes and muttered under her breath that he wasn't welcome here right now. They exchanged dirty looks that suggested they were still in the throes of a previous argument.

Paulussie staggered toward her, oblivious to those watching. Sarah stepped out of his way. He locked his gaze on her as she sat back down in her armchair and proceeded to sew the lining for a pair of mitts.

Undeterred, he walked around the chair and stood behind her. He leaned forward as though he were about to tell her something intimate, heavy breaths ruffling the hairs on her head. Sarah remained upright in her seat, spectacularly uncompromising, jabbing the cloth with her needle, yanking it through with a vigorous tug. All through it she kept her composure. Only after Paulussie got bored and lumbered over to the bedroom to sleep it off did Yasmeen notice Sarah's hands, how they couldn't stop trembling.

The bubble-wrapped package finally arrived in the mail. It had taken so long Yasmeen had almost forgotten about it. She tore it open right there in the post office.

For months she'd done her best to give her students the tools they needed to navigate their future, but what she really wanted was something that would mirror their own story back to them, the centuries of accumulated wisdom that had allowed them to live in harmony with nature. Now she had it in her hands, the celebrated 1922 silent documentary, *Nanook of the North: A Story Of Life and Love In the Actual Arctic*.

Qalingo's eyes widened as he moonwalked into class and noticed the TV and VCR player set up by the blackboard. "Yes!" he said, high-fiving Audlaluk.

The girls pushed their desks together and poured themselves each a handful of Skittles. Yasmeen switched off the lights and pressed Play. The film jumped around and crackled as the opening subtitles filled the screen.

"What the hell," groaned Qalingo. "What's this old stuff? Where's the action?" He crossed his arms over his chest and tapped his toe on the floor, impatiently.

Yasmeen gave his shoulder a gentle squeeze. "Give it a chance." She pointed at the hero of the movie, kayaking in traditional skins.

Qalingo looked away, unimpressed. Yasmeen left him and walked confidently to the back of the class. She glanced around the room and waited. After a while, Qalingo uncrossed his arms and leaned forward, saying *wow* and *cool* during the hunting scenes. "Mamaqtuk," said Audlaluk as the actors gorged on their blubbery kill. The kids watched all seventy-eight minutes of hunting and sledging and igloo-building with record attention. Yasmeen had never been so ecstatic about a lesson.

"Don't tell me," said Elliot afterwards in the staffroom. He was leafing through a pile of test papers. "You wanted to remind them of their lasting connection to the world of their forebears. You wanted to show them that you value their customs, so they should too."

Yasmeen felt the blood drain from her face.

Elliot took a sip from his Batman mug and licked the sheen off his lips. "You *are* aware that a lot of what Flaherty did in that film was unethical, are you not?"

"What are you talking about?"

"I mean, beautiful as it is, a lot of that film was staged. Remember the harpoon? Cute, wasn't it? Did you know they were already using rifles by then?"

She couldn't think of what to say.

"Seriously. I can't believe you didn't know that."

She wanted to tell him he was just a jaded old guy, but she remained positive. She told him she thought it was groundbreaking cinema. "Who gives a shit if the filmmaker played around a little? Sometimes an artist has to exaggerate to get at the truth of something." She told him how much they loved the trading post sequence, when Nanook stared incredulously as crazy sound came pouring out of the gramophone. Qalingo clutched his side, he was laughing so hard. Audlaluk looked like he'd pee his pants. When Nanook put the record in his mouth and bit it, the entire class was in stitches. "Oh, my god, that scene—"

"Entirely scripted," said Elliot. "And things aren't going to go back to the way they were any time soon, you can bet on that. The people here just *love* their gadgets."

"Scripted or not, I'm glad I showed it to them. Most of my kids have grandparents who understand it's up to them to carry the traditions forward. But things are changing so fast, it's hard for them to keep up … we have to help them the best way—"

"That's not our mandate," Elliot interrupted. "That's what the Culture teachers are here for."

Yasmeen gathered her papers in a huff. "We should all of us be putting their traditions on a pedestal! For fuck's sake, *Nanook* was filmed in their own backyard, why shouldn't we show it to them?" She reached for Elliot's tests and dumped them in his lap. "You're a dick," she snapped. "For always spoiling everything."

"Tell me again about the old days," said Yasmeen as she soaked lazily in the bath. Joanasi's hands rinsed the soap from her body. He kissed her hair. He kissed her breasts. He told her things his father had told him about the dogsledding days, how hunters had to keep moving in the hopes of finding caribou, stopping where the snow was soft enough to make camp and lighten the load, how they stored their supplies in the igloo and took off on foot after the herd, turning the sled on its side to keep the dogs from running away with it. He spoke of long winter evenings inside, the man making bracelets or trinkets out of walrus tusk while his wife sewed clothes for the family, the silence only broken by the howling of the dogs. "I love your people," Yasmeen said. "It's like I'm living the end of an age with you, only I never want it to end." Joanasi rested his hand between her thighs, waiting for her to reach down and guide his fingers around and in.

With Christmas in the air, classes began thinning out, students either skipping off or arriving halfway through the day, tousled and sleepy. Elliot and Sam stood around the coffee machine talking about the weather conditions, analyzing the likelihood of plane delays or flight cancellations. The hope, of course, was for clear skies. Neither wanted to be socked in. Neither wanted to be stuck, as they put it, in Saqijuvik for the holidays. "We're expecting a blizzard," said Yasmeen one morning, trying to get a rise out of them.

Through her connection to the sewing circle, she was invited to the holiday bake sale, hosted by the village ladies' association, to raise money for an after-school hockey program. Yasmeen was thrilled to have been the only white teacher officially invited. Annie helped her put the finishing touches on her new alirtiks so she could wear them to the event, show people what she had made with her own hands. Joanasi was so proud he convinced his mother to give Yasmeen her Christmas gift early, a beautiful pair of sealskin boots, so she would genuinely feel like part of the community.

A small committee repurposed the gym in a few hours, festooning it with red and green paper chains and artificial pine boughs. They rushed around setting up tables and arranging cupcakes on aluminum pie plates with little price cards beside them.

Yasmeen arrived with a tray of carrot muffins, hoping to be assigned a task to help out, but the women kept rushing past her with their hands full. She set her tray down on one of the tables and went to stand by the door under the bright red Exit sign, hoping to spot someone she knew. She was grateful when Annie saw her and invited her to be part of their gift exchange. Yasmeen followed her to a large glass bowl already filled with names. She folded her slip of paper and dropped it in, mixing it around with the others.

An elder passing by caught her arm. "Yasmeengai," she said, in the customary way. She was with another old woman who was wearing a floral-print dress over her bulky snow pants.

Yasmeen said, "Aah."

The first woman squatted to admire her new sealskin boots. "Eeee," she trilled. The other one knelt beside her and rubbed her knobbly hand across the boot. She waggled a finger at Yasmeen and burst into laughter.

"What are they saying?" Yasmeen asked Annie.

Annie chuckled and pointed at their feet. "They're saying that you look like the Inuk in your sealskin boots and they look like the white people."

It was true. They were wearing the same puffy Sorel boots with the sturdy rubber soles that she had brought with her from the army surplus store in Montreal. She pointed to herself and joined in their laughter. "*Uvunga Inuk,*" she said. I am Inuk.

"Aah," they chimed in unison, before shuffling away.

She arrived home to the phone ringing.

"I'm throwing a party," said Elliot. "You're coming, right?"

"What's the occasion?"

"The end of the semester," he said. "You've heard of Christmas in July? Well, this is summer in December, a luau. B.Y.O.M."

"Huh?"

"Bring your own margarita. Get it?"

Yasmeen hung up and dialled Sam. "So, are you going?"

"Everyone's going," she said. "Even Jacqueline and Tommy."

Yasmeen mentioned it to Joanasi.

"Why do you wanna go over there?" he said. His back was to her and his head bent like he was working at something that required all of his concentration.

From where she stood, Yasmeen couldn't tell what he was up to. She waited for his answer. She waited some more. "Oh, come on. It'll be fun. Plus, I want to show you off," she said.

They could have been in Jamaica. Or the Bahamas. Yasmeen hardly recognized Elliot's place when she walked through the door. It was a tropical paradise, a makeover created with just a few items ordered through the mail: a life-size mural of a sandy beach at sunset, plastic palm trees, melon-coloured paper lanterns hung from the ceiling. He had fashioned a straw Tiki bar and stocked it with hibiscus-pink tumblers and wine goblets, and full bottles of tequila and rum. Swizzle sticks and miniature parasols poked out from exotic drinks served in coconut shells. Joanasi's eyes lit up.

Elliot bellowed from the kitchen for everyone to grab a drink. No wasn't an option. It's a party. At a party, you party.

Jacqueline was sitting barefoot on Tommy's lap in a grass skirt and halter top and was chewing on a red straw, admiring her toes, curling and uncurling them as though they were the most interesting thing in the world. She sounded slightly drunk, repeating "Tommy just loves kissing my toes," to whoever would listen. Across the room Iris was sipping from a tall glass of ginger ale, her effort at a costume limited to a floppy white flower in her hair and a dangly pair of snail earrings. Sam and Paulussie were partying on the dance floor, hands across each other's shoulders, kicking their feet from side to side to "Good Vibrations."

Yasmeen ducked into the kitchen to say hello while Joanasi stood on the sidelines and lit a cigarette. Elliot was in a loud Hawaiian shirt, his back to her as he slid a tray of ice cubes into the freezer.

"Welcome," he said, pecking her on each cheek. "Let's dance."

"In a minute," she told him. "You didn't tell me we were supposed to dress up."

"Don't get your knickers in a knot." He wiped his hands on a dishcloth and followed her like a puppy into the living room.

Yasmeen grabbed two coconut drinks and curled up beside Joanasi on the couch.

"C'mon!" shouted Elliot. He grabbed her hand, almost spilling her drink on Joanasi. "No one sits on their tush to the Beach Boys! Not in this house!" He took the drink from her and gave it to Joanasi to hold. She waved in protest but he dragged her up and hooked his arm around her waist and swung her in circles, saying, "Excuse us" to the tables and chairs they kept bumping into. She laughed so much she couldn't catch her breath. He told her to calm down or she'd have a heart attack.

"You sure are a lunatic sometimes," she yelled across the music. He reached out and pulled a strand of hair out of her eyes.

Something went click inside her. She pushed his hand away, glancing over at Joanasi. Smoke was shooting out through his nostrils. She blew him a kiss and mouthed the words *I love you.* He smiled without smiling too much, crushed out his cigarette and lit another.

Yasmeen called for him to join them, but he scrunched up his nose and shook his head. "You dance," he said. "You dance with Elliot."

The opening chords of "God Only Knows" came on. She wrenched her hands free of Elliot's and went to plant a wet, deliberate kiss on Joanasi's mouth. "I love this song, Joanasi," she said.

Joanasi shook his head and said, "No, not now." He moved in closer. "Later I'll fuck you really hard," he said. His hot breath in her ear gave her goose bumps.

"What's up with you and Joanasi?" said Elliot, when she returned to the dance floor. "Don't tell me you're an item."

"You could say that." She could see that he was surprised.

They slow-danced at an awkward distance from one another until the song was over and a fast one came on. Elliot pulled her into a corner and sat her down. "I only want a minute of your time," he said. She bobbed up immediately.

"Joanasi's waiting," she said.

"Just one," he said, holding up his forefinger. "Do me a favour." She sat back down and looked across the room at Joanasi, trying to send him a message with her eyes.

"Make it fast," she said. She crossed her arms.

"Okay, so there was this white guy named James Houston. You heard of him?"

Yasmeen stretched and faked a yawn.

"James Houston, Canadian artist. From Toronto." He said Toronto like an American, pronouncing every T. "In 1948, Houston ends up in Inukjuak with the idea he's going to paint. He spends, I don't know, maybe ten years there. During that time he sees these guys making beautiful carvings out of soapstone and he decides he wants to help them out, he wants to do something good for them, you see what I'm getting at here?"

"Not really."

"So he takes some of their small carvings down to Montreal and the people there go bananas and the next thing you know, there's a government grant to send him back up there to get more. By now, city folks are lining up around the block to get this stuff. It's getting shipped out to Europe, South America, the Middle East, everywhere. See what I mean?"

Yasmeen shrugged. "What's your point?"

"My point is they were happy as pigs in shit making their little carvings before Houston came along. I'm saying maybe they didn't need his help. I mean, look where it's got them. When they're sober, they produce these sublime sculptures. But these days, because of Houston, they know that if they need pocket money for booze, they can always just whip up one of those beauties and there's always going to be a white guy ready to pay big bucks for it."

"What the fuck does this have to do with me and Joanasi?"

"What I'm saying is, we're teachers, we're here to teach a few kids math, a little English, that's it."

"Maybe that's it for you, but not for me," she said.

"Let me put it to you this way," he said. "A record album can be skipping at the same spot every single day for an entire month and you ask a guy here, is it gonna skip tomorrow? Nine times out of ten the guy will say 'Aatsuuk,' maybe, who knows, while the white guy says, 'Of course.' It's how we think. And it's how they think ... My advice? Enjoy the experience, take it all in, take great pleasure in going for a walk and breathing in the fresh air," he said. "But crossing over to the other side, that's a whole other ballgame."

Yasmeen rose to her feet. "As usual," she said. "You're full of shit."

❀

Night was waning. Yasmeen yawned into her hand. The Tiki bar looked like the aftermath of a Grey Cup celebration with its moraine of empties and crumb-filled chip bowls. Wall decorations dangled from their filaments. A blue curtain of smoke hung in the air.

Iris had gone home early. Sam's head was lolling drunkenly on Paulussie's shoulder, the two of them snoring on the couch. Yasmeen and Jacqueline were sitting on the floor, backs propped against the wall. The beach music had mellowed into Cat Stevens.

"Tell me about you and Tommy," Yasmeen said, jiggling the ice at the bottom of her glass.

"*Qu'est-ce que tu veux savoir, ma belle?*"

"Well … do you plan on marrying him eventually?"

Jacqueline picked at the ragged label of her beer bottle. "*Honnêtement, je crois qu'non.* Tommy is a beautiful lover, yes, of course. But I'm not here forever."

"You mean he's not the one?" She stared at Jacqueline's ankle tattoo, the antique key that Yasmeen had called the key to her heart. She knew now that it probably had nothing to do with Tommy.

"The world is a big place. *J'ai pas l'intention de rester plantée ici toute ma vie.* Forever is a long time."

Yasmeen hid her surprise. "What'll you do? Will you go back to Shawinigan?"

"Hell, no. I want to move around. There's still Thailand I want to see, and India, of course. *Puis c'est mon grand rêve de faire l'amour avec un Arabe un de ces jours. Tu sais, un bel homme aux yeux noirs!*"

Yasmeen couldn't believe her ears. She couldn't believe how badly she had misread that relationship. Here she thought Jacqueline was a permanent fixture in Tommy's life and all along she'd been fantasizing about the next lover, someone on the other side of the ocean, an Arab with intense black eyes.

"I don't get it. Why have you stayed for so long, then? Four years, that's a big chunk of time."

"*Peut-être*," she said. "But where else in Quebec does a nurse get to be her own boss? I mean, really run the show?"

Yasmeen nodded. She had so many questions, like how was she going to break it to him and didn't she feel the least bit guilty that she was going to hurt him in the end.

But Jacqueline had a bigger picture in mind. She told Yasmeen about one of her cases a while back, a man who arrived at the clinic with blood all over his clothes and hands. The tire of his pickup had exploded in his face. She told the story breathlessly, about how she knew when she saw all that blood she wouldn't be able to bandage him up and send him home, so she called a doctor in Kuujjuaraapik and told him she had an emergency and what should she do. "Oh my god, you must have been shitting bricks," said Yasmeen. And Jacqueline shrugged, saying how the doctor told her to stay on the phone, he would guide her step by step so she could properly sew him up and not have to medevac him out, and she took care of the whole thing without a single slipup. And now that she knew she could do something like that, she was ready for the next challenge in her life.

"I don't know how you do it, Jackie."

Their men were hovering over them, a potent whiff of alcohol coming off one or both of them. Yasmeen couldn't look Tommy in the eye without thinking about the swarthy Arab who would one day replace him in Jacqueline's bed.

"Get your sandals," Tommy said in a gravelly voice. "Let's go." Jacqueline stood and kissed him on the mouth.

Joanasi was wobbling a little but sober. He stretched his hand out to Yasmeen and pulled her up off the floor. "Home," he said.

THIRTEEN

The teachers were headed south again, Christmas less than a week away. A few villagers made it out to the airstrip to see them off but most were busy preparing for their own festivities, or sleeping. Besides Joanasi, a small delegation came out to say goodbye to Yasmeen: Annie and two students, Elisapie and Salatee. The girls waved shyly from the sidelines as a sharp gust of wind from the propellers swept their hair in all directions. They looked like changelings, midway between childhood and womanhood.

"Why aren't you girls wearing hats?" shouted Yasmeen.

They shrugged and came to stand beside her.

"I think that you are the smartest teacher that I ever knew," said Salatee, kicking up snow with the toe of her boot.

"I'm really, really gonna miss you," said Elisapie.

Yasmeen hugged them both at once. "I'm only going for two weeks," she said. "You can't get rid of me that easily!" She glanced over the tops of their heads at Joanasi who was waiting patiently to have her to himself. Annie hugged her and told her to hurry back. Yasmeen pointed to her alirtiks and gave Annie the thumbs up, meaning she couldn't have made them without her. A hand poked around Yasmeen's waist and she turned just in time to meet Joanasi's lips. The girls skedaddled.

He and Yasmeen waited in silence as the plane loaded up, Joanasi's mouth clamped tighter than a bear trap. Yasmeen could tell by the little throbs at his temples that he was grinding his molars again. When it looked like they were about to begin boarding passengers, he dug into his pocket. "I have something for you," he said. He rolled it between his fingers so she could see that it was an ivory ring. He held it for a moment in his palm.

"My god, Joanasi, it's beautiful," she said. He removed her mitt and slid it along the marriage finger of her hand.

She dropped her knapsack in the snow and threw her arms around his neck. "I wish I didn't have to go, I wish I were already back." She felt a lump in her throat, but she didn't cry.

"So don't," he said, his eyelid twitching. "Don't go. Stay here with me instead." He ran his thumb along her upper lip.

"You know I can't. My family's expecting me."

He nodded and walked her slowly to the plane. She hugged him and started up the steps, turning to look at him one last time before leaving him behind.

She settled into the last available seat, beside Elliot, and shoved her knapsack under the seat in front of her. The co-pilot banged the door shut, locked it and went to belt himself into the cockpit. The pilot turned and flashed a Pepsodent smile at everybody. *And now, it's ho-ho-homeward bound,* he called out.

He drove a short distance along the airstrip before turning the plane around. A chorus of phlegmy coughs erupted in the back seats. Yasmeen craned her neck to get a last look at Joanasi waving. A blast of wind blew off his hat but he just stood there, refusing to go after it.

They thundered down the runway, gathering momentum as the plane rose weightlessly into the air. The last thing she saw was Joanasi's black cap tumbling over the white snow, lifting a little, touching down again as it drifted further and further out of range.

Yasmeen stared through the window until the village disappeared behind them. It wasn't long before the flat, snow-covered land grew harsh again and all that was left was a veined hemisphere of ice and rock. She once told Joanasi that she could hardly conceive of so few inhabitants on such a vast terrain. It made her appreciate the concept of the Inukshuk even more, how a small pile of rocks made the inhuman landscape human.

She ran her thumbnail along the band of the ivory ring, wondering whether Joanasi was still lingering at the airstrip. It felt strange to be in the sky so far away from him. She knew that after she switched to the bigger plane in Kuujjuaraapik and then touched down in Montreal, it would feel like they were in two different galaxies. Over there, in what the Northerners called the South, the sad light of neon and office towers would reign over the sky. It would make her wish she could turn back the clock to the first night of Joanasi's hands in her hair.

Now all she had was his ring, its crown delicately raised into the head of a polar bear. She admired how it looked on her hand.

Elliot was chewing gum and leafing through an airline magazine. He cleared his throat, refusing to look up. "So, are we talking?"

"I guess."

"Good." He slipped the magazine back into the seat pocket and turned to face her. "What I've been trying to tell you is that people aren't always what they seem on the surface."

"Tell me something I don't know."

"Okay, then, how about this? Don't trust your heart."

She rolled her eyes. "What do *you* know about that?"

"I just know," he sighed. "I had a wife."

"So you had a wife, big deal. So does half the planet."

He swallowed. "So, she took off with my best friend and then she took me to the cleaners."

"How does that have anything to do with me?"

"I'm just saying, trust me. You aren't the first to fall for someone up north."

"So?"

"So, I've been here longer than you. Eventually, these things ... they go sour."

"Are you speaking from experience? Because if you're not, you have nothing to teach me."

"You're not going to change him."

"I would never do that. I respect him too much."

Elliot picked up the magazine again and opened it to a random page. He brought it close to his face, pretending to read it.

"What is it you want from me?"

He turned and looked straight in her eyes. "I don't want you getting hurt."

"Who asked you to protect me?"

"It's not about protection," he said. "You're a big girl, I know."

"Then what?"

She was drained. The day had exhausted her, the worry over how she and Joanasi would part, their goodbyes, the anxiety over seeing her family again, the uncertainty of how much of her new life she would reveal to them. Would she tell them of Tommy's break-in? Would she mention Joanasi? She didn't have the patience for Elliot's guessing games. She told him to cough it up, stop beating around the bush, just come clean and say what you want to say.

He slapped the magazine shut. "Okay, here's the thing. I lost everything, so I came up here. It's not that easy to start again from nothing, you know." The lines around his eyes softened.

A part of her felt sorry for him.

"You know, my dream was to go to law school," he said. "I could have done it, but I worked to put my wife through school and then, well ..."

"My mother hoped I would go to law school."

The plane hit an air pocket. Elliot's magazine flew off his lap but Yasmeen snatched it before it hit the floor. "Don't worry, things will work out," she said. She passed back the magazine and gave his arm a comforting squeeze.

A flashing cabin light instructed passengers to fasten their seatbelts. Yasmeen raised the blind and gazed out at the wavy point of light in the distance, watching it slowly become a twinkling network of bridges and roads, high-rises, cathedrals, shopping plazas, railway yards, houses. The sound of the engine shifted as the effervescent city filled more and more of her window. She stared as though she'd never seen it before, its blood flow, its swelter of rush and noise, its dirty snow and agitated traffic, its jewelled red taillights that snaked through the busy nerve centre. Sitting where she was, at the wing of the plane, she watched the opening of the landing flaps, stippled with grease and rivets. She closed her eyes and let the jostling aircraft carry her as though she were aloft in the belly of a large bird.

A staticky announcement came on, in French, then English, then in halting Inuktitut. She opened her eyes again, straining to make out the pilot's message—the weather forecast, she assumed. She was right. Something about *damp with flurries*. The rest, except for *happy holidays*, was garbled. This far from Saqijuvik, the Inuktitut registered as something alien to her ears.

It was a smooth landing. Scattered applause filled the cabin. The aircraft droned along the runway, gradually decelerating until it lurched to a halt. Every light extinguished and a dark stillness saturated the plane. Moments later something beeped and everything switched on again.

"I guess this is it," said Elliot, reaching into the overhead compartment for their carry-ons. "Someone meeting you?"

"Mother, probably." She strapped on her knapsack and followed him down the aisle, waving goodbye to Sam and Iris, who were still gathering their belongings.

Inside the cavernous terminal, passengers wheeled squeaky baggage carts toward the rotating carousel to wait for their luggage, while welcoming locals gathered on the other side of the gate, friends and relatives and weary children clutching balloons and teddy bears.

Detouring to the restroom to freshen up, her eyes fell on a tired-looking artificial tree with half its lights burnt out. She couldn't get over how much she was missing Joanasi. At the mirror she searched for a tube of lip-gloss and ran it around her lips. By the time she emerged from the restroom, parka and snow pants draped over her arm, the crowd had thinned out.

Tarek greeted her with a cellophane-wrapped cone of flowers. He hugged her tight. "So, how ya doing, big sister?" he said, mussing up her hair. "You haven't changed that much. Well, maybe a little skinnier."

"Haven't they been feeding you?" said her mother, pointedly. She held Yasmeen at arm's length, looking her over. "And how come you smell so fishy?"

Yasmeen shrugged. She sniffed the hood of her parka but all she could smell was Joanasi's hair.

They trooped through the parking lot, her mother arguing with Tarek over where they had left the car. Yasmeen rubbed the spot on her cheek where her mother most certainly had left a bright ring of lipstick. She sprawled out in the back seat with her knapsack as Tarek backed out and shifted into drive, gunning it to the front gate and out onto the highway, ignoring their mother's advice to slow down and watch where he was going. Yasmeen closed her eyes. She had almost forgotten what it was like to live in her family. As for the city, she knew there would be an adjustment, anticipated it, but she didn't expect it to feel so foreign, so garish, so loud and claustrophobic. So unfamiliar. What was familiar now was riding out toward the horizon and never hitting a tree or house, seeing all of space and time and every star in the sky without a single obstruction.

Tarek made a sharp turn and joined the parade of cars, grey with salt, getting onto the Jacques Cartier Bridge. The radio kept veering off the station into static, but neither he nor their mother made any effort to adjust it until she cried out, "My ears, you guys, don't you hear that?"

"Okay, okay," said Tarek, "don't be so touchy." Her mother ordered him to get cracking, Rose was waiting for them at their favourite barbecue joint, the place her father had always taken them for Sunday lunch. Yasmeen wished they could go straight home, but she knew her mother had the evening planned out and she didn't want to spoil it for her. Tarek turned into the entrance and drove around looking for a parking spot while their mother warned him not to hit anybody.

Rose waved at them from an out-of-the-way booth already set with menus and four glasses of ice water. She jumped up and embraced Yasmeen. There were tears in her eyes. "So glad you're home," she said.

"Me too," Yasmeen replied automatically. Children with greasy faces charged past them with crayons and half-eaten chicken legs, almost bowling them over. Yasmeen thought of dinnertime at Joanasi's place, how much more natural their chaos seemed, the joyful cacophony of belching and farting, everyone just shoving the food into their mouths. When the waitress came, her mother ordered their usual, the same meal for everyone. Yasmeen picked at her soggy slaw and cardboard fries, but left half of it in her plate.

At home her mother cornered her in the bathroom wanting to catch up, but Yasmeen said the flight took everything out of her, maybe tomorrow. Her mother brought a set of fresh towels to her room and chirped, "Sleep tight, don't let the bed bugs bite," the way she used to when Yasmeen was a child.

"You too," she called back through the closed door.

The tree outside her window dragged its spiky branches along the pane like nails on a chalkboard. Yasmeen climbed into bed and closed her eyes. Lying there by herself she felt lonely and cold and alone. She slid her fingers underneath her nightshirt and imagined they were Joanasi's. She thought of their last night together. After her bath, after he towelled every part of her dry, hair, face, breasts, thighs, he'd carried her into bed and tried to make love to her even though she was on her period. How adamant he was when she pushed him away, slightly disgusted by the idea. "I want to love all of you, every single part," he insisted. "*Mamartuuaq.*" Then he went down and swallowed her menstrual blood as though it were the most natural thing to do. Afterwards he propped her head against his chest and asked her to tell him the worst thing she had ever done in her life. She thought it over, though it was hard to think clearly after what she'd just experienced. He raked his hands through her hair.

"Tell me," he pleaded. "I won't judge you." He turned her around until she was looking straight at him.

"I don't know, you might change your mind about me if I tell you," she said. He touched the small depression at the base of her throat and promised that he never would, he loved her too much for that. She covered her eyes so she wouldn't have to see the expression on his face. He wrestled her hand away. She put it back and said, "I've never told anyone this. It's sort of, well, cruel."

"Come on," he said, "Tell me."

"Okay, okay, just give me a minute." She told him it happened while she was doing a grade eight science project for bonus marks, training two hamsters to salivate to the sound of a bell the way Pavlov did, though she didn't mention Pavlov because would Joanasi even know him?

"That's not so bad," he said when she was done. "You didn't kill anybody." Then she told him the other part, about how on the final day of the experiment when she went to check on the hamsters, she found one twitching in the corner, its pale BB eyes staring across the cage to where the other one was lying in a pool of blood, its entire head chewed away. She paused and waited for Joanasi's reaction. When she didn't get one she said, "Don't you see, it was all my fault, Joanasi. I was responsible. I thought I could teach them to do what I wanted but they went crazy instead."

Morgan put the latest Talking Heads album on. She placed a cone of incense on the underside of a jam jar lid, lit it, and rummaged through her purse for her stash. The day Morgan left for grad school her parents announced they were turning her bedroom into a den, but somehow they never got around to it and whenever she came home for the holidays, it was hers again, everything pretty much how she had left it.

Yasmeen was already into the wine when Morgan joined her, barefoot, on the bed. She rolled them a joint, jabbering on about her thesis, something about the role of women in mythology and an amazing professor she had met named Trish. "You've cut your hair short," remarked Yasmeen.

"Yeah," she said. "I'm going for the asymmetrical look. Trish likes it, what about you?" Yasmeen thought it made her look slightly masculine but she didn't say so. She wondered if she'd also grown the hair under her arms, which would have been a big deal for Morgan. The two of them were always trying to look hot and hot girls took care not to have hairy pits. Hot girls shaved their legs and bikini lines and had clean, tweezed brows.

Morgan ran the joint through her mouth so it would burn more slowly. She lit it and took a long haul before passing it to

Yasmeen. Her voice went croaky as she tried to exhale and talk at the same time. She was saying what an ass her ex-boyfriend had been and how she and Trish were tired of men who couldn't communicate properly. "Hey, remember the time I gave you *Bear* for your birthday?"

"My mother wanted to throttle you," said Yasmeen. She was already feeling a buzz.

"Nope, she was too polite for that."

"You're right," said Yasmeen. "She wanted to hire a hit man." They both laughed.

"Gawd, it was just a book."

"Not just any book. A book about a woman who fucks a bear."

"I guess Samiyah the prude found it a little shocking."

"Just a tad."

Morgan played with the fringe of her bedspread. "So what's all this with Joanasi?"

Yasmeen toked and handed back the joint. "Wasn't it you who said the rules of life don't apply when you're elsewhere?"

"Nope, that was you, I believe. I said real living involves some genuine risk, but you still have to have a backup plan."

"Well, I like my philosophy better."

"I suppose these new rules mean fucking your brains out? Don't get me wrong, I'm all for casual fornication. What is he, some kind of Inuit fuck machine or something?"

Yasmeen took the joint from her. "It's not really like that. Not exactly." She inhaled and held the smoke in her lungs for as long as she could before exhaling. She stared at her feet, remembering the hunting trip with Adamie and afterwards in the igloo when he massaged each of her toes, how it had opened her up to the idea of being with an Inuk.

"Well, what then?" said Morgan. She poured herself more of the red wine and held the glass to her cheek, peering closely at Yasmeen.

167

"Don't look at me that way."

"What way?" She took a thoughtful sip. "Holy shit, your letter, it's true. You weren't exaggerating."

It wasn't the reaction she had hoped for. Yasmeen knew she could explain everything if Morgan would just listen. She could tell her how sex with Joanasi wasn't just sex, it left her feeling full, unlike the guys Morgan always talked about who missed the mark each time, getting her to the brink and then spoiling it with some off-putting grunt like *I'm coming, come with me babe* while they touched her in exactly the wrong place, taking her right out of the mood. Morgan would be jealous if she knew how it worked so naturally with Joanasi, how just the heat of his fingers made her wet. She wanted to tell Morgan everything, her desire to become his wife, his seamstress, the mother of a whole slew of his children. She wanted it all out in the open, how she would spend the rest of her life gutting and cleaning the animals he killed for their food, how she would cook and sew and tend to the house and not need anything of the outside world ever again. All of this was bubbling up inside of her but she remained silent, the dope and the fear of Morgan's reaction having constricted her throat.

Morgan stubbed out the joint. She had a weird look in her eye when Yasmeen complained that the dope was making her feel shitty. A song called "Burning Down the House" was playing. Morgan rolled off the bed to examine a blackhead in the mirror like it was the most critical thing that needed doing while Yasmeen lay there almost puking, pretty sure she could hear Morgan saying loud and clear *Have you lost your mind?* and *You said you'd wait on this.* After a while she realized that Morgan wasn't talking to her at all, she was actually on the phone with someone else, screaming over the music.

First thing on her agenda was the tattoo she wanted to get, Joanasi's initials just above her shoulder blade, a Christmas present along with the new Mötley Crüe album she had promised him. She didn't warn him ahead about the tattoo; the whole idea was for him to find it on her during a hot night of love and then just burst with total desire for her. She had it done in the seedier part of town, blinking with sex shops and peep shows and decrepit rooming houses crusted with the residue of their heyday. It hurt, but she survived. Afterwards she ducked into Sam the Record Man. She had zero interest in visiting the flashy department stores with their jumbled clothes racks, their bouffant-haired saleswomen waving smelly perfume swatches, their basement bins of holiday kitsch, yards of tinsel, metallic wreaths and garlands, jumbo candy canes and aerosol cans of fake snow.

Tender from the tattoo, she hurried home to wrap gifts and slice her mother's desserts into dainty squares to lay out on platters lined with lace doilies. She and her sister dusted and vacuumed and tidied up while their brother sat with his feet up and a bowl of chips in his lap and criticized what they were doing. They scrubbed the toilets and polished the silverware. Just before the stores closed, her mother handed her a fifty-dollar bill for soft drinks and a large sack of ice for the freezer. She threw Yasmeen the car keys and said, "Get it washed and filled up with gas while you're at it." It was exhausting. She dropped into bed and fell into a deep sleep and when she woke again it was Christmas Day.

"Habibti!" her aunts cried in unison, making a big scene of hugging and kissing her. They arrived, as always, newly coiffed and streaked and accessorized in 18-karat gold, each with a Hermès scarf draped across her bosom. They brought hummus and desserts bandaged in tinfoil—sweets glazed with honey or powdered in flour and stuffed with dates, *ghoraibee, maamoul, pistachio baklawa.* They wanted to hear all about the snow ("That much? How on earth did you survive?"), polar bears ("God forbid, did you ever run into one?") and raw meat ("*Ya'Allah*!).

"It's a little like our *kibbeh nayee*," Yasmeen explained, trying to reassure them.

Meanwhile her brother played the wandering waiter the way her father used to, pouring each of the uncles a stealthy shot of Arak, their traditional spirit of aniseed and grapes.

"*Sahha*!" said Uncle Ramzi as Tarek dropped an ice cube into his glass with a pair of silver tongs.

"*Ya'Allah, salute*," echoed Uncle Boutros. The silver-haired men stood by the Christmas tree talking business as they savoured their drinks.

"How does it feel to be back among the living again?" said Uncle Ramzi, wearing the same plaid sweater he always wore, a little too tight across the stomach.

"Okay, I guess."

"You guess? You should be ecstatic, my dear."

She shrugged her shoulders.

He wanted to know how a tribe of "piss-poor people with grade school education" had the smarts to "finagle such a sweet land deal" from the government. "I don't know much about that place, but I've seen a few of them downtown begging for money, real sad cases. They're always three sheets to the wind, and if it weren't for the fact that all they're gonna do is go buy themselves another bottle, I'd be glad to help 'em out, you know?"

"It's not their fault, Ramzi," said Yasmeen's mother. "It's their constitution. They lack that whatchamacallit … the enzyme that breaks down the alcohol."

"All I know," he scoffed, "is that our parents worked hard when they came here from the old country. They didn't just sit on their precious behinds waiting for a government handout."

Yasmeen gritted her teeth and made a beeline for the tea wagon her mother used as a serving table. She passed out the cocktail napkins and circulated with a *mezze* dish of pickled turnips and spinach-filled *fatayer.*

The aunts shouted for her from her mother's kitchen, the place where they always congregated to exchange the latest family gossip. Yasmeen recalled how happy she was when she was first allowed into their circle. She understood early on that the women held all the real power in their family; that the kitchen was the place where all the machinations and manipulations were conceived to trick the men into believing *they* made all the important decisions. But Yasmeen felt disconnected from all this now. She felt more of a kinship with the ladies in her sewing circle.

The aunts with the Hermès scarves, Jameela and Dunya, were already tying on aprons, congratulating her mother on her new acquisition, a mahogany dining table with elaborate, Louis Quatorze-style legs that she had bought with some of the life insurance money.

"*Mabrouk,*" they nodded, with envious approval. They praised her ultra-modern refrigerator with its door that made crushed ice, her smart row of cooking pots arranged in descending order of size. They watched in awe as her new, electric garburator digested a sinkful of cucumber and potato peelings.

"The cream needs whipping," Samiyah told Yasmeen. She put the carton and the electric beater in Yasmeen's hands. Yasmeen installed herself at the end of the counter, away from the women. She focused her eyes on the frothy peaks accumulating under the spinning blades. They reminded her of Joanasi's snow-draped village. She dipped her finger for a taste, wondering what he was up to, certain the talk in Pasha's kitchen was not about expensive furniture and appliances. She longed to be there.

Samiyah instructed her to invite everyone to the table. Uncle Boutros unbuttoned his suit jacket and hung it on the back of his chair, at the head where her father once sat. He poured everyone a glass of wine while Samiyah loaded up the plates with turkey and stuffing, butternut squash and fresh cranberry. He snapped open his linen serviette and stuffed the tip into the collar of his shirt like a bib. "*Ahalan wasahalan* and Merry Christmas," he said with his glass raised. "I'd also like to thank God for bringing Yasmeen home to us safe and sound." He winked across the table at her. "Welcome back to civilization, kiddo."

Yasmeen felt her cheeks flush as everyone's gaze turned to her. "Hear, hear," they toasted.

Ramzi cleared his throat and proposed his own toast, eye whites exposed as he glanced upwards at the ceiling. "And we remember Ed in our prayers, two years gone. God rest his soul." There was a quiet murmur around the table before people picked up their forks and began to eat.

"So," her mother said, passing the *tabbouleh* around, "why don't you tell everyone what it's like living with the Eskimos."

"Inuit."

Her mother glared.

Rose jumped in, deflecting the awkwardness. "I remember, we learned that at school. They call themselves Inuit now, not Eskimos. It means 'the people.' Right, Yaz?"

"That's right."

Dunya stabbed the air with her fork. "Very, very interesting." Her earrings jangled as she spoke.

Uncle Boutros pulled off his bib and loosened his tie. He propped his elbows on the table. "They don't live in igloos any more, that much I know."

"The people??" said Uncle Ramzi, through a mouthful of rice. "What's that crap supposed to mean? And what are *we* anyway, chopped liver?"

"For Christ sake, Ramzi," said Uncle Boutros. "It's Christmas. Can't you just relax?" He looked at Yasmeen. "Do they really suck the marrow out of the seal intestines or is that all just hooey made up by us ignorant whites?"

Her brother shovelled a wedge of pita into his mouth, trying to talk at the same time. "If they rub noses instead of French kissing, I'm guessing they don't suck face, they suck snot."

"Tarek, we're eating here!" Samiyah reprimanded. She glanced at the aunts, checking to see that they registered her disapproval.

"Hold it, just hold your horses," Ramzi interjected. "I mean, hell, do these people"—he faltered on the word people—"do these people even know who the prime minister is? How on earth do they get the right to vote if they don't know anything about what's going on in the real world? They should have a law against that."

It was the usual family banter, loud, critical, people passing food back and forth, gesturing for refills, no one listening to anybody else. This time it wasn't about the Middle East or the Jews or the lazy, unionized workers. It was closer to home.

Yasmeen excused herself. "I'm not really feeling well."

Dunya glanced at Samiyah. "Give her some *kishk*. That'll fix her up."

"Cod liver oil," interrupted Jameela.

Yasmeen threw the napkin into her plate. "Would you mind if I went upstairs to lie down?"

Her mother nodded, turning to the aunts with her nose wrinkled. "It's those flimsy planes, you know. Nothing between you and the atmosphere."

Yasmeen dropped her food into the garburator and took the stairs two at a time to go call Joanasi. She could hardly dial fast enough. He answered on the first ring. "I just want to be back home with you," she whispered into the phone.

FOURTEEN

"You're not to mention Annie today," said Joanasi as he opened the door to his mother's place for her. Yasmeen stamped the snow off her boots and hitched her sewing bag over her shoulder, eager to be back after two weeks away. "Not a word," he repeated.

"Why not?"

"Shh." He pecked her on the lips and disappeared into his old bedroom to listen to music.

With Annie missing, Pasha's living room was conspicuously silent, the women keeping their hands busy, stitching, cutting, knotting, no one uttering a word.

Sarah glanced up from her sewing. Yasmeen lifted her eyebrows and Sarah shrugged her shoulders as if to say God knew a heck of a lot more than she did, what could she do? Yasmeen settled into the empty seat beside her and whispered hello. Sarah nodded half-heartedly. Nobody else acknowledged her. She searched through her bag for her needle and thread and the half-sewn mitt she had started before Christmas, conscious of the noise she was making. She hoped that one of them would recognize she needed help but no one did, so she just blurted out, "I'll need a hand with these," hoping to spark a little interest. "Since Annie's not here, I mean." She looked around the

174

UNCORRECTED GALLEYS

room, but there were no takers. Sarah frowned disdainfully and shook her head.

Later that night in bed Joanasi discovered her tattoo. He put his hand on it and traced the inked initials with a finger, pleased with it but not overjoyed.

"I'm permanent here," she said by way of explanation. "I'm not a guest or visitor or tourist."

He shrugged and said, "Good, I'm happy for that." He brought up the time when his father was a child and the RCMP arrived in the community to register all the families, who belonged to who, etc. "Most of the people here didn't have last names, so they gave them a necklace with a number on it, like a dog tag." He said her tattoo kind of reminded him of that. His reaction disappointed her but she tried not to let it show.

"Tell me more about your father," she said, flipping onto her back.

He kissed one of her nipples. "Well, he definitely improved my English," he said.

She made a face that indicated she didn't understand.

"I had to spend a year down south with him when he got sick with the cancer and had to go to the hospital ... I ate a lot of chocolate bars back then."

"You must miss him. I know I miss mine."

"First time I saw a tree it reminded me of my grandmother." He smiled shyly. "The branches were like all the veins on her hand."

"The first time I saw the tundra and all this wide open space, it reminded me of a desert, except the sand was snow. My ancestors came from the desert. Weird, eh?"

"Yeah, weird," he said with lukewarm interest. He stroked her hair. It was a pleasant conversation until she asked about

Annie. His expression changed rapidly the way the sky changes before a storm, dark clouds arriving unannounced. He sat up with his back to her and lit a cigarette. "I told you," he said, sitting naked on the edge of the bed. "No more talk about that."

A small, sweet-looking boy crossed Yasmeen on her way to the Co-op, a kid she had never seen before. She smiled at him. Something about him reminded her of Tarek at that age. The child made a gun with his hand and pointed it at her. It shocked her. She lowered her head and continued walking.

A dozen Skidoos were idling outside the Co-op. The store manager that the locals nicknamed Aupartuq, or Red, because of the colour of his hair was outside chopping up the ice on the steps. "Hey, Stewart," she called out. He looked up and nodded. He was a gentle-looking man. She remembered what he had told her when she first arrived, about how the old store managers were trained to deal with all sorts of emergencies, and how villagers used to go to them for tooth extractions. She couldn't imagine Stewart pulling anyone's teeth out with a pair of pliers.

She zipped through the store with her cart, collecting what she needed for the week. At the checkout line, she recognized Annie's amautik. She was just ahead of Yasmeen in the line. Yasmeen was about to tap her on the shoulder when she realized that the guy standing with her wasn't her boyfriend. He was speaking to her in a gruff tone, signalling with his head that he would wait for her outside. He slid a cigarette out of his pack and clomped toward the door. Annie turned her head slightly and in that instant, catching her profile, Yasmeen saw that it wasn't Annie after all. But why was a stranger carrying Annie's kid in Annie's amautik? It was definitely Annie's kid in there. Curious, Yasmeen gently bumped the woman, issuing a swift apology. When the woman turned around Yasmeen almost puked. The woman *was* Annie. Annie, not even hiding behind a pair of dark glasses. Annie, with a full-blown lip and hollows for eyes. Yasmeen glanced quickly away, grateful for the groceries in her friend's cart, a frozen dinner, a Jumbo Coke and a pack of cigarettes, something other than her blue, swollen face to look at.

Yasmeen never expected Annie to call. She hoped she would, but she didn't wait for it. When Annie finally phoned, a week later, Yasmeen was flattered that she trusted her enough to unload. She assumed it was because of Joanasi. Being his girlfriend gave Yasmeen credibility among the Inuit that the other teachers didn't have. It conferred on her a certain status—she wasn't exactly one of them, but almost. As it happened, Annie wasn't calling for that. What she really wanted to tell Yasmeen was that she'd just baked and could she interest her in a fresh loaf of bannock.

"How much?" Yasmeen asked, trying to mask her disappointment.

"Maybe twenty," said Annie. "How about you come here?"

Yasmeen knew the price was high, but she also knew that Annie wouldn't ask her if she weren't desperate. That was beside the point. Yasmeen already had a rough idea of what had happened to her. As a first responder, Jacqueline always had the gruesome details of what happened around town. Yasmeen felt slightly guilty going over Joanasi's head to get the gossip when he refused to budge on the issue. Tight-lipped, he kept telling her to butt out, it was between the couple, how would you like everyone knowing all *our* private business? She saw his point but she went behind his back anyway.

"I'm not really authorized to talk about it," said Jacqueline.

"C'mon, she's my friend."

"You're putting me in an awkward position."

Yasmeen promised not to breathe a word to anyone. "Besides, all the villagers probably know, anyway."

"But *you're* not—"

"Jackie, this is me, Joanasi's girlfriend. I have a right."

Jacqueline sighed heavily.

"C'mon."

"What I *can* tell you is that it was terrible," said Jacqueline. "At least the guy's in jail down south."

Yasmeen pressed her for more details.

Jacqueline shook her head in defeat. "Okay." She lowered her voice. "Annie came here for Pampers and milk because her boyfriend used all their money for booze. Then when he found out, he went after her with a hammer."

It was impossible to believe, especially of him, that boyfriend who always seemed to be sleeping or watching TV or playing tenderly with their kid. The same guy who every so often made an exquisite carving and sold it down south for a pretty penny.

Yasmeen lingered outside Annie's door, working out a strategy for how to conduct herself. Should she pretend everything was fine or get her to talk? There was still blood on the snow outside the house, a congealed spatter on the porch and a few dribbles down the steps where Yasmeen supposed Annie had slipped and slid, running for her life. Why hadn't anyone cleaned it up? She picked up a shovel and tried clearing it away but the snow was iced over and impossible to chop. She leaned the shovel back against the house, thinking at least she had tried. There was still all the business about what to say to Annie. She decided that saying nothing was maybe the best thing. Wait for her to bring it up herself. She knocked once and entered. The television was blaring and Annie and her son were laughing their heads off at a silly commercial for dog food. Yasmeen stood by the entrance, waiting for Annie to acknowledge her. When nothing happened, she cleared her throat, loud enough to be heard over the television. Annie turned briefly to look at her, hugging her son closer into her chest. Yasmeen flashed her the money, laid it on the counter and left immediately with the bannock.

On Valentine's Day, a dump of snow blanketed the village. The school bus didn't make it out of the parking lot, the driver and half the students still home asleep when the bell rang at nine o'clock. Yasmeen waited patiently in her brightly lit classroom of particleboard and drywall. She waited for her students to shuffle through the heavy steel door with the push bar and the key-scarred lock. She waited with a pot of barley soup and raisin muffins. She waited at her desk with a hot cup of coffee, staring through the big window that cut the sky into four grey rectangles. One by one they trickled in sleepy-eyed, and helped themselves to breakfast. On the board she drew a large heart.

"Poetry, we've said, is about language. Being the day of love, I'd like you to think of words you love the sound of."

Savouring his muffin, Qalingo shouted "*mamaqtuq.*" Crumbs spilled out of his mouth and onto his desk.

"Excellent. I wonder if you can think of some English words?" She handed him a napkin and nodded at Elisapie to get the ball rolling. Salatee retreated shyly behind her bangs. "I can think of one you might like. How about beluga?"

Everyone smiled. Qalingo smacked his lips. With the chalk she wrote beluga at the centre of the heart on the board. "Anybody else?"

"Sewing!" cried Elisapie, taking the chalk from Yasmeen to add it to the list.

"Hunting!"

"Seal!"

"Polar bear!"

By the end of the period, the heart was filled with all of their words.

Yasmeen never let on what she knew about Annie. She just went about her days loving Joanasi, whose ancestors embraced the glacial land a thousand years ago. When he touched her, she wanted to melt inside of him.

"Our grandparents didn't believe in love," said Joanasi over their candlelight dinner. "The elders decided who would marry who when the children were very young. Sometimes it was arranged between families."

"The parents, you mean?"

"Yeah, the parents decided who would make a good match."

"What if the kids grew up and realized they didn't like each other?" said Yasmeen. "I mean, it must have happened at least once."

He shrugged. "That's how it was back then. I heard from somebody that the aunt of my aunt didn't want to marry the guy they chose for her. When she was around fourteen, her father strapped her to a *qamutik*, a sled, and sent her to him. She kicked and screamed all the way." His look grew stern when he told her that any husband could exact revenge on a wife who had relations outside the marriage when the couple hadn't agreed to it. He'd be justified, he said.

"Oh my god."

His eyes bored through her.

She didn't know where to look. "It's a little barbaric, don't you think?" When he didn't answer, she tried to backpedal. She went to say something, then thought carefully before rephrasing. "I would never cheat on you."

"I hope not."

"A man needs a woman," she said. "*Aliappunga,* I'm happy with you."

"*Uvangalu.*" He smiled with little emotion, pulling a bead of hash from his shirt pocket. Did she want to get high, he asked.

"Sure," she said. "Why not?"

He broke it up into teensy pieces and folded them expertly into a rolling paper with a small amount of tobacco. He twisted the end and twirled the joint around in his mouth.

"I didn't know you were a pro," she said.

He lit it and flashed a smile. Even his teeth showed. "I like sex when I'm stoned."

"So it seems."

"Put your hand here," he said. She felt him harden. "You make me strong."

Yasmeen felt her own pleasure awaken too, instinct kicking in, telling her that his was the only body capable of giving hers what it needed. He held the joint for her while she inhaled and continued rubbing him until he got so big she had to release him. "Aippaq" he said—which she understood as partner—"Aippaq, I have to come right now, I can't hold it in anymore" and they dropped to the floor and she moved underneath him with her mouth and let him drain all over her.

FIFTEEN

It was Yasmeen's first visit to the Pentecostal church. Its congregation, about a quarter of the population, believed it was the only real church in town, the one place on earth they could repent for their sins. They believed, as Sarah intoned, that Jesus would come again to receive those who were saved.

Sarah had called several days earlier to remind Yasmeen about the special baptism, her voice echoing through the receiver. "A true miracle is about to take place."

Since Christmas the village had been buzzing with the gossip that Paulussie, Sarah's own insolent husband, was the new convert. Jacqueline had heard it directly from Annie when she was at the Nursing Station getting her wounds attended to. When Sarah learned that it was Paulussie who had sold Annie's boyfriend the booze that led him to beat her with the hammer, she issued him an ultimatum, the Good Lord or the front door. Even Yasmeen figured out he would never give up his children.

The church was overheated, people fanning themselves with their hands, ignoring the gaggle of children crawling around under the pews. Up front, a man with shoulder-length hair and an earnest face strummed his guitar while a woman in a knit dress, chartreuse with shiny gold buttons, jangled the tambourine, her long, loose mane waving behind her. Eyes closed, they swayed with abandon as though they were experiencing an extraordinary visitation.

Yasmeen spotted Paulussie standing in the first pew, shifting his weight from foot to foot. The only one in the entire row, he was dressed in the same collared shirt and trousers he had worn at the school opening. Sarah rustled over to him in her priestly robes, signalling the start of the ceremony. She lifted her eyes up to God and laid her palm on his crown, murmuring a prayer.

Yasmeen glanced over at Joanasi. She adored being out in public with him, loved broadcasting their relationship, the electric charge between them, how it was impossible for them not to touch one another. Being in church with her lover, a holy place, a sanctuary of symbolism and human connectivity, had even more meaning for her. She was certain it raised her worth in the eyes of the locals, who surely saw the difference between her and those living at arm's length from them, Iris and Sam and Elliot. She longed for the day when she would stand with him in her own amautik, their love child nestled in its hood.

As the congregation prayed aloud in Inuktitut, her mind wandered to the time she and Morgan dropped acid and went to the votive chapel of St. Joseph's Oratory to trip on all the auras. It seemed like a cool thing to try. She was so high that day she almost got down on her hands and knees and prayed with all the invalids with their canes and crutches and wheelchairs, hoping to be healed. Now that she was with Joanasi and had stopped taking the pill, she hoped her foolishness hadn't damaged her chromosomes, ruining her chances for healthy babies.

Sarah's chanting intensified. The service veered into English. "The love of Jesus flows through me. Pray to Jesus. Praise the Lord."

Yasmeen closed her eyes and prayed for herself too, though she'd always been a skeptic, like her father. Even in his final days he refused to give in. For him it was always "a whole lot of malarkey," the idea of a benevolent God who'd step in to pardon him for his sins. As for the religious Christians, they were just a blind flock fleeing eternal damnation. Holy rollers, he called them. But what if they were right, thought Yasmeen. Wasn't it better to err on the side of caution?

Energy built inside the modest church as pockets of the congregation rocked back and forth and side to side, their faces flushed with exaltation. Rapturous, they moaned and wailed in several registers at once. Some had their arms outstretched to a higher being, asking for protection from the hostile spirit of Satan. "Amen," they cried, "Amen," each time Sarah invoked Jesus. Yasmeen obsessed about her reproductive organs.

"And, Brother, do you understand?" said Sarah, fire and brimstone rising in her voice. "Do you understand now that there is a better way?"

Paulussie nodded weakly, lifting his face and hands to God. His shirttail, damp with sweat, slipped out of his pants and hung behind him like a loose appendage. "I want the Lord to lead me wherever I go," he cried out. His hands flailed like a couple of doomed fish twisting in a net. Yasmeen could hardly recognize his voice, its flat, false note.

Robes swishing, Sarah led him to a large font filled with water. She helped him down onto his knees, racing through the blessing. "Just as Peter said unto them, 'Repent, and be baptized every one of you, in the name of Jesus Christ, for the remission of sins, and ye shall receive the gift of the Holy Ghost,' I say unto you today, repent! Let us raise our hands and say that we are not ashamed of the gospel of Jesus Christ." Jubilantly, she dunked his head and lifted it out. "We baptize our brother in the name of Jesus."

The holy rain slithered down his face and neck. Outbursts erupted here and there like little forest fires, rapidly spreading through the church. A young, slender woman with a single braid down her back leapt from her pew, repeatedly pounding her chest. She was breathless and hysterical. Yasmeen thought she saw a wave ripple through her body. The woman scratched her limbs as though vipers were overtaking her. The torture went on for some time—the clawing, the repeated blows to her body, the intermingled sweat and tears—until she crumpled to the floor in a heap, drained of everything, her swollen lips trembling but serene. "Amen, amen, thank you, Lord, a-men."

Light surged through the high, narrow windows of the church. The congregation nodded. "Thank you Jesus, hallelujah!"

Yasmeen was stunned. Her head was spinning. What was running through Paulussie's mind, she wondered? How had Sarah managed to convince a man who adored his whisky that if he prayed twice a week on his hands and knees and denied himself the pleasures of the world, he would have eternal life? She thought of how devastated her own mother must have been the moment she realized she couldn't do a thing to save her husband from the bottle.

Joanasi took Yasmeen by the hand and led her to the front of the church, where the other worshippers were already rejoicing and sipping grape juice from Dixie cups and calling each other brother and sister.

Paulussie's conversion didn't take. For about a week everything was fine and then Yasmeen got the call. He wanted his firewater. Not tomorrow or the day after, he wanted it right fucking now.

Yasmeen twisted the phone cord around her finger, cutting off the circulation. What was she supposed to do? He'd know she was lying if she told him she was out of stock. Everyone knew that white people always had a stash of it somewhere in the house. And where was Sarah, anyway? Why wasn't she keeping tabs on him? She wished Joanasi were home, he would have known how to handle it. But he was out hunting with Tommy.

Paulussie rambled on, promising her a day off school, a couple of fish from his freezer. "I'll pay you—a hundred dollars for a mickey of whatever you have." When she didn't answer he upped it to two hundred. "I'll pay you anything you want, just name your price." His voice was hoarse. There was a pause and static at the other end while he lit himself a cigarette.

Yasmeen considered hanging up when his crusty voice came back on the line. "Arright Little Lady, are you still there? You are?" He lashed her with obscenities, much of it garbled. "Are you fucking there, you bitch?"

Her silence wasn't a strategy, she was simply dumbfounded. She couldn't understand where all his rage was coming from. What had she ever done to him? And where was his newfound Jesus, why wasn't He kicking in to help him through his troubles? When Paulussie switched into Inuktitut she hung up on him, mid-sentence. In her rattled state she tried to think who to call. She dialed, misdialed, hung up, redialed.

"Slow down," said Elliot.

"Sorry." She motored through her story, stopping only once to catch her breath.

"He was here watching the Super Bowl," Elliot confirmed. "We had a couple of beers. When he left he was in a foul mood, but sober."

"He called me a dumb fuck."

"He didn't mean it. Forget about it."

"Right. Sure. Easy for you to say."

"He's probably already passed out on the floor by now. I wouldn't worry about it."

"Well, would you, uh, mind coming over, anyway? In case he shows up."

"Sure, kid."

She hung up the phone and double-checked the lock on the front door. She drew the blinds and turned off all the lights and crouched low to the floor, listening to the twisted wind. It blew for a long time. Where the heck was Elliot, anyway? Why was he taking so long? She checked the jerking second-hand of her watch.

When he got there, she exploded. "What the hell? It's been at least half an hour!" She yanked him inside and slammed the door. She slammed it so hard the embroidery Annie had sold her fell off its wall hook. She stooped and hung it back up.

"Annie, right?" said Elliot.

She nodded.

"My god, she's been trying to sell me that thing since last year."

"I happen to like it. Anyway, that's not the point. Where were you all this time?"

Elliot winked at her. "Suddenly she wants me."

"You idiot, I was worried."

"I thought I'd take a walk and see for myself."

"You could have let me know."

"I take it you missed me, then? That's a good sign." He reached into his pocket and pulled out his green-and-orange Phentex slippers. He stretched them over his feet. "Anyway, I went over there." He hung his parka over the doorknob but kept his *nassak* on, the tapestry crocheted hunter's hat with its wide double band and oversized tassel that a student had made him. "I could sure use a coffee." He headed for the kitchen.

"Never mind the coffee. What did you find out?"

He pulled out a kitchen chair and sat on it backwards while she stuck two cups of leftover coffee in the microwave.

"So?"

"He let me in for a while. The door was bolted and he had his big chesterfield pushed up against it. To keep Sarah out, apparently."

"And?"

"And then Sarah showed up. She started banging on the door like a lunatic, scratching and clawing and kicking it with her feet. She kept screaming 'Devil be gone!' at the top of her lungs."

Yasmeen poured the coffee. "And?"

Elliot paused a minute to blow his nose. He lifted his hip off the chair to stuff the tissue into his back pocket and sat down again. "Paulussie waited for her to go away and then he told me to leave."

"He kicked you out? Seriously? You're, like, his best white friend."

"Seriously."

"Were the kids in the house?"

"I didn't see them. But that doesn't mean they weren't there."

"I don't get it. Barely a week ago we were celebrating his baptism."

"Isn't it obvious?" he said. "He and Sarah, they don't see eye to eye. He loves his booze and she loves her God and never the twain shall meet."

A week before the alcohol took its toll, Yasmeen's father called out from the upstairs landing of their house. It was a crotchety cry of panic. "Samiyah, help me." He'd fallen again and probably soiled himself. Her mother was downtown running errands. Only Yasmeen was home. She ran upstairs and helped him onto his feet. He'd gotten so thin he was almost weightless. His hair was down to a few snowy wisps. She felt to see if he was dry and lifted him back into bed. It wasn't a thing a daughter should have to do. She hated him this way, wondered what was so great about the Great Beyond that he wanted to rush to, out of her life, before his time. When you were dead, you were dead and it was final. Everything disappeared in a flash, the pulsing world, flavours, sights and sounds, the shiver you get when a lover touches you in a certain way.

"Do your old man a favour," he said, looking up at her. A soupy film covered his eyes. All the courage was gone from him. "The bottle, it's under the bed." His pointing finger trembled. "Please."

She turned to leave, unwilling to walk him to the edge of the cliff and push him off. He called her back, begged her. His voice cracked and she could tell he was crying.

"Habibti, please," he whimpered. He looked her straight in the eye.

"Daddy, don't." She propped him up and helped him blow his nose, trying to think what to do. Either way, she failed him.

Everything after that, after she fluffed his pillows and arranged him comfortably in the bed, got jumbled up in her mind. Time filled in, days and weeks and months, until she hardly remembered being in his room at all, hardly remembered reaching for the bottle under his bed. There was just one thing that stayed with her, the last thing he ever said while he could still talk, a sort of riddle about the end being the beginning and the beginning being the end.

SQUALL

SIXTEEN

The snow was blowing hard. Joanasi still wasn't back from his hunting expedition. At three in the morning, Yasmeen couldn't wait any longer. She rang Jacqueline, apologizing for the hour. What? No, Tommy's here in bed with me. Missing? I doubt it. There was a long pause. Yasmeen heard static and muffled talk and then Jacqueline was back on the line with more information, her grogginess waning.

"Tommy told me they split up and took two different routes home, they do it all the time. One usually wants to get back sooner than the other. I'm sure he's fine, go back to bed. When you wake up, he'll be there beside you like a warm piece of heaven."

But Yasmeen didn't believe he was fine. It wasn't in Joanasi's nature to make her panic unnecessarily. The plan had been for him to come back to her place for a shower and then a quiet supper in front of the TV. It wasn't like him to miss Saturday night hockey.

After she hung up the phone she thought of putting in a call to Pasha but reconsidered. There was no point in alarming her as well. Besides, the few words she could string together in Inuktitut wouldn't have sufficed. Instead of explaining the situation, she would have triggered more worry. Pasha, like many of her generation, still believed in the Wind Spirit, how it could level everything on earth.

She slid a movie into the VHS player and tried to focus on the lives of fictional characters whose predicaments were settled in a couple of hours. But she couldn't concentrate. She kept coming back to Joanasi, ruminating over worst-case scenarios, letting their poison work on her. She noticed his jean jacket slung over the back of a chair, its empty sleeves waiting for him.

She paced absently. Noticing his half-smoked joint in the ashtray she picked it up and took a few tokes. Desperate for some noise in the house she turned on a replay of the earlier hockey game. She watched for a few minutes, unable to concentrate, then shut it off again, the announcer's voice grating on her. The kitchen light drew her like a beacon. She walked toward it and then forgot why she'd gone in there.

She saw the kettle and filled it and decided it was as good a time as any to clean her cupboards. She reached under the sink for her sponge and rubber gloves and went to work scrubbing and rinsing and drying. She rearranged the dishes and mopped the floor. She emptied the fridge of iffy foods, withered vegetables, an expired container of furzed yogurt. Even after all that work, the stove clock had only advanced an hour.

She reheated the water in the kettle and poured it over a teabag, remembering a visualizing technique she had read about. She also recalled Joanasi once telling her how people in the North used their words sparingly, because words, he said, had the power to create what was spoken of. If the words were about something bad, then bad things could happen, he explained. Yasmeen decided if she chanted a hopeful mantra it would keep Joanasi out of harm's way. If she imagined the oneness of the universe, if she prayed hard enough, if she did it all with reverence, if she solemnly uttered the right words, then somehow he would feel her presence, and she his, and this would be enough to keep him safe. She squeezed her eyes shut.

Concentrating, she willed Joanasi into the doorway of her mind, his hardy silhouette cutting the snow for an igloo while she waited for him on the qamutik. She imagined a squalling storm and their child whimpering in her hood. The apparition, Joanasi, walked toward her and fed her a spear of raw fish from his hand. He licked the oils from his tongue onto the baby's lips.

When Yasmeen opened her eyes again, the tea had cooled and Joanasi was still missing. It was already dawn and though she clung to a feather of hope, her brain reminded her that life in the Arctic was harsh and unpredictable. Brief. You took what was given. People were specks in the shape-shifting snow, each of them at the mercy of one Great Spirit.

On Valentine's Day Joanasi had surprised her with a special gift, an elegant but chilling sculpture of a mermaid. He told her that he began working on it the day he decided to give himself to her. He held it in his hand while he peeled back the layers of cloth like the delicate petals of a flower. His thumb had a slight tremble. "Do you know who this is?" he asked.

She nodded. It was Sedna. Most of what she knew about his mermaid came from books. She knew she was the Goddess of the Sea, one of the most feared but revered figures in their culture, the one who determined which hunters would eat and which would starve.

"Some Inuit call her Takanakapsaluk. It means 'the terrible woman down there.'"

He told her about Sedna's beautiful hair and how every man in the village desired her. How she wanted none of them. He told her about the mysterious suitor who arrived in stylish furs but was really a raven in disguise. "The guy took her away to an island and beat her and ordered her around," he said. "He warned her that she would never be free again."

"How violent," said Yasmeen, without missing a beat.

He continued as though he hadn't heard her. "Eventually, the father arrived in a kayak to save her. He felt really bad about sending her off with this terrible guy." He described how she scrabbled aboard while the raven's dark wing ruffled the sea and sent huge waves smashing over the boat's edge and how in his panic, the father threw her back into the water. "Then the wind stopped. The waves stopped."

"I know the rest," said Yasmeen, happy to report what she knew of his culture. "She grips the side of the boat and begs her father to take her back. Only he slams his oar down on each of her fingers and breaks them one by one. But this woman is tough as nails. She doesn't give up. She keeps holding on until she can't anymore, until her father slices off the last of them and then she slips underwater and disappears forever, her hair floating like seaweed behind her."

"That's not the end."

"I know," she said. "I want *you* to tell it."

"What's the point if you already know?"

"Tell me."

"Okay, okay." He took her hand in his, stroking it gently. "The end of the story … her fingers float down to the bottom of the sea and turn into all the food hunters need to feed their families, seals and whales and walruses. Then Takanakapsaluk becomes the underwater queen."

"The decider of everything," said Yasmeen.

Yasmeen woke with a start. She was surprised that she had fallen asleep. Bed sheets tangled in her fists, she wondered where

Joanasi could be. It was already morning and she had begun to fear the worst.

Everything seemed quieter than the night before. The wind had died down and an immense snowdrift had backed against the house. She pulled on her parka and boots and waded through the snow, sinking to her thighs with every step. Her breaths were shallow and she couldn't get enough oxygen, her heart drumming too fast for itself. Was it a panic attack? She had heard of them, but wasn't she too young? Paulussie's upsetting phone call kept coming back to her. Where on earth was Joanasi, why was he doing this to her? She clutched her chest, choking back tears as she walked to wherever she was going. She let the will of the boots carry her forward. They led her to straight to Pasha's. She burst through the door.

She climbed over a sprawl of children playing with action figures in the lambent light of the television. She followed the vapoury trail of boiling food straight to Joanasi's mother hunched at the kitchen table, cleaning and scraping some meat with her ulu. Pasha cocked her head up.

The sight of his mother carrying out her household chores without a single worry reassured Yasmeen. She wanted to fall apart right there, wanted to sob uncontrollably so that Pasha could comfort her, the woman who had made Joanasi for this world, who had carried him in her womb and fed him her milk. She wanted Pasha to hold her, wanted to feel the woman's flesh against hers, this woman who had finally made her understand her role as a nurturing force, something her own mother had never been able to do. She needed to inhale Pasha's winter skin.

Pasha laid down the knife and wiped her fingertips on a dish-cloth. She opened her bearish arms to Yasmeen as the flood of her emotions took hold. "*Sulirqit?*"

Yasmeen wept. "*Anaana.*" It flew out of her mouth before she realized it. The word for mother. She wept and wept, while

Pasha stood as still as a mountain in a hurricane. She rubbed Yasmeen's back and combed her hair with her fingers. She sniffed Yasmeen's neck the way Joanasi did before they made love. After a while, Pasha said "Shhh," and released Yasmeen, brushing away her hot tears.

Yasmeen didn't know how to communicate. She repeated random phrases in Inuktitut, not quite sure what they meant or whether she'd made them up. *Sivanirumavunga,* she said. Pasha nodded and brought her the telephone. Yasmeen didn't know what she was expected to do with it. How could she call Joanasi when she didn't even know where he was? She tried another word. *Natsiq.* Pasha pointed to the inert mound on floor and then to the pot of boiling water on the stove. But Yasmeen wasn't hungry. She hadn't been able to eat anything since Paulussie's call. She kept thinking of Joanasi dead on the ice somewhere. Everyone knew that Skidoos weren't as reliable as dogs. They could break down or run out of gas. They were useless in an emergency.

She resorted to English, speaking in a very loud register as though somehow her message would get through to Pasha. "Joanasi!" she shouted. "Where? Where?" She articulated like a teacher speaking to an ornery child, moving her face very close to Pasha's. "Where's Joanasi?" she repeated. "You must know something."

Just then the light in the room turned rosy-gold. The sun they hadn't seen in days was pouring through the window. Pasha smiled, revealing each of her decayed teeth.

"What's going on here?"

The familiar voice was coming from behind her. Yasmeen spun around. Her tears were unstoppable. They soaked her face and neck and reduced everything to water.

"*Ullaakut,*" said Joanasi, leaning against the wall, freshly showered, a towel knotted around his waist. The light hitting him in a way that made him look almost otherworldly.

Joanasi sat her on the edge of his bed and wiped her face with the tips of his fingers. He pulled her head gently toward him. "Do you really think that I would ever leave you?" he said. "Do you? You're all I care about, you and the babies we're going to make together. *Tukisiviit*—do you understand?"

After that she didn't want him to say another thing, she just wanted their bodies intersecting on the bed and never coming undone. She wanted to seal the space between them until it was nonexistent, until they were interlaced and nothing could pry them apart.

His voice dropped an octave. "You're a bad girl for thinking what you thought. Don't ever doubt me again. I know about the land. I know how to judge things by watching the moon and the tides. I know how to find the right animals to keep our bodies warm in winter." She could smell the sweat along his hairline. He pulled his shirt up over his head.

The vast relief that he loved her, the certainty of it, woke her desire. It made her want to push further, whatever that could mean. She slid his belt off and touched the cold leather lightly to her neck. She coaxed him to lie on top of her. She put an end of the belt in each of her hands and pressed down against her throat. Her breathing quickened. She took his hands and signalled for him to take the belt from her. She liked its hard edge against her throat. She liked how he held it there, how easily he agreed to her terms. "Keep going," she told him. "Do whatever you like." She wanted him to take her to the brink. She wanted to free-fall. He drove his fingers into her cunt and carried them back to her mouth.

"Now taste yourself," he said. "Taste how good you are." She licked the offering, listening to the far-off sounds of his little brothers and sisters in the kitchen. A baby was crying.

He rose and stepped away from her and said, "Get up, we're going to finish this later." He dressed her in his mother's fringed amautik and told her she should take his cousin Maggie's baby for a walk before lunch. His taking their sex away, withdrawing it abruptly and replacing it with a rigid directive, appealed to her sense of pleasure. She'd never known the thrill of being compliant, bound to a man who laid down orders and expected you to follow them.

"You'll just want it more later," he said.

She liked his understanding of her body, his control over it, the power he exercised over her. It made her want more of him. She wondered whether he would give in if she teased him, camisole purling off her shoulders. If she pushed his buttons. A part of her wanted to test him, this virility, she wanted to know her own capacity to seduce him. She wanted to take him to his point of no return, weaken him all over so that all he could think about was rising like a serpent inside of her.

"Hey," he said snapping his fingers. "Let's go."

Wearing the coat was like wearing the sacred skins of the past. They walked side by side, Joanasi smoking a cigarette, leading the way. She realized he was right about waiting. This brief interlude, sharing a baby so tiny for this world, would be just the thing to open her up, to moisten her enough for him to push deeper inside of her. She felt an absolute joy walking with him on the land that belonged to everyone and no one. There was only this.

Maggie appeared at the door in sweatpants. She couldn't have been more than fifteen. Little seeps of milk had leaked through her cotton top. She went to get the baby from the crib.

The child was naked. He was crying. Yasmeen could see the soft spot of its head that hadn't closed over yet. Maggie jiggled him in her arms, the mauve nub of his penis rubbing against her neck. She cooed in his ear. She stooped over and cranked a music box, trying to soothe him, but nothing would.

Joanasi ordered Yasmeen to kneel, bearing down on her shoulders until she was on her knees. From her position on the floor she watched him wrap a blanket around the fussy child. Joanasi kissed him on the forehead and walked behind Yasmeen to settle him into the spacious hood. It gave her a flutter of excitement, the newborn's pattering heart against her back, the little hot breaths at her neck. Joanasi came around the other side, reached for her hand and pulled her up. He waited for her to find her balance.

They stepped out into the stark white snow. Yasmeen couldn't get enough of the sun's brilliance on her face. Her forehead tingled. The village looked different than it had on the walk there. Even the old shacks and neglected outbuildings were singularly beautiful. Her eyes registered everything they passed as though they were miracles from on high—boys slapping around a hockey puck, the idling sewage truck, the dog nipping at her heels that Joanasi kicked away. Through the soles of her feet she felt the drifting sea creatures under the immense cathedral of ice. Whether it was true or it was her mind playing tricks, she had the odd sensation of seeing the thumbprint of creation in every snowflake. It helped her see that when it came right down to it, everything was about skin and bone and the tides of the blood, everything was either life or death, nothing more. Nothing less.

The baby's cry flattened out until it stopped altogether. Through the duffel of the amautik, Yasmeen detected the small, sucking muscle of the baby's mouth, like the pull of the moon on the tide. She understood that if she had had the right anatomy, a darkened nipple and a mother's aureole, she could have nourished him. She could have taken him to shelter and given him her milk. "I think he's hungry," she announced to Joanasi. It was the first time in her life she had said anything so meaningful. It was a sign. Her body was supple. It was ready.

March 30

Dear Yasmeen,

I got your letter about Annie, and you know something? It scared the shit out of me. Do you have any idea what you're dealing with? I don't think so.

I was doing research for a paper (that's my excuse, I was actually checking up on you) and I stumbled on an old myth from the Kivalliq region. It was very telling, especially after hearing all that Annie business. Basically it's the story of a cannibal who kills and eats his wife's parents and then goes after the rest of the community. The wife is afraid he wants to eat her too, so after a few choice manoeuvres she gets the hell out of there and takes off for her brother's village. Meanwhile, the cannibal is so hungry he rips off a piece of his own leg and eats it. Of course it doesn't even occur to him that others must have felt that same pain while he was gorging on them. After a while, he tracks her down. She's playing a tightrope game with her family and he joins in. When it's his turn and he's hanging from the rope, the wife's brother rams a harpoon through him.

I won't go on except to say the other stories are equally horrific. People are mercilessly clubbed to death, there's absolutely no logic behind any of what they do. Their actions are guided by pure emotion, jealousy, anger, despair. Action-reaction. I'm positive that their violent temper where alcohol is concerned is built into their genetic code. Annie and the rest are probably used to it by now. But, you? Come on. What are you thinking?? Come home. I'm afraid for you.

Love,

Morgan

Morgan,

You have to stop this lunacy. You don't even know what you're talking about. These incidents are isolated cases; they can and do happen everywhere, and in the South too! Check out the statistics on violence against women perpetrated by entitled white men.

Consider the snowflake, small but unique, that lands between your eyelashes, liquefies and changes the look of everything. One of those touched me and now things are different. People change. I never thought I would say it (or even think it) but I kind of see now what my mother's been trying to tell me all these years.

About Joanasi. There will never be anyone else for me. Every day I thank God that I found him. How would we have ever met if I'd stayed in Montreal? What would the chances have been? We always said that half measures were for everyone else. Remember?

I ask again for your understanding rather than your judgment. If you feel you can't accept what I'm doing, I don't know if we can stay friends and that would really suck.

Be happy for me instead.

Y

SEVENTEEN

After their walk with Maggie's baby, Joanasi said, "Come and be with me, I haven't had enough of you today." He popped the buttons of her shirt and loosened her jeans. He removed each of her socks and all that she was wearing, until she was down to her underwear. It was quick rather than erotic. His eyes travelled up and down. She crossed her arms in front of her. He pushed them away. "Don't do that," he said.

She was vaguely aware of Pasha in the kitchen, preparing the seal he had killed for their supper. She didn't care what his mother could hear of them. She wanted Pasha to know that she had surrendered her body to him. It felt like the perfect gift to give a mother, the knowledge that her son was with a woman wholly devoted to his needs.

Yasmeen wanted to make him promise never to leave like that again unless he took her along with him. But she knew she had no right. Saying it would have been selfish, childish even. This was what it meant to live in a place where one mistake can send a hunter off course. This was how it would be to wait for him at home with their children while he fought for their subsistence. If she stayed, she would have to get used to it. Joanasi was a hunter. He was made for the weather. He was made *by* it.

The spirit of his ancestors pulsed through his blood and gave him the resources to adapt his rhythms to the shifting seasons.

He led her to the dresser and slid down her briefs. He stood behind her and swept her hair aside and murmured something into her ear. "I don't understand," she said. He knocked her into the dresser with the back of his hand. His jeans were already pooled around his knees and he was rubbing himself up and down the back of her. She slit her legs apart in a yes.

He nodded. His dry, rough fist entered her. It left a fire burning along her tiny infolds. She thought about feigning a whimper, partly to make him stop and partly to incite him to push harder. He pulled out his hand and dropped his pants completely. She gripped the dresser, preparing for the pain she endured whenever they did it this way. He grunted and slid his arms around her waist and drove his full weight into her, forcing a widening rent. He kept at it without a break, her forehead thumping against the mirror until all she could see in front of her was a jeweled zap of stars. She tried to whisper for him to go easy on her, but he covered her mouth with his hand.

"No talking, I said." He pushed harder. She wanted it to stop but he didn't seem to be reading her and she began to understand that this was what it was like to be treated like a northern woman. The man doing what he had to for satisfaction. The woman accommodating. She wanted to cry out with happiness. She wanted him to flip her around and press his face against hers and say her name very, very slowly before doing it to her again from the front. For an instant, while he was still shoving into her from behind, their eyes locked in the mirror. She grunted her pleasure like an animal. His bone stiffened inside her and then he released everything he had with a moan, falling on top of her, holding a fistful of her hair. They remained that way in an exhausted heap, limp, exposed, sated, until Pasha called them in to eat.

"Kaapaa," said Yasmeen, cross-legged on the floor. Pasha showed her how to cut with the ulu. The blade had blood from the animal on it. Yasmeen made a ritual of bringing the silky, glistening chunk of meat to her mouth, grateful for what nature had brought them. She tore its flesh with her canines and ground it into a mash, chewing and swallowing until it found its warm place in her belly. She put her hand there. "Mamartuuaq." She smiled at Joanasi, picking the gristle out of her teeth. "Aliappunga."

Yasmeen woke with a start, pain spearing through her lower back. She curled into a ball, squirmed around and straightened out again. Rolling onto her side she pressed the cold soles of her feet into Joanasi's thighs, unable to get relief. She wondered if maybe the seal at supper hadn't agreed with her.

Lifting her head off the sweaty pillow, careful not to wake Joanasi, she reached her toes down onto the cold floor. She eased off the bed and groped her way through the darkened house. A rancid animal smell coming from the kitchen made her gag. She lifted her pyjama and sat on the chill seat of the honey bucket, trying to pass whatever was pressing on her organs. She hoped it wasn't a kidney stone. Her Uncle Ramzi was always ranting about how painful that was.

When she saw the livery-red discharge in her underwear it shocked her the way her first menstrual blood had the night Harrison tried to have sex with her. For weeks afterwards she blamed him for setting off her ovaries. But this was different. She didn't blame Joanasi. She had wanted their intimacy, the boundaries dissolved, nothing separating them. She had wanted their rough sex.

206

She fashioned a pad out of Kleenex and stuffed it like gauze between her legs, trying to soak up all that was draining out of her. Rising, she turned to see what she had left in the honey bucket. It was worse than she imagined: a veined sac the size of a small plum. Her heart sank. She pressed her thighs together and tottered back to the bedroom.

Joanasi cupped her face in his hands. "*Suviit?* What's happening?"

"Nothing, go back to sleep." She didn't want to tell him what she had seen in the honey bucket. The cramps were intensifying. She felt the downward pull of gravity as though her borders were wide open and life was flooding out of her, taking everything with it, like a powerful river tearing the trees from their roots.

Joanasi insisted on waking his mother. "No," she winced. "Let her sleep. I'll be fine."

He lifted her head to fluff the pillow and laid her back down, stroking her hair. His eyes lit up. "Maybe we have a baby in there."

She had to admit the thought had crossed her mind. Earlier in the week she had gone for a pregnancy test but an emergency came up at the nursing station and Jacqueline told her to come back another time. Then things got crazy at school and she never got around to it. Now she wondered whether she had been negligent.

Joanasi guided her back to the bathroom. She leaned into him, terrified at what was raining down through her. "I'm gonna pass out," she kept repeating. Joanasi eased her down onto the floor where she choked up a river of mucus and something that resembled the tip of a sausage. She tried but couldn't slow down her breathing. A droplet of perspiration slid down the side of her face into the folds of her ear. The last thing she heard was her head against the cold tile, like the muted whump of a melon hitting.

Yasmeen opened her eyes. They skirted left to right, left to right. People were hovering over her but they seemed very distant, as though a cloudy windowpane were separating them from her. They all had lips like duckbills and they were talking to her with their hands on their hips. The one she took for her mother pointed a single, scolding finger at her. Her duckbill was flapping. "That cat belongs to someone. We can't just keep it." The man beside her with a baritone voice said, "Dear girl, you have a big heart but you can't be inviting every damn animal into the house." At first she thought it was her father but then she saw it was her Uncle Ramzi in his holiday sweater with the Scottish Black Watch pattern on it.

The two were shaking her. They shook her so hard she thought her arm would break. Their garbled faces moved in and out, sharpening and blurring, it was like looking up through the wavering surface of a lake. At some point she realized it wasn't her family at all.

It was Jacqueline wearing a mask and a stethoscope around her neck. She was poking Yasmeen's arm, talking like she had marbles in her mouth. Yasmeen tried to turn her head to see who else was there, but she had no strength in her. Her head felt heavier than a boulder. Jacqueline was slapping at her arm. It felt like a hundred wasps were landing there. One squeezed through her skin and didn't come out. When Yasmeen tried to cry out, the water level began rising, pooling in the small depression of her throat, rising over her mouth and ears and nose, pulling her down past the swaying tendrils of ancient sea organisms. Down, down, down toward the ocean floor.

Yasmeen was right on the money. She'd been pregnant. The strip would have come out blue. It would have kissed its lucky stars, donned its tap shoes and belted out a tune. *Hello, ma baby, hello ma honey. Hello, ma ragtime gal.* The whole world would have known about it.

One minute she was, and then she wasn't.

Jacqueline was holding a clipboard and trying to keep everything professional. It had been a boy, with detectable body parts, eyes, a tongue, fingers and toes. Jacqueline kept reassuring her that none of it was her fault. These things were all about probability and about nature regulating itself.

Yasmeen wanted to see it, but Jacqueline advised her against it. Anyway it was only a clear sac with fluid inside. Yasmeen refused to listen. She stared ahead in a stubborn daze until Jacqueline told her Inuit co-worker, a girl named Alacie, to go bring it. Jacqueline sat Yasmeen up and smoothed her pillow. It felt cool on her back.

Alacie returned with the cloth-wrapped bundle. She handed it over to Yasmeen. It hardly weighed a thing. After holding it she decided she didn't want to see it after all. It was enough to know she had failed at being a woman. She had failed a natural, simple task, one that every day, in every corner of the world, in opulence and squalor, others had succeeded at, some just squatting naked over the earth. Doing it on autopilot, a dozen times or more.

Non-viable was how Jacqueline kept referring to Yasmeen's child. Not a human name but a scientific term. No different from the vocabulary used to signify a grotesque deformity like webbed fingers or a cleft in the toes, or a single eye in the middle of the forehead.

"Just toss it into the honey bucket," said Yasmeen with cool detachment. She didn't want to think about it anymore. She just wanted to get on with things.

Jacqueline ordered Alacie to take it away. She prescribed painkillers and asked if Yasmeen was ready to see Joanasi. "He's really anxious. I've never seen him look so scared."

Yasmeen nodded weakly. The room was swimming.

Elliot stepped forward and cupped her hand in his. "You had us all scared shitless, kiddo." His face was so close she could smell his mouthwash. It made her feel sick to her stomach. She turned away from him. "Iris and Sam both wish you a speedy recovery. They're at school holding down the fort."

Paulussie poked his head out from behind Elliot, looking like an old toy that someone had left out in the rain. He was gaunt and unshaven and his eyes had little red veins floating in them. He patted her on the arm. "Don't worry about school," he mumbled. "Sarah can fill in for a couple of days."

"*Nakurmiik,*" she said, straining to see where Joanasi was. "Thank you."

Jacqueline bustled back in her scrubs and hospital shoes. She shooed everyone away with her hands. "*Enweille! Décrisse!* Time to give this lady some rest."

Once they were gone Yasmeen spotted Joanasi standing near the exit, sipping from a Dixie cup. His black cap was pulled down over his eyes. Jacqueline dragged a chair to the gurney and waved him over. "She's all yours."

Joanasi pushed the chair aside with his foot. *"Aippangai."* He stood over her, gripping the bed rail. His eyes had a teary sheen. He removed his cap and leaned in close to her face, sniffing her eyes and ears and neck. "*Tutigumallipaa,*" he whispered. "I want to kiss your small brown rose. I want to make it better."

She squeezed his hand.

"We almost had a baby in there."

She brushed her thumb over his lips, unable to face his disappointment. Her arm was heavy from the sedative. "Shhh," she said. Her eyes fluttered, unable to stay open. Each time they closed, he disappeared.

EIGHTEEN

She awoke suddenly to the shatter of glass. The hairs on her nape were standing on end.

Joanasi was still asleep beside her, serene, slack-jawed, a long dry rattle in his breath. Blankets kicked away, his penis was resting across one thigh.

She checked the clock, thinking maybe she'd imagined it. The exploding glass. Since her miscarriage, she'd been having unsettling dreams. Sometimes they felt so real she thought the bright, waking world was the fictitious one. Sometimes, just after she woke up, she felt the ghost of what had attached itself, briefly, to the wall of her uterus.

She and Joanasi never discussed the baby she had lost. They never made a plan not to, they just sort of carried on as though nothing had happened. They took on activities that lasted most of the day, like ice fishing or going out for fresh drinking water, chopping up the ice and hauling it back by Skidoo. They watched TV and played Monopoly and had weekend Yahtzee tournaments. Whenever Yasmeen tried to bring it up he got very quiet or changed the subject. She couldn't tell whether he blamed her or just accepted it as one of life's inexplicable hardships, a devastating experience to live through and bury. Once, not long after it happened, she whispered an apology while he was sleeping, an emotional "sorry I disappointed you." A baby in the North was a celebrated event—even more so than back home. She said she hoped she could do better next time. She knew he heard her because he nodded with his eyes still closed and then rolled over and went back to sleep and they never talked about it again.

She turned on her side and closed her eyes, hoping to drift off. The next time she awoke Joanasi was nudging her in the ribs. He ordered her to stay put while he zipped up his jeans and disappeared barefoot down the hall.

Yasmeen found his T-shirt on the floor, poked her head through and pulled her arms gingerly through the sleeves. Tender from her ordeal, the slightest exertion was still an effort. She went to the window. An orange pall hung over the village.

"I told you not to move," said Joanasi. His voice caught her off guard.

She turned around. "I was just, I just wanted to see what—"

"You don't listen very well."

He flopped down on the bed to pull on his socks. "My shirt," he said, holding out his hand.

She shrugged it off quickly, ignoring the discomfort it provoked. "What's happening out there?"

"Put something on, you'll catch a cold." He cupped his hand to light a cigarette while she wrapped herself in the blanket.

"It looks like a fire," she said.

"Stay here. I'm going out to see." He left without kissing her.

It was 3:30 in the morning. With all that was going on around her she knew her chances of getting to sleep again were nil. She decided to get dressed. Just as she was dragging a comb through her hair, the phone rang.

The way Elliot was shouting she had to hold the receiver at arm's length to decipher what he was saying. "It's fricking insane!"

"Is it a fire?"

"Yeah, it's Sarah's church and it doesn't look good."

"Oh my god."

"How can you sleep through all the fuss?" he hollered. "Almost everyone in town's out watching the spectacle. They can't get it under control."

"I'm up now. Where are you exactly?"

"I just came home for a sec," he said, "to get some sweaters and blankets for people. There aren't enough out there and the kids are freezing."

"You don't have to scream, I can hear you." She held the phone to her ear with her shoulder while she rummaged through the drawers for her long johns. Focused on the fire, she almost forgot her pain. "I'll meet you at the church."

She joined a stream of people headed for the billowing columns of smoke, some on Skidoos, some on foot, still half-asleep. Approaching, she saw the water truck parked just far enough from the flaming structure to avoid being consumed by it. Three men with hoses were struggling to contain the blaze, but their lacy arcs of water kept freezing on contact with the air, tinkling down every which way. One of them was Tommy, she was almost certain.

Only a week ago there had been a fire in Kaivittuq, just north of Saqijuvik. It destroyed an entire house in three hours. News of it spread through the communities as quickly as the fire itself. It didn't take long for the authorities to call it arson. Elliot's version put all the blame on a teenager who'd been hot-knifing hash all night. At some point, the kid ran around the perimeter of his house squirting gasoline while his blotto girlfriend sat on her Skidoo hollering, "More fire, more fire!"

Yasmeen couldn't shake the image from her mind, the bright embers of the flicked cigarette skipping across the fuel, the drawn-out millisecond of absolute stillness before the blue woof of combustion.

213

By the time she arrived on the scene the church was engulfed in the blaze, bright flames pouring through the windows like lava. Embers fell from the sky like orange snowflakes, snagging their points on neighbouring houses and telephone poles before seething into ash and fizzling out altogether. Yasmeen put an arm around Sam, gave her a squeeze and said, "Hey."

"Holy crap," said Sam.

"Yeah, I know."

"Should you even be out here in your condition?"

"I'm okay." A sudden updraft sent glass and other bits of debris shooting out of the building. She shuddered. "God, I hope no one's inside."

"I doubt it, not at this hour," said Sam.

Yasmeen spotted Elliot out of the corner of her eye, distributing blankets while Jacqueline trailed behind with her tote of medical supplies. Though Yasmeen and Sam kept talking, her attention was more focused on the crowd, scanning over people's heads, trying to locate Joanasi. "Sarah must be devastated. Where is she, anyway?"

"I heard she's home, praying," said Sam. "The sister took the kids."

"And Paulussie?"

"Nobody knows."

By 5 a.m. the church had dwindled down to a skeleton of itself. Yasmeen waited until the last wall collapsed and decided it was pointless to stay out in the cold while the rest grizzled to ash. There was still no sign of Joanasi.

On her way home she passed a woman carrying an infant on her back. The woman was walking at a rapid pace, too distraught to notice the baby squirming precariously in her amautik. Yasmeen worried that if she didn't stop her and say something, the child would tumble backwards out of the hood. She retraced her steps, smiling in a gesture of great compassion. "Your baby, it's upset."

The woman stared gravely.

Up close, Yasmeen saw that she was much younger than she had originally thought, a teenager. She removed her mitten to shake hands, but the girl scoffed and kept walking. Yasmeen couldn't understand how she had possibly offended her when all she had done was reach out to a fellow human being. How could the girl not have seen that her intentions were pure? The reaction baffled Yasmeen. It was a slap in the face. Yasmeen shook her head and slid her mitten back on. Continuing on her way, she ran through the scene again and again, wondering how she could have played it differently. All the way home she registered a foul taste in her mouth, the sooty residue, acrid and granular, of the demolished church.

At dawn, the faithful and the curious returned to the ghostly ruin to see what was left of it and to salvage whatever they could. The cooled relics were collected into heavy-duty garbage bags along with charred prayer books, a coffee machine that had melted into a smooth black lump, a single claw of the baptismal font. Here and there, red-hot coals seethed and glowered, but mainly it was a repository of ash and rubble.

Later that afternoon, officers from the Sûreté du Québec arrived to investigate. They wrapped the site with reams of yellow plastic tape that said "Police Line: Do Not Cross." They went door to door with a notepad asking if anyone knew anything about how the fire started. By the end of the day Sarah's church—or what was left of it—was officially identified as a crime scene.

Iris asked Joanasi to make an announcement over the FM that school would be closed for a couple of days to give everyone time to recover. She offered Sarah the gymnasium for the next few Sundays to hold services if she felt like it.

"What were you doing there," said Joanasi, "after I specifically told you to wait at the house?" He was searching impatiently for something to make a filter with, not caring what it was as long as it did the job. He tore a strip off the back cover of her book of crossword puzzles.

"Everyone in town was there."

"I told you I would take care of it."

"What's the big deal? Elliot called and asked for help passing out blankets. I met him there."

Joanasi retreated into silence. He pinched some tobacco from a cigarette and rolled it into a paper with the hash, refusing to look up. "You're lying."

"I'm not. He called me to come."

"I mean about the blankets. You weren't helping, I saw you talking to Sam."

"What, you were spying on me?"

He stuck the joint between his teeth, rummaging through his pockets for the lighter. His eyes swivelled up at her while his thumb spun the little wheel to ignite the butane. A tall flame shot up, casting him in an orangey glow. "The point is, you didn't listen," he said. "Did you?" He tossed the lighter on the table, but it ricocheted off and landed on the rug.

Yasmeen kneeled to retrieve it. Joanasi took three quick hauls on the joint, half of his face in shadow. When he offered it to her she wrinkled her nose. "No thanks, I'm not into it tonight."

He shrugged his shoulders. "Okay. More for me then."

"I don't appreciate you accusing me of lying," she said after a long pause.

He blew a wall of smoke at her.

"Look, I know you're upset, but that's no reason to—"

"To what? To be mad when I ask my girlfriend to do one simple thing and she disobeys?" He smoked the rest of the joint until it was down to the filter and then crushed it in the ashtray.

She stood up.

He glared at her. "Aippaq, where are you going? We were talking."

"I feel like coffee."

A peculiar look came over him, as though he were trying to recall an important fact he had once heard. She could almost see the gears of his brain on overdrive. After a while his face brightened. He went to slap his knee but missed and hit his thigh instead. "Funny, you don't look like coffee." His laughter echoed throughout the room.

She rolled her eyes and disappeared into the kitchen.

"Did I say I wanted any?" he grumbled, when she returned with a mug for each of them. He stretched his legs out across her coffee table.

She put a cup in front of him and went to sit on the floor with hers. "So leave it." She tapped out the cards and dealt herself a hand of solitaire. "More for me."

He stood up and lit a cigarette. "Hey! Am I invisible here?" He bent down and mussed up her game.

She remained poker-faced through his little tantrum. She reached for her cup and took an extended sip of coffee. "So, let me get this right. You're allowed to come back late from hunting and make me worry all night but I can't go outside in plain sight to help out when there's a fire?"

"I told you already!" He let out a loud, fish-smelling burp.

"Uh huh, right. You got home late, so you went to your mother's instead. You didn't want to wake me." It was their first real argument. She hoped he would see that he was being unreasonable. How could he not?

He flopped back down onto the couch. "Every time I got my head turned you're with that guy, Elliot. Does he turn you on or something?"

"What? We work together, we're colleagues."

"He's always flirting with you."

"Don't be ridiculous."

His eyelid twitched. "A fire—since when is that work?"

"I told you *he* called me, I didn't call him. And, anyway, Sam was there too, along with Jacqueline and Iris. We weren't out there, the two of us, alone. Christ, the whole town was there!"

He stared vacantly, flicking his ashes into the coffee that he wasn't drinking. "*Yasmeenaapik,*" he finally said. "*Qaigit.*" His eyes had shrunk to BBs. He looked half-asleep, which was how he always looked when he was stoned.

"What?"

"Just come." He pressed his nose into her forehead and inhaled her deeply. He scissored his legs apart and gestured for her to sit between them. "Let's forget about all this fire business."

She leaned back into him as his hand reached around to unzip her. He dipped three of his fingers inside her and moved them around until they were coated with her glaze. He brought them out and slid them under her shirt, lathering her nipples. "Now isn't this better than talking?" he whispered in her ear.

She rolled down with him onto the floor and went to remove her clothes but he grabbed her by the wrists. "No," he said. "Me, not you. You *owe* me." Like an Arabian prince he sprawled out while she slowly pulled off his jeans, socks, shirt, while she lowered his boxers to release him. He spread his legs apart and said, "Put it in your mouth." She moved onto all fours and lowered her face over him, his smell so concentrated she almost gagged. He steered her closer to him. He used both of his hands. "What are you waiting for?" he snarled. His fingers dug into her scalp. She parted her lips as he pushed in, gently at first and then with exhausting resolve, struggling to get hard. They waited impatiently for his tiny spasm, the single, essential, involuntary jerk, but instead he went limp and slid out of her mouth. He blinked up at her.

She reached behind to unclasp her bra, hoping the sway of her breasts would give him some relief. The more effort she put in, the angrier he got, until finally, sulking, he gave up altogether. She massaged his temples and blamed it on the weed, but nothing could call it back. She rolled off and covered them both with an afghan. When she made a move to fondle him he turned on his side, away from her. As though what he really wanted was for night to end, the sooner the better.

NINETEEN

Joanasi bolted awake. He pulled on his briefs. Someone was walking around Yasmeen's house, he was sure of it. "Just stay here," he instructed. When she opened her mouth to talk, he shushed her and closed the door behind him.

Since the fire, Joanasi couldn't sleep through the night anymore, waking four or five times, usually in a bluster over some dream he had had.

The stranger's voice was familiar. She strained to make it out. It was shouting and Joanasi was shouting back. She tiptoed to the door and opened it a crack, as mouse-quiet as she could be. She didn't want Joanasi stomping back to their room in a spitting rage.

It was Tommy.

"Suviit?" Joanasi repeated, gruffly.

Jacqueline flashed into her mind. Yasmeen prayed she was all right. She wondered if maybe they had had "the talk," if she had finally confessed to Tommy that she didn't plan on sticking around forever. From the sound of it, it was a possibility. He seemed mad enough. Maybe he'd lost it and punched his fist through the wall, or trashed the nursing station, or worse, struck Jacqueline across the face.

Yasmeen eyed the phone by her bed. She figured she probably had enough time to put in a quick call to Jacqueline, the way Joanasi and Tommy were going at it. On the other hand, if Jacqueline was in serious trouble what help could Yasmeen be from her bedroom? What use would she be to her if Joanasi returned and found her plotting something behind his back? After he'd specifically ordered her not to get out of bed.

"*Salluputit!*" shouted Joanasi. "*Sallutuuraaluvutit!* You're a goddam liar!"

The shouting escalated. She trusted Joanasi, but Tommy—he was another story. She knew from experience that he was like a fuse that could go off at any time, without warning.

The front door slammed. It rattled the jewellery and coins on her vanity. She heard Joanasi run the tap in the kitchen and then bang his empty glass down on the counter. Footsteps pounded down the hall. She flew across the floor and dove under the covers. When she got there she realized that in her haste she had left the door ajar. It was too late to get up and close it.

Joanasi appeared in the doorway.

"What's happening?" she said, with a calm that surprised even her. "Who was it?"

"None of your business."

She felt the sting of his words like a slap across her face but was relieved that he hadn't noticed the door. He sat on a corner of the bed as though she were invisible. Preoccupied, he lit a cigarette.

In that moment Yasmeen saw beyond his tough exterior to the vulnerable man that he was. Though no one had instructed her in these matters, she considered it her duty, as his lover, to go and comfort him. He was a man with feelings. He needed her. She wrapped the sheet around her and sat cross-legged beside him, synchronizing her breathing with his. For a long while he ignored her. She waited.

"I'm sorry, Aippaq."

Her hand reached up protectively. Careful not to stoke his ire she rubbed his back. "What happened out there?"

"Tommy said he knows who caused the fire." His hand trembled as he lifted the cigarette to his lips.

"Oh," she said noncommittally. She didn't understand why Tommy would even care about the church burning down. He'd never given a hoot about religion, least of all Sarah's.

Joanasi turned to look at her. He looked gaunt, sleep-deprived. "He said it was, it was … he blamed my uncle."

"Your uncle?"

"Yes, my uncle." The blood drained from his face. "Paulussie."

"Missing in action," Elliot announced a few days later. "No one has a clue where Paulussie is. The police turned the place inside out for a couple of days, then figured it was a lost cause."

Though almost everyone in the village was a cousin to somebody else, it was the first Yasmeen had ever heard about Joanasi being Paulussie's nephew. Their fathers had been brothers, she discovered. When Joanasi's father died, Paulussie became like a surrogate father to their family. He fed them from his kill. He provided Joanasi's mother with hides to sew. After Joanasi told her, he'd let his head fall into her lap. She stroked his hair and reassured him that it must be a mistake. When he realized he had revealed too much, exposed his weakness, he'd wrestled himself from her, snatched his coat and left without a word.

Sam scavenged around for a frozen pizza to pop in the microwave. The teachers had congregated at her place, even Iris, who usually spent evenings locked up in her office doing paperwork. It had been a difficult week. A cloud hung over the village as people went about their usual routines, trying to put the fire behind them. Mostly they wondered about Paulussie. Could he have started it? If so, to what end? Unable to sit around waiting for news, Joanasi set out with a small search party, vowing he wouldn't return until he found him. He and Tommy made peace but it was fragile. Sarah prayed day and night, waiting for him to turn up. In public, she acted as though everything was fine. She kept insisting that deep down he was a good soul, the father of her kids, that all he needed was the Lord to shine His light on him. She told everyone with stone-faced certainty that he'd be back.

Iris crossed her knife and fork neatly on the plate and dabbed the corners of her mouth with a napkin. "What do they figure happened?"

"Nobody knows. The cops told me that if he's disappeared into the interior no one will ever find him, he's that good a hunter," said Elliot. He popped the cap on his beer bottle, frost smoking off the lip.

Yasmeen hardly touched her food. Tommy's accusation kept cycling through her mind. She replayed all the names Paulussie had called her in his drunken stupor, the night he would have sold his own kids for a bottle of antifreeze. It wasn't so far-fetched to think that he was responsible. He could have come unhinged. Something could have short-circuited in his brain. It wouldn't have been the first time something like that happened to someone. She hated herself for going down that road, but she couldn't help it. Or could she? She could try harder. She would have to if she wanted things to be right again. Turning on Paulussie meant turning on Joanasi too, and he would never forgive her betrayal.

Yasmeen collected everyone's plates, piling them noisily one on top of the other. "How does anybody know for sure *he* did it? Why? Because Tommy said so?" Her chair legs screeched across the floor as she got up to carry the dishes to the kitchen.

"And we all know how stable Tommy is," said Sam. She lit a cigarette, aiming the smoke away from the table.

"Point taken," said Elliot.

Yasmeen scraped the leftovers into the garbage. "We just have to work harder," she mumbled under her breath. "We're not doing any good here if we only teach the southern values."

"We don't," said Elliot. "We adapt the curriculum. We try to show how it relates to their world here. We give them ways to defend themselves against the shit we dumped on them. We show them what's out there so they can make educated decisions about their futures." He smiled at her. "I know you're doing it in your class, too."

She refused to back down. "And what do we do about the other ones, the ones who've already been damaged by those who preceded us?"

"Nothing. Not our problem."

Yasmeen glowered. "Not our problem?"

"Okay, forget it. I take it back. It was callous of me."

"Thank you. Anyway, I can't believe Paulussie would go and do something like this. It doesn't add up."

Elliot held out his beer as a peace offering. "You and me both, kid. There's nothing I'd like better than to find out he didn't do it."

She nodded.

"But I'm starting to come to terms with the fact that very little here adds up."

Yasmeen watched Joanasi transfer gasoline from a large canister into several plastic jugs. He poured it slowly from one to the other, careful not to spill any. She was remembering how he had said her name the first time they met, as though it contained the answer to a riddle he'd been trying all his life to solve.

"I'm quitting my job at the radio station," he announced, screwing the cap tightly on one of the jugs. He was on a brief stop home to restock before resuming the search for Paulussie. The others, including Tommy, had bailed on him. He was the last holdout.

Yasmeen wondered what he was thinking as he made love to her that night, indifferently, as though somehow in his hazy mind she were another of his many tasks to take care of. All she had managed to say, with little enthusiasm, before he stripped off her clothes, was, "Quitting your job, that's a huge step."

He shrugged and said what was the point of working when he could line up with everyone else and collect the government cheque, and go hunting whenever the spirit moved him. "An Inuk has to be out in the cold," he said. "If I'm not, what am I? Just a voice on the radio, playing white man's music." He sounded like someone trying to convince himself.

She wanted to ask what would happen when his babies came and they didn't have her teaching job to rely on anymore. How would they live, all of them, on welfare? But his mind was somewhere else already, or maybe nowhere at all. He was remote, hardly aware of her. Their lovemaking reminded her of the land, its repetitive sameness. He didn't bother removing his shirt. He lowered his jeans only partway, enough to get inside her, jerked his hips and didn't stop until he was done.

TWENTY

Yasmeen stared out the window. With spring on its way everything had begun to change, the quality of the light, the glacial earth shifting incrementally. Days were lengthening. Soon the bay and its many rivers would be a jigsaw of ice and water and Saqijuvik would look again as it had the day she arrived all those months ago.

It felt like a lifetime had passed.

"So, what's your decision?" said Iris.

Yasmeen pretended not to hear the question. She shuffled through the documents before her on the desk.

It had been weeks since the last search party and Paulussie was still missing. After the police exhausted every lead, they permanently closed the file. The village went back to its regular routine. Over time the giant crater where the church had stood morphed into a playground for toddlers who gathered there until the pinking twilight with their shovels and plastic trucks. Rumours of a new building bristled over the airwaves while Sarah continued nursing the hope that her man would return one day to atone for his sin. By now everyone, including Joanasi, accepted the grim fact that Paulussie had caused the fire.

Iris leaned across the table. "The commissioners are holding a meeting and I have to let the school board know your decision."

226

Yasmeen put down the contract. She looked up. She thought of Joanasi and her new life in the village, all her friends from the sewing circle, who assured her that soon she would have the skills to make her own amautik. She thought of Elisapie and Salatee and all her other students who were finally beginning to trust her the way they had trusted all their previous teachers who abandoned them in the end for a job down south.

"What are *you* planning to do next year?" said Yasmeen.

Iris retreated in her chair. "Well, to be frank ..." She removed her eyeglasses and rubbed them with a tissue, looking through each lens before putting them back on. "To be frank, I'll be resigning at the end of the year. My parents ... they're not getting any younger, you know."

Her words came as no surprise to Yasmeen, who already suspected months ago that Iris was at her wit's end. There had been too many episodes, beginning with Tommy and the cancellation of Halloween. The fire, though unrelated to school, was more than she could handle emotionally. Iris, she thought, was no different from every other white whose adventure in the North had an expiry date. Yasmeen sat upright in her chair. "I'll be staying," she said firmly.

On her way out she paused outside Paulussie's office. It was exactly as he had left it the day of the fire, a full ashtray of cigarette butts, the top drawer of his filing cabinet pulled out, his desk cluttered with paperwork and disposable coffee cups and an open tin of Maxwell House. She saw the deflated Happy Birthday balloon he had kept as a souvenir from the official school opening. The room's aliveness gave the impression he was only home for lunch. She pictured him seated at the kitchen table, jabbing a toothpick into his mouth after a big meal while Sarah criticized him for a trifle. As soon as she imagined it she excised it from her mind—Paulussie, the alcoholic vestige of a monumental fuckup. She wanted to remember a different incarnation, the great hunter eating with his family on a cardboard mat, on his knees, on the floor, relishing the earth's bounty.

"Where were you?" said Joanasi, informing her by his tone that he had been waiting an excessively long time. He was smoking by the window.

"I had a meeting."

"With who?"

Yasmeen pulled the *kamiks* off her feet.

"I said, with who?" He came within a hair's width of her face.

Yasmeen stepped away from him. "What's the matter with you?"

"You said you'd be here to make supper." He ground his cigarette into the ashtray and lit another.

"I was with Iris. Why is this even a problem? I have a job, you know, I have responsibilities. I can't just leave work when the spirit moves me." She said it, knowing full well that the Inuit teachers worked to a different set of standards. They came and went as they liked. If they slept in, they slept in. People excused and accepted it, but not from the white teachers.

His eyes narrowed. "The bell rang a long time ago."

"Yes, and as I said, I had a meeting. Anyway, what's wrong with *you*?"

"What's that supposed to mean?"

"It means you're home all day, why can't *you* cook dinner for once?"

He studied the coal of his cigarette, weighing her criticism.

"It also means you don't trust me. You're here all day long doing nothing, you don't even hunt anymore. You get stoned and then your mind starts playing tricks on you, telling you that I'm looking for someone else."

"I don't *need* to hunt," he said. "And I don't need to work. I have money coming in."

"I get it," she said.

"So you were with Iris?"

"Yes, Aippaq, I was signing my contract for next year." She gave his shoulder a squeeze. "And as for the rest, you're imagining things."

"Okay," he said, his bluster waning. "You signed?" He lit up like a child getting special privileges.

"Of course I did," she said. "Now come and help me make dinner." She went for quick and easy, macaroni and cheese with a tossed salad. They prepared the meal side by side, Joanasi slicing tomatoes, Yasmeen shredding a block of Parmesan. She uncorked the leftover wine and poured two glasses. "Chin, chin."

"*Nalligivagit*," he said. He tapped the rim of his glass against hers.

"I love you, too." The pasta was boiling vigorously. She lowered the temperature, using a fork to dislodge the bits that had stuck to the bottom of the pot. He popped his favourite Kitty Wells tape into the cassette deck.

"Let's forget supper," he said. He switched off the stove and wrestled the fork from her hand. It felt like the old days, his tender words, the longing in his eyes. Before she knew it they were in the bedroom.

He set her glass on the nightstand. "Undress for me while I watch," he said, pulling off his socks. He propped the pillows against the headboard and leaned back, sipping his wine. She knelt to put his toes in her mouth. "No, Aippaq. I said undress." He jerked his foot away.

She stood.

"Turn around so I can see you from behind," he said. A familiar edge crept in to his voice. "Yes, there. Like that." She felt his searing eyes on her. The cool air hardened her nipples. "Now walk over here. Qaigit." Her pulse quickened. She pretended he was a stranger with a quick temper and rough, callused palms. She thought of them holding a length of rope as she moved slowly toward him. She glanced out the window into the grainy darkness. "It's just you and me," he said.

THAW

TWENTY-ONE

Spring was floating in the air. Yasmeen could tell because the students had begun teasing her, mainly the girls. They didn't want answers to useless questions of math or grammar, they wanted to know the details of her love life. Elisapie drew hearts on her jeans in permanent marker and made up a jingle, *You and Joanasi, you and Joanasi, gonna have a ba-by, gonna have a ba-by*. Earlier, someone had drawn a heart on the board and written Yasmeen Haddad loves Joanasi Maqaittik in three different colours.

Yasmeen felt her cheeks flush. Resting her fingers in the hollow of her throat, she tried to be firm. "Girls! Taima! Cut that out, I said!" But she wasn't very convincing. Somewhere deep down, she knew their behaviour was a sign they had accepted her into their world. Joanasi had handed her the key to the front door and now she was inside. In some ways she considered them her children.

"Are you gonna marry him?" Salatee asked, staring at the floor.

The boys groaned and pulled their baseball caps over their eyes.

"When are you gonna make a baby together?" said Elisapie, unaware she was opening up an old wound.

Yasmeen pasted a smile on her face and drifted into thought. For a minute she forgot where she was.

"Hey, teacher," shouted a voice from the back of the room.

Their resounding laughter snapped her back to reality. "Pardon? What?"

Audlaluk's hands were waving for attention. His eyes gleamed. "I solved the equation! Can you check it?"

Yasmeen walked toward him.

Overjoyed, he tilted backwards in his chair, balancing precariously on its hind legs—a habit she could never break him of.

"How many times have I told you never to do that?" Yasmeen snapped. "Someday, you're going to fall and hurt yourself and then you won't be laughing anymore."

Every radio in the village was tuned in to the afternoon program. The general tone was bleak but unemotional, callers rehashing facts, stating opinions, repeating gossip. The new announcer, an older man with a droning voice, lacked Joanasi's expertise on the controls, making for a crackly, uneven broadcast. Transitions between songs and the ongoing update of information produced intervals of dead air that were longer and more dragged-out than usual. During those breaks Yasmeen stood up, stretched her legs or shifted her position on the couch, a hint to Joanasi that she would appreciate a translation, however abridged. In the beginning he translated, begrudgingly, but the longer the program went, the fewer details he provided until eventually he gave up altogether, staring catatonically into space.

"I have a bad feeling," he mumbled.

The phone rang.

Yasmeen almost tripped over her feet, running to answer it. "They think they found Paulussie," she whispered breathlessly into the receiver.

Elliot sighed. "Where?"

"I didn't get that part."

"I should spread the word then."

Yasmeen eased the phone back into the cradle. "It was Iris," she said, though he hadn't asked. The lie surprised her, the way it slipped so naturally out of her mouth, unprovoked. "Just something about school." She swapped the full ashtray for a clean one and sat beside him, kneading his shoulders to loosen him up.

"I have to go," he said, pulling away.

She fetched two slices of bread and a banana from the kitchen. "Take some food. You need your strength."

He turned away from her, the door slamming behind him.

Paulussie's body was discovered near an Inukshuk about sixty kilometres from town. He hadn't shot himself, though he might have. He hadn't been ravaged by a polar bear. There was no evidence of a great fight to survive. He had simply removed his clothes and lain down stark naked in the snow, waiting to be taken. Leaving the world the way he came into it. Alone. With nothing.

A small party of hunters from Kaivittuq found him buried under a snowdrift. One of them recognized him and sent for a qamutik to pick him up and take him back to Saqijuvik. Their solemn procession arrived in the failing light of dusk, Paulussie strapped onto the sled, covered with a tarpaulin.

The blue tinge of death settled over the village. Sarah finally accepted the bitter truth of what had happened. Putting aside her pain she became a mother figure to everyone in the community, her face like granite, grave and expressionless, as though all along, deep down, she had half expected it.

Preparations for a proper burial began. Joanasi and Pasha sponged his body down and displayed him in bed in his good suit, the one he wore for his baptism. Mourners came and went around the clock, paying their respects, reminiscing about Paulussie as a boy, as a hunter, as a dedicated father. A hardworking man with a respectable job, a pillar of the community. Pasha served them tea and bannock while Sarah graciously listened to their stories. For an entire day people crowded into the small bedroom to lay a hand on Paulussie's cheek and murmur their goodbyes. Some wailed, some sat in a private corner in silence. Outside, the village looked as desolate as the moon.

The teachers gathered at Sam's, no one leaving to go home except to shower or change their clothes.

"I can't believe he's really gone," said Iris, dabbing her eyes with tissue.

Yasmeen shook her head, tears sliding down her face and chin. "How could he just give up like that?"

Iris passed her the box of Kleenex.

Elliot hooked his arm around Yasmeen and hugged her into him. "He sure was a man of extremes." She let her head fall against his shoulder.

Sam nodded. "How's Joanasi holding up?"

"He's barely said a word to me. I don't know how to help him." Yasmeen blew her nose and went to pour herself a glass of water.

"So what happens now?" said Sam.

All eyes were on Jacqueline. "Time," she said, pragmatically. "It happens. People deal with tragedy here all the time. And then they go on."

It was an unlikely day for a funeral, the sun out in mesmerizing splendour, a potent, blinding swirl of incandescence. By the time the truck delivered Paulussie's body, everyone was gathered at the cemetery, a hillock of lopsided graves on the shifting perma-frost. Fenced off with a line of whale ribs, it was a modest resting place dotted with artificial flowers and cheap plastic wreaths, everything tattered and sun-bleached. Many of the dead were children or teenagers who had succumbed to accidents on the land or drowning or substance abuse.

A small front loader had already broken up the land in prepa-ration for the interment. On the count of three, Joanasi and Tommy lifted out the simple coffin they had nailed together out of plywood. Together they lowered it into the hole.

"*Ataata,* my father! We will never forget you," cried Jimmy, the eldest son. Joanasi knelt beside him and whispered some-thing in his ear, probably the very thing Paulussie had said to him after the death of his own father. Yasmeen was pretty certain that's what it was. That he had to be strong now that he was the new man of the house.

Silasie wailed as Sarah gathered them into her bosom for the closing prayer. Her voice was resplendent. "John 11, 25. I am the resurrection and the life. He who believes in me will live, even though he dies."

Yasmeen stood away from the burial site with the other teachers, studying Joanasi from a distance. The funeral was an Inuit thing, he had said, and even though it hurt her, she respected his wishes. At least he had broken his silence and spoken to her. Sam leaned into Elliot, wiping her tears with the back of her hand. Iris stood slightly apart from them, next to Yasmeen. Together they mouthed the Lord's Prayer.

Through the crowd Yasmeen spotted Adamie in sunglasses looking very solemn. She remembered the ptarmigan smell on his hands the time he handed her his cigarette, the time they went hunting and stopped at the old igloo to warm up. Her heart sped up a notch and she realized she still had a soft spot for him, the boy who had first introduced her to the land. He wore a brown tweed cap tipped slightly forward on his head. He and his grandfather were standing together, arms interlocked. A pretty young girl with a child on her back was standing on the other side of Adamie. Yasmeen squinted and saw that it was the same girl she had passed on her way home from the church the night of the fire, the girl who had scowled and rebuked her.

Yasmeen turned her attention back to Joanasi and the others. It was the most sadness she had seen in Saqijuvik since her arrival. She marvelled at the community, how they took it, stoically, gracefully, how resigned they were to the great will of the universe, how, faces lashed with sun and wind, they carried endurance on their backs and forged ahead into the next calamity, and the next, with dignity. She thought of her Syrian forebears, nomads who endured similar hardship in the arid desert, sometimes going days without a single drop of water. People who thrived against impossible odds, as these people did, in their interminable wasteland.

TWENTY-TWO

After the funeral Joanasi disappeared again. He didn't touch base with Yasmeen, tell her where he was or what he was doing. He didn't leave her small gifts or folded notes slipped under her door reassuring her that he was okay. Annie told her not to worry, he'd be back. Like all Inuk men, he just needed time to clear his head. Yasmeen missed him but knew Annie was right. He was suffering, she realized, and it didn't seem she had any of what it took to lift his spirits. She understood that to give him up was to get him back. It was what the other women would have done.

Still, Yasmeen spent her time waiting for him. And worrying. She hardly ate. She was distracted at school and grumpy with the students. Nights before bed she scrolled through her memories of him, their initial awkwardness when Elliot introduced them that day on the airstrip, their first kiss, the time he confessed that he once almost killed a guy and how, rather than frighten her, it turned her on. She never mentioned it to Morgan out of fear of what she might say. Yasmeen closed her eyes and imagined his hands carving the soapstone mermaid for her, rubbing its natural grain to a fine polish. She tried to piece together what had gone wrong between them but kept coming up with nothing. Restless and exhausted, she got pills from Jacqueline to help her sleep through the night. Then, unpredictably, he turned up.

239

She was rinsing her supper dish when she heard the squeaking hinges of the front door. Before she knew it he was behind her, slipping his arms through hers. He rested his cheek against her head. For a long time, neither of them moved.

"Nalligivagit," she whispered. "Tell me what I can do to help you." She could hear the cries of children pattering through the spring slush outside. Though it was evening, the light was abundant.

He twirled her around until she was facing him. She stroked his hair with her wet, soapy hands. She could tell by his expression that he was stoned.

"Are you?" she asked.

He raised his eyebrows, sluggish.

"It's not going to help you feel better, you know."

He held his hand over her mouth. "Aippaq," he said. "Touch, not words." The desire rushed out of him. He backed her against the cold fridge and cleaved open her jeans. She felt the earth about to fall out from underneath her—"Slow down," she whispered, though she didn't want him to—and his cock was already bristling into her as though it had been too long. He held her in a vise-like grip. Her head knocked against the refrigerator. The first time it hurt and afterwards she wouldn't close her eyes, afraid they might never open again. She imagined a swallow flying into a barn door, missing the opening, flying into it again, and again. It wouldn't stop. Her mind clouded over and floated away, far beyond anything she knew, where the air was thin and nothing grew and nothing was recognizable except for the monstrous disturbance quaking first through him and then her. The darkness lasted forever.

The air stilled. His eyes cracked open. They were both breathing as though their hearts would explode. She stared into his dead pupils. They made her think of the ragged holes in the ice where the seals push through.

Spring turned everything brown. What the pure snow had masked all winter was now rearing up through the muck, sodden, warped, corroded. Cigarette butts, gnarled antlers, dog shit, dirty diapers, scraps of corrugated siding, twisted nails and two-by-fours, desiccated, unrecognizable animal carcasses. Every shrieking Skidoo on the road belched black fumes of gasoline.

Even though Joanasi was back, something had changed between them. She no longer got the same thrill strolling through town with him, each like a trophy on the other's arm, his cocky swagger making her feel like a well-loved possession. Now that spring had arrived, his addiction to her mutated into pathology. It was as though a permanent particle of death hung over them. Some nights he was inconsolable, conjuring up the worst scenarios of jealousy Yasmeen had ever heard. No one was above suspicion, friends, cousins, those on a brief stopover, usually construction workers or cops or government officials checking on the progress of a new social program. He smelled a lusty cocktail of testosterone in almost every updraft, a lurking man who wanted her between his legs no matter who she belonged to. He started to make unreasonable demands. She wasn't, under any circumstances, to be left alone. He escorted her to and from work. Except for her sewing circle, no outside activities were permitted unless he was present. Each day Yasmeen was hopeful that his true nature would resurface, that eventually he would loosen up and she would gain his trust again.

"We're going to the Co-op," he said one afternoon. "Get dressed." He ignored her suggestion that they wait until the plane arrived with a fresh shipment of food.

Outside the store a dozen trucks and Skidoos were idling noisily, their owners inside stocking up on the necessities of life, cigarettes or diapers or bingo tokens. A pack of surly teenagers in shirtsleeves stood at the door bumming money, pretending not to be cold, while the bully among them scratched "Fuck you shit" in red ballpoint on the facade. Joanasi pushed past them, strong-arming Yasmeen into the store. He ordered her to get a grocery cart and forced her to walk beside him as he wheeled up and down the aisles, mindlessly filling it with foods that caught his attention, frozen pizza, soda pop, chocolate pudding, an Oh Henry bar.

"How about some yogurt?" she said.

He scrunched his nose.

"Let me go grab some bread, then. We've run out." She pried her fingers from his. Immediately he spun the cart around and followed her into the next aisle, where they saw Elliot whistling to himself, squeezing the different loaves of bread for freshness.

Joanasi almost crashed into her with the cart.

"Well hiya, you two," Elliot chirped, a loaf in each hand. "So what do you think, raisin or whole wheat?"

Yasmeen shrugged her shoulders.

He dropped both into his cart, making a joke of it. "I have to watch my calories if I want to keep my girlish figure." He modeled his hips for them.

Joanasi snorted.

Yasmeen stepped around Elliot in a wide arc, avoiding eye contact. "Why ask me, you're the one who'll be eating it." She reached for the nearest loaf and dropped it into their cart, interlocking arms with Joanasi, helping him to steer past Elliot.

"Bye, Joanasi," Elliot called after them.

Joanasi ignored him. He growled into Yasmeen's ear. "I didn't know he was going to be here. Did you tell him we were coming?"

"What, seriously?" She couldn't believe his reaction. Hadn't he noticed her absolute neutrality around Elliot? Her efforts to avoid stirring up trouble? She remembered how, right from the start of their relationship Joanasi held all the power, how she wanted it that way, how it turned her on. She thought of the night he smoked her up and zipped her inside his parka and took her outside under the velvet sky where a single star glowed above them. How deliriously happy she was. And now, this. His instability, his irrational extremes. Was he trying to goad her, force her into a false confession so that he could say he had been right all along?

"Did you?"

"And why would I do that?"

"You can't fool me," he said, steering the cart into the check-out line. He unloaded their groceries under the harsh glare of the fluorescent light.

The flirty cashier smiled at Joanasi as she entered his account number into her ledger. They exchanged pleasantries while she bagged their items, ignoring Yasmeen altogether. Joanasi mumbled something to the girl and told Yasmeen to take the bags. He rushed her out of the store by her elbow and warned her they were going right home to straighten things out once and for all.

Outside they passed the same half-dressed teenagers. One of them begged Joanasi for a cigarette but he ignored him. He tightened his grip and picked up speed, his boots spraying slush everywhere. Yasmeen had to run to keep up with him.

Elliot passed them briskly on the road without looking back.

"Aippaq, it's me who should be mad at you," Joanasi said, as though he were having an epiphany. "You already fucked him, didn't you?" His persistence reminded her of a spoiled child who won't stop until it gets what it wants. "Yes, you did. You fucked him. While I was taking care of the funeral you fucked him, I can tell. You fucked him behind my back, didn't you?" He snarled and spat in the snow.

She wrenched herself away from him, but he yanked her arm back with a fierceness she had never felt outside their bedroom. It was proprietary, the way she had seen village huskies rip into a carcass, asserting their ownership of it. "Just stop this now, Joanasi!"

"You did, didn't you? You fucked him, you fucking bitch!"

She tried again to wrestle her arm loose but he clamped onto her wrist, cutting off her circulation. Villagers on the road looked away or stepped aside, knowing better than to meddle in a man's business. She decided not to make a scene, mostly out of embarrassment.

For the longest time she had refused to admit, even to herself, that he was different, that their relationship wasn't what it had been in the beginning. But his behaviour was becoming harder and harder to justify. Most of the time he was stoned, walking around the house with his sunglasses on, drinking some sugary drink and spilling his chip crumbs everywhere for her to pick up, in the bed, on the couch, in the bathroom. He blew his government cheques on bootleg alcohol whenever he could get it. Nights, he fell asleep as soon as his head hit the pillow. No kiss goodnight, nothing. Their talk was limited to a few mumbled words punctuating the prolonged silence. She began to understand that conversation hardly mattered to him at all. Out on the land, under cruel conditions, his instincts had served him well. For months she had praised his faculties, his acumen and skill at keeping them out of harm's way. She had gladly left him the responsibility. She had surrendered. How could she change her mind now? How could she account for her sudden about-face? Would she not be sending him mixed messages? *I love it when you protect me, but I will decide what dangers are real.*

"I said, did you like it?"

She glared. "I'm not having this conversation."

"Why not? Because you're a liar? Because you fucked him? I can smell him on you!"

It seemed pointless to continue. Was he even listening? Or did he just want to repeat the same things over and over, punishing her because he couldn't stop feeling so bad? She thought of Annie who had gotten a beating simply because she went to Jacqueline for diapers. Joanasi had more sense. He would never work himself up into such a lather that he would attack her.

When they reached her place, he pushed her and she stumbled, hitting her shin on the porch step. She dropped the grocery bags, food spilling everywhere. "Get up," he ordered. She could hardly believe what was happening. "And pick all this up. Now!" His face told her he meant business. She reached down to retrieve everything. He strong-armed her up the steps.

"Joanasi, stop," she begged. "You're ruining us."

"I'm ruining us? *I'm* ruining us?" He twisted her arm behind her back and held it there. "I'm not one of your hamsters that you can tell do this and do that. I'm my own boss."

He was out of control and she knew it. "Joanasi, you're hurting me." It horrified her to hear those words out of her own mouth. She knew she had to get away from him at least until he calmed down. It was her only option. She didn't stop to think what could happen if she bungled her escape, if in a moment of dithering he caught her by the scruff the neck, angrier than ever. She gathered her courage and shoved him as far away from her as she could and ran inside and bolted the door, thankful they had left it unlocked. "Come back when you're rational!" she shouted from inside the house. Her hands trembled. Her breathing was shallow and quick. The more she tried to calm down, the less air she got into her, until the room started spinning.

Blam, blam, blam.

He pounded on the door. Trying to drown out the sound she talked to herself, rambling on about nothing, until the idea to sing "Climb Every Mountain" came to her.

He kicked and hollered and kicked again. "Quit fucking around!" he screamed. His aggression triggered her animal instinct for survival. She tried to forget that the only thing that separated them was a cheap, hollow door that anyone could put a fist through, the way Tommy had. The vomit was rising in her. She stuck her fingers in her ears and sang louder, another verse and another, until she was hoarse, making up words as she went: "Fol-low all the mad-ness—la, la, la, la, laaaaah!"

Eventually his fury subsided. She put her ear up against the door but couldn't hear him anymore. She wondered whether he was sulking or if his ego was just recovering, taking a short break before firing up again. Sweat trickled down her neck. She thought of his tattooed initials on her skin, a forever reminder of him no matter what happened between them. She remembered their baby, Joanasi's son, and thanked the gods it hadn't made it to term. Was he even ready to be a father? She slid down to the floor and hugged her knees to her chest and rocked herself, humming a tune her mother used to sing to her. She stayed this way, rolled into a ball and barricaded inside, for a long time, until she heard his retreating footsteps over the granular snow.

TWENTY-THREE

Dear Morgan,

Nothing grows here. Not trees, not grass, not hope. If anyone says it does, they're lying. My father was a liar. He lied about everything. He lied to himself. He lied to me. I know you always thought that he was A-okay. But here's the thing—that sweet, A-okay guy, my father, he spent his entire life encouraging me, saying go for it, don't give up, don't look back, reach for the stars, and then he goes and kills himself. I mean, he didn't actually do it physically or anything, he fucking drank himself into a stupor and just never woke up again. He never woke up! What kind of truth is that? I think people—all of us—are born liars. We lie to each other. We lie to ourselves.

Okay, what am I trying to say here? That I'm losing my mind, that you might be right after all?

The people here are fucked up. Sometimes they're the most beautiful beings in the world. They're the truth of what humans are, what we could be. But other times, they're animals. I include myself in that. And I'm afraid. Of them, of us, of myself.

M, I need your strength to pull me through this. I don't think I can do it alone. I'm exhausted. Mostly I'm tired of living with all this shit.

Y

There was an urgent knock. Yasmeen had been expecting it. She squinted through a gap in her door and when she was positive the coast was clear, she let him in. Elliot stood with his hands on his hips, coat unzipped to his waist.

"What happened?" she said.

"We talked."

"How was he?"

"What do you think? He had a bottle in one hand and a joint in the other."

Yasmeen sighed. "What did you say to him?"

"Never mind that, it's what *he* said first. He looked me square in the eye and said, 'You don't like me, do you?'"

"And you said?"

"Damn straight. I don't like you, and you don't like me."

"So?" She could hardly breathe. The walls were closing in on her.

Elliot laid a hand on her shoulder. "I told him he should consider himself warned. And you, Sweetheart, much as I love having you around here—and this hurts to say—you should probably think about getting a transfer next year."

Yasmeen looked away.

"He's never going to be the guy you want, you know."

She didn't want to believe him. Elliot didn't know the Joanasi she knew, the provider who wanted her to make his babies, the lover who fell asleep with his hand resting in the small of her back. Elliot had always disapproved of their relationship. She instantly regretted asking for his help. He probably wasn't the best person to consult. She needed someone more objective, someone who could see the big picture. "I think you should go. If he finds you here, it'll only make everything worse."

"I know. I'm done here, anyway. Except to say one last thing."

"What?"

"I'm not too sure how to say this, so I'll just go ahead and say it."

She waited.

"You know, Yasmeen, I care as much as you do about the work we're doing here."

"I know."

"It's just that sometimes, well, it's just that I see things and I don't always know how to deal with it, so I say stupid things without thinking them through."

She shrugged. "You're a good person."

He stopped looking at the floor and focused on her instead. "I wondered whether maybe … I wondered if it's possible that you might feel, well, like we have something in common." He rested a hand on her shoulder.

She took a step back. "I appreciate your friendship," she said as neutrally as she could. "I know where to find you, don't worry."

After he left she leaned against the door and crumpled to the floor, tired of Joanasi, tired of Elliot, tired of school, tired of everything. She twisted off her polar bear ring and threw it across the room.

Yasmeenaapik,

I'm very sorry I got a little mad at the Co-op the other day. It's hard to believe that you're doing this to me. It hurt a lot that you said those heartbreaking words and slammed the door on me.

I've been very down. I never cried from missing anyone before. Last night I was crying a lot and praying too. But I don't know if prayers work. I never missed anyone this much before.

You made me a very happy person, like I've never been happy before. You turn me on more than anyone ever did. I hope someday we'll have our children. Please say you feel that way too. Please, please. Aippaq, I want to keep going. *Paingupagit.* I miss you. I would like to come back. My bed is too big without you.

Kiss inside this circle, for I also kissed it.

Your Joanasi

It was late when he showed up at her door, hands in his pockets, no jacket, no boots, just his contrite self. After eight long months of snow and ice, it was strange to see the rosy blush of sky at night, to hear the piercing cries of schoolchildren splashing through puddles with their hockey sticks when they should have been fast asleep.

Joanasi didn't walk in unannounced. He knocked lightly on the door. Uncombed, stubbly, looking as though he hadn't slept in days, he refused to look at her.

"Look me in the eye," she said. She made him wait a long time before asking him in. She wanted him to see that she had the upper hand.

Opening the door to him so soon after he had been so rough with her would mean that the slate had been wiped clean, that she forgave him, and did she really? She didn't think that enough time had passed, wasn't convinced he understood the full repercussions of his actions, how his unchecked rage had destroyed the underpinnings of her faith in him. These were the thoughts chipping at her as he looked deeply into her eyes, trying to make her forget everything. The thing was, although the little voice inside her was skeptical, she really, really wanted to be with him again. She wanted his animal presence. She wanted his hands on her as he whispered the thing he always whispered into her ear: "Aippaq, I want to put a baby in there." When she stepped back and waved him inside, he flew into her arms.

"We have to start again," she said, resting her head against his shoulder.

Without wasting another minute he carried her to the bedroom and undressed her. She cupped his shoulders while he rose over her and down and up again. As the bed creaked, she felt the pleasure of motion, felt the rocking sensation of water and the pure bliss of light. The two of them floated in and out of sleep until morning.

"*Maqailaurluuk,*" Yasmeen whispered in his ear. "You're best when you're out on the land." She kissed his mouth. "Let's go. Let's go hunting again like we used to." It had been months since the night in the igloo when it was only the two of them for hundreds of miles. When he told her how much he loved the snow.

He blinked up at her, eyes full of sleep, and said it was the best idea she had had in a long time.

"I really think if it's just us for a while, away from everything …"

"Yeah." He nipped her with his teeth, first her upper lip and then her lower and then both at the same time. He sat her up and climbed behind her, stretching his legs out on either side of her. He began braiding her hair. "You know what?"

"What?"

"Your Inuktitut is improving." He turned her head so she could see that he was smiling.

"It must be the teacher." She could see the sparkle of her reflection in his eye.

"Must be."

She had never heard him make such an effort at small talk. She kind of liked it. "You're babbling."

"I'm happy," he said. He apologized again for putting her through what he did. He promised he'd get his old job back at the radio station and that everything would go back to the way it had been in the beginning. "*Auka*," he corrected himself. "It will be better."

She said she believed every word out of his mouth and that she would never doubt him again. Desire was stirring in her and she veered the conversation in that direction. She hinted that he was making her wet and horny, that she was a very bad girl, a slut even, for thinking of sex while they were having such an important discussion. She reminded him that sluts were usually punished. They were punished hard. They were spanked or their tits were pinched or they were licked and fucked in small, dirty places where hardly a finger could fit. She waited for him to pin her down but instead he held her tenderly against him.

Spring breakup officially arrived, the estuary heaving in a jigsaw of ice and melt water, colossal chunks dislodging and charging against the shoreline, forcing the old snow upward into the shapes of winged gods. The ephemeral sculptures shimmered in the sun while feathery clouds drifted overhead.

Joanasi went back to doing all the things he did best. He studied the weather and kept tabs on the wind's inflection, affirming his connection to the natural and spiritual worlds of his people. Yasmeen was exuberant. She could hardly wait for the black, open water to carry them away together. All she wanted to do was be alone with him in the stillborn quiet, away from all that had gone wrong, the melancholy of being apart, the foul slop of spring, the conjoined stink of dog shit and diapers and rotting carcasses. She wanted him all to herself, away from everybody and everything.

She opened her eyes one morning and Joanasi was sitting on the bed, dressed and ready to go. A soft apricot light pulsed on the horizon. They paddled out, everything fresh, new, unbegun.

Listening to the gentle whoosh of the canoe cleaving the water, she fell into a trance, watching him with awe, the strength in his shoulders, the perfect rhythm he kept with the paddle. He had a beautiful face. Elliot was dead wrong about him. He was a just man with pure needs and desires.

Yasmeen had thought a long time about what Elliot said the day he weakened and professed his love for her. His arguments were convincing: "We've got fingers, opposable thumbs, the ability to reason. It's not just hunger and lust and Neanderthal displays of affection." It was true that Joanasi had knocked her into the stairs. It was true he had ordered her onto her hands and knees to pick up their groceries. He had humiliated her and it would have been a mistake to let him get away with it. Elliot made perfect sense. But then Joanasi came back with his tail between his legs. He made promises he intended to keep. No more booze and no more dope, he vowed. He promised her a real life. How could she refuse after all she had invested in him?

A flock of geese fluttered overhead as a single cloud slid across the sun, casting everything in a bluish light. Joanasi laid the oars down on the floor of the canoe and they drifted aimlessly, water lapping against the boat. After a while he removed his dark glasses and inspected the water around the hull. He squatted behind her. She felt his warm breath on her shoulder where the tattoo was. The cloud moved away and sunlight poured over them.

"Over there, do you see it?" he asked.

She shrugged. All she could make out was a swift current of energy.

He signalled ahead to a dark outline skimming underwater and handed her his rifle, fitting it against her shoulder like an appendage of her body. She gripped it awkwardly, its wooden stock digging into her. Joanasi repositioned her arms and told her to relax and just get a feel for it. Her finger caressed the trigger as she looked down the barrel into the thin black crosshairs the way she had seen people do it in the movies. She trained it on the small point of life in the distance.

"Shoot," he whispered into her ear.

The seal's glistening head broke through the surface of the water. She watched it glide into range, the rifle weighing in her arms.

"Don't think, shoot."

His words reverberated. Shoot. Shoot. Shoot. There was only the immediacy of the moment. A deafening bang roared through her ears. It was over. She dropped the rifle onto the floor of the canoe, the aftershock of the explosion rippling through her body. The animal skirted away. "Damn," she said, rubbing her shoulder. She turned and looked apologetically at Joanasi, his eyes dazzling in the sun.

"Good try."

"I didn't realize how hard it would be."

"For you, maybe." He put his sunglasses back on and kissed her on the nape of her neck. He reached for the oars and continued paddling.

By late morning they made it to a small island patchy with snow. Joanasi pulled the canoe up onto the beach while Yasmeen unloaded their supplies, the sun spanking her face. They hunted for a dry spot to lay down the blanket.

"Back in a minute," he called over his shoulder. He picked up a musk-ox skull, bleached from years of wind and sun, and pretended it was his own head. It was out of character but she liked it. He clowned around, dancing light-heartedly with it until she laughed out loud, and then he put it back down on the ground and continued on his way. She watched while he disappeared over the hummock.

Her stomach was growling. She knelt on the blanket to lay out the lunch they had packed that morning, sliced apples and cucumbers, cold cuts and bannock and a full box of Whippets. She set the thermos on a flat rock just as Joanasi arrived back from his short walk with a handful of something. She saw that he was smiling.

"What?"

"Dessert," he said. "For later." He tucked it into the knapsack and cuddled up with her on the blanket. He took a slice of cucumber and circled her lips with it. He bit off a piece, rolled it around in his mouth and tongued it back into hers.

They laid on their backs and gazed up at the sky, reading animal shapes into the clouds.

"I see a whale," he called out.

"That's no whale, that's a caribou!"

"Qallunaaq, you know nothing."

"I feel like I could sleep here until next summer," she said, sprawling across the blanket. She kicked off her boots and popped open the button of her jeans. What she really wanted was to be naked with him under the beautiful blue sky. She wanted him to mount her in nature, out in the open. She imagined Adam and Eve as they bit into the apple, swelling with the knowledge of what they were about to do. It made her want to touch herself.

"I have a present for you," he whispered, reaching for the knapsack. He rolled up on his elbow.

"I have everything I need right here," she said.

"Close your eyes."

She stared curiously at him.

"Do it," he repeated.

"Okay, okay."

His cool hand fumbled with the zipper of her jeans until they were open in a V. Finally, she thought. She could think of nothing better than being at the brink, dilated, ready to spill over.

He rolled back her shirt, exposing her belly to the air. She felt a rush of goose bumps as his tongue, dry and scaly, circled her navel. He drooled saliva onto her skin and mixed it with a paste that felt like crushed sea urchins in glacial melt water.

"What IS that?!" she shrieked.

He shushed her and insisted she keep her eyes closed. "This is serious," he said. "I want you to imagine a baby in there."

It was more erotic than any fantasy she could imagine. She let her body go limp and followed his instruction the way she followed his commands in bed—without question. She pictured a nebulous spirit, a kind of benevolent raven working to release the flood of her loins.

Joanasi ordered her to shut off her thoughts and to be hungry the way an animal is hungry. "You have to want it," he said.

She pictured squatting over the rocky tundra, her belly carrying the weight of the moon, an immense tidal wave rolling through her, gathering momentum, pushing against her uterine walls. She thought of intense pain and then respite and the flooding heat of a baby's head against her blue-veined breasts, a boy, Joanasi's boy. Joanasi continued talking her through it, but she wasn't listening to him anymore. She was in a world of her own imagining, the shaman arriving to place a miniature ivory carving of a whale inside the infant's mouth, good luck for his life as a hunter. When she opened her eyes, the warm light of the sun had dried the mystical paste on her belly.

"For you and me," he said, scraping the desiccated remains into his cupped palm. He dug a small hole where the earth was soft and poured it in, covering it over with moss.

The air was pressing down on her. Bloated with desire, Yasmeen could hardly sit up. She would have done anything for him, without the slightest reservation, if it made him happy. If it were the old days when the Inuit had more than one woman, she would have shared him around. She would have joyfully watched him put his seed into another if it meant populating the tribe with more of him. "I need you," she said, guiding his hand all the way inside her. "I need you to stop talking and do it to me."

TWENTY-FOUR

Joanasi crammed every kind of loving he could imagine into their final week together. He wanted to make doubly sure that by the time she got on the plane, they had a baby growing inside her. His light-filled smile returned and he acquired a spring in his step. He put a stop to the excesses, dropped down to three cigarettes a day, stayed sober and was better on the radio than he had ever been. There were no empty promises, no resolutions to do better. There wasn't a need for them. Once he put his mind to it, his volatile behaviour became a thing of the past. He was even cordial to Elliot.

She pitched out the wall calendar, each day an unhappy reminder that their time was running out. She rid her mind of all previous misunderstandings, the fights, the toll that the fire and Paulussie's senseless death had taken on their relationship. They concentrated on getting the feeling back again. They made love two and three times a day in whatever part of the house they were in when the urge struck, kitchen, bathroom, leaning against a wall. Before they knew it, it was her last night in Saqijuvik.

Sam offered to host the farewell bash. She decorated her place with streamers and the leftover paper lanterns from Elliot's Christmas party and strung up a large poster wishing everyone a Happy Summer. With the extended hours of daylight and the night sky as bright as a coin, she had to tape black garbage bags to her windows to create a party atmosphere and ensure privacy.

Iris looked more buoyant than Yasmeen had seen her all year. Golf sweater tied around her neck, she managed the potluck dishes as they arrived, inventive casseroles and salads and desserts people had thrown together to use up the last ingredients in their fridges and pantries. She transferred cans of beer into the fridge, filled bowls with pretzels and chips. Her demeanor spoke volumes. "I'm so glad it's over," she said.

Yasmeen was certain Iris's floors were already swept, her luggage tagged and waiting by the door. What a waste of a year in someone's life, she thought. She poked her head into the fridge for a couple of beers, swinging the door shut with her hip. "Sorry you feel that way."

"Well, I didn't always. I really loved my time in Chimo. But this place ..." She shook her head. "This place is something else."

"Oh, come on, Iris. Can't you at least pretend to enjoy your last day?"

Iris removed her glasses and looked Yasmeen in the eye. "I just don't believe in the work we're doing anymore. To be frank, I think we're failing miserably."

Yasmeen shrugged. "Well, I don't agree. I can list a ton of locals who've done well here."

Iris put her glasses back on. "Yes, that's what I told myself my first couple of years. But I was wrong. Why not save yourself the trouble and benefit from my experience?"

Bailey darted into the kitchen, frightened away by the loud music and dancing in the living room. Yasmeen shoved past Iris with her beer bottles, bending down to comfort the dog. "I don't think I want to have this conversation with you."

"You're a smart girl, look around you."

"I suppose you're talking about Tommy and Joanasi?" She gave Bailey an affectionate pat and stood up.

"Well, am I wrong?"

Yasmeen refused to engage. Iris was too cynical, a bitter old maid who drank soft drinks and wore cushioned orthopedic shoes with little breathing holes in the sides, someone who'd forgotten what it was to dream and love somebody. She felt sorry for her.

It didn't seem to matter to Iris whether or not Yasmeen was listening. She continued with her lecture anyway. "We coop them up in desks and make them pass exams in subjects that are completely irrelevant, meanwhile they can't build igloos anymore." She stared into the bottom of her glass. "One day you'll see it. I'm sure." The light in her eye changed abruptly. She forced her mouth into an awkward smile.

Yasmeen spun around and saw that Joanasi was standing there.

"Aippaq, I missed you." He took the beer bottles from her hands and stood them on the counter. He cupped her chin and tilted her face up toward his.

"Nalligivagit," she murmured in a syrupy voice, pressing her hips against him. She rolled her tongue into his mouth and moaned with delicious excess, relishing Iris's discomfort, the defeated setting down of her glass, the unlatching of the door to flee as far from them as she could.

A week earlier there had been another party, a surprise for Yasmeen. Joanasi kept telling her not to blow off her last sewing circle but she insisted she'd rather spend the whole day in bed with him trying to make their baby. He kept at her. "No, go, it's important, I'm sure little Joanasi is already in there." He patted her belly. Afterwards, she understood what all the fuss was about.

She made a point of arriving early since Annie was hosting and with all that had gone on in the village since the fire and the funeral and all her effort trying to patch things up with Joanasi, she hadn't been much of a friend to her. Yasmeen called and asked if they could get together over coffee, before the others showed up.

Annie was glad to see her. Her wounds were healing nicely, though she was experiencing excruciating headaches.

Yasmeen hugged her and asked how she was doing besides all that. Annie told her she was looking forward to her boyfriend getting released from prison in a year or so. Her son missed him terribly and was starting to act out. She made a sideways movement with her head indicating that both her kids were in the back room sleeping so they could have a real visit without any interruptions.

"Coffee?"

"Sure," said Yasmeen.

"How's our Joanasi?"

Yasmeen smiled with her whole body. "Good … very good."

"Well, that's a good news."

Yasmeen watched her pour boiling water over the instant coffee crystals in their cups. She wanted to ask how Annie forgave her boyfriend so quickly but held back, hoping she would come forward on her own. She didn't. They talked about little things instead, the new wool at the Co-op, the latest donation of fresh meat to the community freezer, whose boats were getting ready to leave for the summer. Annie showed Yasmeen a pair of beaded earrings she had made and offered them to her at a good price.

The women started arriving in dribs and drabs, all empty-handed, without their usual sewing satchels. Only Pasha came carrying a small cloth shoulder bag. They congregated in the kitchen until most of them arrived and then Annie clapped her hands and ushered everyone into the living room where she had cleared away the mattress to make enough room for chairs and a small coffee table. Women yattered to each other while Annie came and went from the kitchen with trays of coffee and a hodgepodge of spoons, creamers and sugar packets. The meeting seemed generally disorganized until Pasha began rummaging through her bag rather noisily, a sort of signal for everyone to stop talking. Right on cue, Joanasi walked in wearing his black leather jacket and sunglasses angled upwards on his head. All eyes turned to him. He shrugged his shoulders at Yasmeen, pretending not to know what was happening. After a prolonged, exaggerated search through her bag, Pasha pulled out an ulu and presented it to Yasmeen, and Annie started everyone off clapping. Stunned, Yasmeen hugged her and Pasha sat back down and cleared her throat to say a few words in Inuktitut, which Annie translated into halting English.

Yasmeen mouthed her thanks to Joanasi. Arms crossed, he nodded and smiled proudly. She turned her attention back to the gift, running her fingers along the smoothness of the metal blade. She marvelled at the beautifully carved handle. Eyes damp with thanks, she bowed her head at each of the women.

Later that night she and Joanasi lay on their stomachs after making love, legs intertwined. She told him how much the gift had meant to her.

"My mom likes you," he said. "She didn't at the beginning, but now she does."

Yasmeen tried hard not to smile. She didn't want to let on how secretly pleased she was that she had won them over. "What changed her mind?"

"She sees you. She sees the real you."

"I love your mother, I love your family, I love everyone who's related to you, even the ones I don't know yet."

He leaned in and kissed her with his tongue. She could have had him inside her again, but he wanted to tell her a story. "My great-grandfather gave my great-grandmother her ulu as a wedding gift. A real old fashioned one with a sharp stone blade and a carved handle made out of caribou antler." His voice shook a little as he spoke. "When she died, they buried her with it like they used to in those days, so it didn't get passed on. My mother was very sad about it."

"My father used to buy my mother purses every birthday and Christmas but she never liked them."

He furrowed his brow as though he had never heard of such a strange custom, giving people gifts they didn't want. "Why didn't she just tell him?"

"Well," she said. "You had to know my father. He was in the accessories business. There wasn't a day that went by that he didn't check out a store window or the newspaper ads to see what was what in the fashion world." She saw that Joanasi still looked bewildered and realized she hadn't really answered his question. "So, there was this purse guy he used to meet for lunch and every time, the purse guy would tell him he had a real deal for him, rock bottom prices, at those prices he was almost giving them away."

Joanasi shrugged.

"You have to understand, my dad could never resist a bargain, sometimes he'd buy two or three at once and stash them away. One year, every woman in my family got a purse."

"I don't really—"

"What it means," she said, "is that my mother could never hurt him; he was a salesman, that's who he was. Selling accessories was at the very core of his being. She loved him for who he was, even though sometimes it was really hard, like at the end."

Abbey Road had stopped playing and they'd been talking straight through the silence for who knew how long, maybe an hour or two. He noticed that she was sniffling and used the pads of his fingers to wipe her eyes.

"I don't know if they ever had our kind of love."

"Those ladies, they didn't give you that ulu just to be nice," he said.

⬧

There was no sign of the plane yet. But it was coming. She couldn't imagine how it would be, the leaving part, knowing they'd be separated for eight long weeks. At the airstrip, they clung to each other. Yasmeen wondered how she would feel the next day and the next, waking up in her old bed, sad and alone. "Don't go," he begged, rheumy-eyed. "You don't have to go. How will I live without you?"

She bonked him on the head with her glove. "Don't be silly," she said in her most reassuring voice. Secretly she loved that he was making a big deal of her departure. It made them special in a world that wanted everyone to feel small and ordinary.

Eyelid twitching, he lit a cigarette.

"What's a couple of months when we have our whole lives ahead of us?" She heard the false note in her voice, thin and reedy.

"Maybe we don't have to wait until August, maybe I can visit you this summer." He looked gravely at her. "I have money."

The idea came out of nowhere. It brought a flood of panic. Joanasi visit? There wasn't a way in hell it could work. How would she explain her "Eskimo" lover to a mother intent on marrying her off to a Syrian boy with a promising future, a lawyer or doctor or dentist? How would Yasmeen ever have the courage to tell her about all that Joanasi gave her?

All what? her mother would want to know, shaking her head in disbelief. What could there be from a man who barely had an education? No way would Samiyah ever let him put a toe in Yasmeen's bedroom. Maybe she'd agree to a cot in the basement, set up beside the laundry room. A decent woman with Christian values, she would never turn away anyone who arrived on her doorstep, especially a friend of her children. But she'd be a cold bitch about it while he was around, distantly polite, disgusted down deep. She'd convince the aunts he was an interesting arte-fact, just a girl's frivolous whim, not to be taken seriously, and certainly not for the long haul.

The fact that Joanasi was a good provider, that he embod-ied the wholesome values of home and family, wouldn't have made a difference to her mother. She would have only seen somebody unsuitable, someone from outside their social class, outside their world.

Just thinking about it infuriated Yasmeen. It was poisoning her last minutes with him. If Joanasi was willing to come, she wasn't going to stop him. She'd just have to find them a secret oasis. "I could get us a hotel room," she proposed enthusiasti-cally. "A luxury suite where they turn down your bed sheets and leave foil-wrapped squares of European chocolate on the pillows. Something classy. I think after everything we've been through we deserve it, don't you?"

He half-smiled as though he were trying to figure out why the scenario suddenly included a hotel when she had a good home with a family they could stay with.

"We could have bubble baths and order room service and then take a *calèche* ride through Old Montreal. Now, that would be romantic." She imagined being downtown with her erotic hunter, spreading their scent, a signal to everyone that they were more than just hot in bed, they were insatiable. Yasmeen wanted the envy of other women, she wanted the monopoly on love. "If you visit, we'll drive up to the mountain when the city's all lit up at night. You'll see how gorgeous it is."

He slid his tongue into her mouth. "Nalligivagit."

The airstrip hummed with energy as people hugged and shook hands and noisy four-wheelers pulled up with last-minute boxes and suitcases to load. Yasmeen looked up as the plane flashed into view, a silver bullet of light in the sky. She wiped a tear away.

Joanasi tried to lighten the mood, teaching Yasmeen a new phrase in Inuktitut, but she couldn't concentrate. She swatted something away from her ear and Joanasi reminded her she was lucky to be missing the black flies.

The plane cast its ominous silhouette over the runway as it came in for the landing. It bumped along the mud and stones, driving gusts of wind, gradually decelerating until it got to the end of the airstrip, turned a half-circle and taxied back.

Elliot helped the pilots load up while passengers hurried to get on. Joanasi rested a hand on her belly. "Maybe, just maybe, there's a baby in there," he said. She wanted him to be right.

The twirling propellers coughed a swirl of dust. Everyone except Yasmeen had already boarded. Glancing up at the plane, she saw Sam's camera lens aiming through the window. She was mouthing for Yasmeen to smile. Yasmeen ignored her and the intrusive camera. She kissed Joanasi's soft, warm mouth, their coats flapping in the noisy wind of the plane. The co-pilot waved impatiently at her, waiting to pull up the steps. Yasmeen pried herself away but Joanasi grabbed her by the collar one last time and wrapped her in his arms. He wouldn't let go. "Don't," she said, "don't make it harder," and she wriggled away and climbed on board without looking back.

TWENTY-FIVE

July, I don't know what
Dear Aippaq,

This place is a ghost town when you're not around. It's like I don't know anyone from here. I don't see anyone. All I care about is you. You're so beautiful, I can't forget about you. I miss going to parties with you. I really miss having sex with you. Paingupagit.

I cried after you called. I could not help it 'cause hearing your voice on the phone tells me you're really far away. I'm gonna try to go down and see you before August. You're worth going down for, you're worth everything to me.

I called an old friend in Montreal today, a guy who came up to the fishing camp when I was working there about three or four years ago. He said he would like to see me if I go down. That guy I gave a whalebone carving to and he never paid me. It was the best carving I ever made, it was real nice and big like the face of an Inuk. It was an iceberg with a bird on top. He only sent me one bottle of whisky. He was going to send me 10 but he never did. I think if I see him I'll ask for more than just one bottle, even if it was two years ago or three. Don't worry I'm not drinking a lot a lot, just sometimes a tiny bit when things are really boring and I can't stop thinking that you are so far away.

I'm very pooped now so I think I'll just go to sleep. Remember I love you very much and I'll see you maybe around the third week of July.

Your Aippaq

Yasmeen opened the first newspaper she had held in months and read most of the articles with serious attention. It felt strange to be reading an entire paper filled with stories about people and places that were alien to her. She read a couple of long editorials about a failed coup by cocaine growers in Bolivia and Pierre Trudeau stepping down as prime minister. She read the Hollywood gossip pages and a light summer piece with suggestions for bored, housebound children.

The café waiter was hoovering the rug underneath the table where her feet were, sucking crumbs through a long thin hose, a not-so-subtle hint he wanted to close up. She lifted her feet and continued leafing through the newspaper, scanning the book pages, the horoscopes, the concert and movie listings.

She swirled the cold dregs of her coffee, considering whether to drink or leave it. Her thoughts drifted to Jacqueline. The last time they had talked, at Sam's potluck, she was still undecided over how much longer she would stay with Tommy. Another year, two tops, she had said. Yasmeen didn't see the point of dragging it out but wished her well anyway. "You know," said Jacqueline, shrugging her shoulders. "He's a great lay. And for now it's enough."

The waiter glared at Yasmeen, checking his wristwatch. He unknotted his apron and hung it on a hook behind the cash. She decided to drink the rest of her coffee. She took her time the way she had learned to take her time in Saqijuvik. She folded the newspaper, section by section. She dug through her purse for a dollar and wedged it between the cup and saucer. As she got up to leave, the waiter beat her to the door with his jangling ring of keys. He unlocked it and locked it again, snappishly, behind her. He flipped the card in the window from Open to Closed.

Outside, a wall of humidity slammed into her, a huge shock to her system after the refrigerated coffee shop. It felt strange seeing the darkness of the nighttime sky again. It felt strange being back in a world obstructed by billboards and office towers, a world dominated by the ugly and the manmade, jittery fluorescence, air conditioners, the blasting exhaust pipes of buses and honking cars.

It was late to be out. All the restaurant patrons had left. The awning was rolled up and the moulded patio chairs and tables were chained together for the night. She tossed her newspaper into a wire garbage bin overflowing with cardboard takeout trays and Styrofoam cups. Heading toward the Peel Métro station, she passed a sullen, middle-aged musician dressed in black from head to toe. He was strumming under a dim streetlight, trying to impersonate Leonard Cohen. She tossed a quarter at the satin lining of the guitar case, dyed the same purple as the innards of an animal she had once eaten with Joanasi.

Her reaction to being back in the city surprised her. She was melancholic but she didn't miss the bitter cold days, the metric dumps of snow, walking around with a persistent chill in the bones. She was glad not to have to deal with her faulty shower nozzle, sporadic water delivery, meagre pickings at the grocery store. Her stove with only two working burners. She didn't miss having only one television channel.

The one thing she couldn't do without was Joanasi. Had they never met she would have eased back into her life—with some difficulty, but it wouldn't have been so lonely. She would have floated along until summer's end, hanging with friends, shopping, going to the movies. She would have racked up debt on her credit card. She would have partied right up until the last day and repacked and said her goodbyes, signing on to Year Two with the confidence and clarity Elliot had had on the rickety plane when he pushed the stick of chewing gum into her hands. Wiser by a year. Ready to greet the new teachers with a smile and a whack of practical advice.

But Joanasi made her return to Montreal unbearable, having had such an intense relationship and abruptly cutting it off for the summer. Feeling him as a shadow presence and a palpable absence, she hated being back in her mother's home in the suburbs, where the wind whistling through the trees was a constant reminder that she was here while her lover was fifteen hundred kilometres away. She stayed clear of Morgan, which by now had become a cakewalk given Morgan's polite but nuanced excuses—"I so wish we could get together but, um, you know ..."—meaning that the outside world, the world they'd once trashed and ridiculed together, had become more important to her than Yasmeen. Trish and her graduate courses and whatever radical experimentation she was into these days.

Yasmeen did whatever she could to keep busy. She decided she preferred the boisterous metropolis to the quiet suburb. She sat through movie matinees and fell into lock step with the anonymous masses traipsing through the labyrinth of the city's underground shopping concourse. She bought herself little things to give her a lift, the latest of the *New York Times* bestsellers, a new bottle of Yves Saint Laurent perfume, the Kitty Wells record she and Joanasi always listened to, the one with their special song, "The Winner of Your Heart." She went to noisy restaurants, where she ordered triple espressos with steamed milk, or frosted glasses of white wine, depending on the hour. She spent hours at the same table writing love letters to Joanasi, tapping her cigarette ashes into a tinfoil ashtray. She told him she missed the arches of his feet, the feel of his hands;

she missed his tensed jaw when he mounted her to make love. Nights she slept with his shirt against her cheek, infused with layers of his outdoor sweat. She remembered a sky dotted with geese, the hardy wind with the sea on its breath.

She eavesdropped on people's private conversations, lively, coffee-drinking students arguing about art and philosophy as though they were the only intelligence on the planet. Their earnest sounds drifted toward her, offering a kind of unintended camaraderie. It brought solace. It passed the time. She sat in sunny cafés and on park benches, watching the bustling day unfold, businessmen scurrying with newspapers under their arms, beggars scrounging for spare change, parking inspectors writing tickets, city workers jackhammering around a steamy dump of asphalt. Every block seemed to have a pinging arcade, greasy hamburger joint or Triple X peep show on it. The air grizzled with *patates frites* and Coke. As the days passed, Yasmeen grew to appreciate the madness of the city again, its flashy, abrasive, king-size distractions.

A week after she got home a brown envelope arrived in the mail. It was from Sam. There was no note, only a yellow Post-it stuck to a snapshot of Yasmeen's protracted goodbye to Joanasi on the dingy airstrip, the one Sam had taken through the window before the plane took off. "You're welcome," it said. It resembled all of Sam's photos, out of focus, usually with the people's feet cut off. She couldn't understand why Sam had bothered to send it except that maybe she felt any souvenir, even a bad one, was better than none at all. Yasmeen stared longingly at it, even though she and Joanasi were off-centre and their faces were so blurry they were hardly recognizable.

Yasmeen went with her original plan not to mention Joanasi's visit at all, not to her mother or her siblings or even Morgan, though Morgan wouldn't have cared less. The last thing Yasmeen needed was people's criticism to deal with. She wanted to love Joanasi as freely as she had in Saqijuvik, and negative talk would have only spoiled it. At this point anyway, why did they need to know? Once she returned there in the fall she would write them a letter telling them her decision about staying for good, how she adored the North, how she had finally found her true calling. Joanasi could remain completely out of the picture. There was only the loose end of Morgan to consider, whether or not she would mind her own business and keep quiet about him. It seemed plausible given her history with Yasmeen's mother, their absolute dislike for one another. Of course there was still the slim chance she might blow the whistle, saying she was doing it for Yasmeen's own good. But Yasmeen weighed it in her mind and bet on their long-time friendship and solidarity.

Not only did she book a room at the Queen Elizabeth Hotel, Yasmeen checked in early and ordered up a bottle of Dom Perignon and an overflowing basket of fruit. She was sure he would get a kick out of sleeping in the same hotel where John and Yoko had held their celebrated bed-in. She rearranged the furniture to make the room more inviting, sprayed the sheets with an essential oil, and laid the fluffy hotel towels on the bed. She pushed aside the heavy drapes to let a bright square of sunlight into the room. It bounced and shimmered off the wine goblets she had set down on the bedside table.

His plane was due at 6:30 in the evening but she arrived at the airport two hours early to avoid rush hour, her stomach in knots. She ducked into the restroom to freshen up.

Someone had scratched *All who wander are not lost* on the stall door. Regardless of its author, she connected with the message. She slid off her underwear and stuffed it into her purse. She couldn't wait to stroll with him through the airport, gliding with a confidence that would indicate to every onlooker that the manly man on her arm was the one who had had the brawn to win her over. She flushed the toilet and went to the basin to wash her hands and kohl a dark line around her eyes. She teased and fluffed her hair and adjusted the straps on her new sundress. She smoothed the dress with the hand wearing the polar bear ring. Standing in three-quarter profile, she ran her hands slowly down her breasts and torso, wondering whether he would find her attractive in clothes that publicly revealed more of her skin. Probably, she decided. Most men enjoyed showing off the fact that they had conquered a certain type of woman. They liked to broadcast their success to the world, parade the trophy they had nabbed and gotten into bed, the woman with the beautiful face or the seductive body or the whatever magnetic thing she possessed that lured them to her. She was sure this ritual would appeal to her new-and-improved Joanasi.

She glanced at her watch. Only fifteen minutes had passed. She sat and watched waves of people wheel their towers of luggage past her. Her attention settled on an Indian family with four toddlers, their toys and belongings monopolizing an entire bench plus a good part of the floor. The mother wore a periwinkle sari and a wrist full of silver bracelets that jangled whenever she tried to rein in their noise at the behest of the father, who sat with an open newspaper, surveying them with his stark eye whites. He signalled and she popped open a Tupperware container, lacing the air with a strong bite of curry. Her brood congregated around her as she spooned the yellow mash into each of their mouths.

When Yasmeen tired of watching them she wandered over to the flower shop and inquired about the black roses on display. The clerk pursed her lips and cocked her head sideways with a look of sympathy and said she'd come to the right place. The black ones were popular here at the airport where people were always breaking up with their lovers. Yasmeen ignored her and went to the glass refrigerator and chose a red one still folded up tight, petals brushed with tiny beads of water. She said no to the cellophane wrap, the usual tangle of greenery and baby's breath. All she wanted was the single long stem. "Oh, and just so you know, I'm not breaking up," she hissed.

She wondered why time played those terrible tricks, why it always inched forward when you wanted it to speed up. She wondered whether the reverse were true, whether you could slow time down when you were running out of it, say if you had a galloping terminal cancer. Could you sit at the oncologist's office, for example, where the appointments were always two hours late, and postpone your demise? Her eyes kept roving to the overhead panel board where the arrival and departure times were constantly being updated.

She visited the airport shops, tried on deerskin gloves and fur hats, sprayed different perfumes on her wrists. She read the dust jackets of paperbacks and leafed through the movie star magazines until the clerk declared in a very rude French that they were for paying customers only. She bought a soft drink to make a sarcastic point, and went back to watch the comings and goings of businessmen and backpackers and regular suitcase-toting tourists. She sat on a bench with her flower, sipping her drink. A gaggle of stewardesses with upswept hair and silk scarves rushed past, pulling bags behind them. Then came a man in dark glasses tapping his way with a white cane. Yasmeen closed her eyes and listened to the ambient sounds of the airport, wondering how she would feel if she were blind and whether Joanasi would still love her if she were. She sprang out of her chair when the garbled intercom announced that the Nordair flight from Great Whale River was in. Her heart pounded, he's here, he's here, he's here.

In her hurry to go meet him, she pricked her thumb on the rose. "God dammit," she yelped, squeezing the skin together, forcing a bright bloom of blood to the surface. She stuck her thumb in her mouth, dreaming of how Joanasi would look after a month of hunting and fishing, bronzed by the sun and wind.

Racing to the gate, she cursed the slowpokes who had difficulty walking at a normal pace. Her mind flooded with questions. Would he be smiling from ear to ear or shy, as he was at the airstrip the day Elliot introduced them? Would he be cautiously confident, knowing she was a sure thing without taking her for granted, the way he played it the night of the school opening when they ended up making out on her couch for the first time?

People streamed into the baggage area. She scanned their faces but couldn't see Joanasi among them. Patience, she told herself. She knew he wouldn't have missed the flight. Not after all his letters to her. He would have arrived at the airstrip early even, overwrought, eager to see her. She studied the crowd, eyes catching on a shirt or jacket that looked like one of Joanasi's— that could have been his, something his style and colour. Then, no, it wouldn't be him after all, and then wait, maybe, and then no and then, stop—was that him? One of those times it was *really* him. Her whole body tensed up. The balls of her feet pressed excitedly into her sandals.

He was wearing tan slacks and an open-collared shirt, looking a little smaller than she remembered. She waved at him from a distance. He smiled a half-smile and followed all the others to the revolving luggage carousel. Shy was what he mostly seemed. He watched the bags go around in circles until he saw his and reached for it and stumbled in his attempt to wrestle it off. The white woman standing beside him offered her assistance and he nodded her a thank you without looking happy about it. He shuffled toward Yasmeen, popping a mint nervously into his mouth. Up close she saw he was badly in need of a haircut.

275

His eyes had the same glazed look they had when he was on a weeklong bender. "Aippangai … qanuipiit?" He flashed her a warm, lazy grin.

"I'm … good … and you?"

"Qanuingngi."

They swam in the awkwardness of the moment until Yasmeen handed him the rose and kissed him on the mouth. They hugged clumsily.

"You look like a different person in your high heels and fancy hairdo," he slurred. "I almost didn't recognize you." He gripped the rose cautiously, between the thorns, unsure what to do with it. She took it back to hold.

"You've been drinking."

He pinched open his thumb and forefinger to indicate "this much only," a negligible amount, hardly anything. She detected a slight movement in the eyelid that twitched when he was nervous or excited or lying about something. She locked arms with him and headed to the nearest coffee shop, where they joined a long line of customers waiting to be served. She handed the rose back to him.

"Crowded," she said. "What a drag."

He nodded dutifully.

She wondered what the veiled Arab woman ahead of them had on under all her robes. She had heard that many wore sexy lingerie as a way to prove that they, not their husbands, controlled their bodies. It was in an article she had read.

By the time it was finally their turn, the nasal cashier was in a foul mood, twice having had to change the Arab woman's order due to a mix-up in communication. Yasmeen carried their tray to a quiet corner table and went to the dispenser for napkins and a handful of sugars. Joanasi dragged the chair out to sit down, scraping its metal legs across the floor. He was starving, he said, and folded the entire donut into his mouth.

"You didn't eat anything on the plane?"

He shrugged.

She poured a packet of sugar into his coffee and stirred it around.

"No," he said, pushing the cup back at her. "You have it." Waves of coffee spilled over the lip and splattered across the table.

She jumped back to avoid getting it on her dress, then quickly sopped up the mess with a handful of napkins. "It's good with a donut," she insisted, trying to encourage him.

He narrowed his eyes. "No, I said. I have what I need right here." He bent down to unzip his duffel bag and rooted through his clothes until he found a bottle of *Smirnoff.* "We're back together again. This calls for a celebration." He cracked it open and poured some into the same thermos cap they had used for tea the day he rubbed her belly with the fertility paste. He transferred it slowly, careful not to spill a drop. He screwed on the top and tucked the bottle back between his socks and underwear, without offering any. Not that she would have accepted it.

For a while neither of them spoke. Yasmeen drank Joanasi's coffee, occasionally sneaking a glance at him. She didn't remember him looking so gaunt.

"I'm thirty-seven, but I'm ancient," Paulussie had confessed the night they arrived at the campsite before it started to rain, before he called her a fucking bitch over the telephone, before the frightful winter caused a power surge in his brain and made him set fire to the church and run.

Yasmeen couldn't wait for Joanasi to finish his vodka so they could leave the hectic airport and start over in their quiet, secluded hotel room. She was homesick for her tiny house by the sea, where the air was so palpable the night he first touched her, the night of the school opening and the battering squall, the night that had sealed everything between them.

※

She located her car in the parking lot and popped open the trunk. He shut it without putting his bag inside, indicating the back seat was good enough.

Mischievously, he pinned her against the hood of the car, gripping her wrists the way he used to. The feel of her body against the vehicle stirred a familiar response in her. It awoke her passion and erased the irritation she had felt about his drinking in the coffee shop. "I missed this," he blurted, pushing his nose into her hair.

"Me, too," she said.

The earlier reaction was just her ugliness rearing up, the attitude of people like Morgan and her mother and her Uncle Ramzi, whose poison sometimes seeped into her when she wasn't being vigilant. She decided that Joanasi's little cocktail wasn't really a relapse. He wasn't falling down drunk all over her. It was just something to steady his nerves and give him confidence. Something to help him make the adjustment. After everything they had been through together, she could excuse that small thing.

She felt his erection through her dress and closed her eyes and imagined him as a bear circling in, licking her with his dry, whiskery tongue. Her toes curled in their sandals as she received his full weight against her.

It wasn't exactly the reunion she had planned, but whatever. The kinks seemed to be working themselves out. The thought of the bunched up underwear in her purse made her additionally horny, the idea that she had walked past hordes of people in the airport, straight-faced, totally exposed; the idea that she had left the balm of her vagina on every chair she had sat on. She slid his hand between her thighs.

"What are we waiting for? Let's get going," he said impatiently. He flopped into the passenger seat.

She wondered what he was thinking as they drove toward the downtown core. She hoped he was working out a good fantasy between them. "What happened to the rose?" she asked, realizing she hadn't seen it since the donut shop.

He looked at her and shrugged.

"Oh well," she said, trying to hide her hurt. "Some other handsome fellow will get it. No big deal."

Secretly she was disappointed it hadn't had the impact she had hoped for. If it had been the other way around, if he had brought her a flower, she would have understood the symbolism and treated it accordingly. She would have hung it upside down in a safe place to preserve it. She would have pressed the petals between the pages of her journal, a keepsake for their children and their children's children.

Yasmeen followed the steady river of traffic, narrating the city landmarks as they presented themselves, but Joanasi had no interest in anything but her. He hoisted her dress up and wrested her legs apart, making it difficult for her to concentrate on the road. She batted away his hand. "We'll be there in twenty minutes," she promised. "Let's wait it out." When he agreed, she got pouty and dangled a hand provocatively between her legs. He pushed it away and rested his finger on her tiny orb.

"I said I missed this."

"Me too, Joanasi, but I need to focus." She didn't know why she was sending him mixed messages, saying no but meaning yes. His hand didn't budge, as though it could read her perfectly. Somehow the car floated along, almost by itself. Her eyelids dipped for just a second. She raised her arm up over her head, arching backwards, willing herself to spill into his hands. She wished he would stop but she didn't have the strength to ask him to.

A horn blared and a shriek of light bounced off the side mirror, treacherously close.

"Holy Fuck, Joanasi! Cut it out!"

The other driver slammed on his brakes and she swerved, barely missing him. He gave her his middle finger in retaliation and she could only imagine what his railing mouth was accusing her of through the sealed window. She pulled down her dress, horrified by the close call, and swatted Joanasi's hand away. She gripped the wheel with both hands, disoriented, counting to ten to regain her composure.

She thought she heard him mumble something, so she asked, "What?" and he answered "What?" back.

"Never mind," she said. He slid out a cigarette, lit it and snapped the lighter shut. Smoke shot through his nostrils.

She opened the window and slid out the ashtray drawer, not wanting his ashes all over her mother's car. He flicked them anyway, without taking care. Some of it sprinkled across the steering wheel.

She exited off the expressway and made a right off Guy onto Dorchester, east past Crescent Street and de la Montagne and Peel, until they neared their destination. She idled the car on the busy boulevard, beneath the floodlit statues of Mary Queen of the World Cathedral.

He squashed out his cigarette. "Is this the hotel?"

"No. I wanted to show you one of my favourite buildings first. It's a replica of St. Peter's in Rome."

He shrugged his shoulders.

"If you look up you can see the thirteen patron saints of Montreal, including John the Baptist." She shifted into park and cut the motor, leaving the keys dangling from the ignition.

He asked why she was stalling. She said, "I'm not stalling." But something in her was resisting him. She couldn't put her finger on it. Maybe a combination things, the slight dip in her libido in the aftershock of their near collision, excitement, anxiety, fear that one or the other wouldn't measure up, that their long-awaited reunion would be less than adequate.

"You're tired," she said. "We both are. Maybe you should get some sleep. I can always come back in the morning when we're both fresh."

"The hotel first, I need to see you." He burped the kind of burp that slithers out before a person realizes it. He told her he wanted to fuck her like there was no tomorrow. She knew he was just repeating what he'd heard in some movie; it wasn't in his nature to talk that way. Usually he just did it to her, without labelling it this or that. He did it in a way that left a lingering reminder that he had just lit a fire there.

Yasmeen couldn't help feeling that her perfect night was slipping away from her. She couldn't stop thinking about how he had arrived drunk off the plane, and how a good percentage of the alcohol was probably still in his blood. She knew that no matter what they did together while he was still under the influence, it would feel like so much less. "It's going to be alright," she said, touching his cheek. She didn't really know what she meant by it.

Joanasi read it as a softening, an invitation back into her good graces, not that he had ever fallen out, and what else was there to do now that she was wet with anticipation? He fumbled around until he unsnapped her seatbelt. Her yes was spontaneous and decisive. They would lock up the car and make a beeline for the hotel where he would push her onto the floor and hold her in a head lock and she would wait with her eyes closed, half expecting something terrifying to happen, the other half knowing that when he thrust into her, a feeling would wash over her like warm water, an intense happiness that came from being his.

She felt his quickened pulse as he rotated his right hip and lifted his leg around to mount her. He cursed and smashed the steering wheel for getting in his way, bumping it repeatedly as his mouth filled up with her hair.

She shoved him off. "Not here! What's wrong with you?"

Just then a slow-moving squad car materialized in the side mirror. Yasmeen turned the ignition key once. She pressed the button in the door handle until the power windows sealed shut. Sweat was rolling down her face and Joanasi was staring vacantly ahead, shoulders rising and falling with each intake of breath. She straightened her hair, trying to appear normal as she waited for the cruiser to accelerate past. She wasn't afraid of this Joanasi and they weren't in unfamiliar terrain. Countless times she'd been the object of his scorn. She'd tolerated his dark moods and cool silences. She knew from experience that with him there was a tipping point and that they often came dangerously close. It was part of the thrill. It was also the cause of their troubles.

Joanasi was knuckle-white. He took a deep breath and bellowed into her ear. "WHAT did you say?"

Yasmeen recoiled. What *had* she said? She couldn't remember, why couldn't she?

"Don't you listen when I say something?" He rambled like someone desperate, someone who knew deep down that things were spiralling out of control and he was helpless to do anything about it.

Yasmeen was beginning to see it, too. Since he had arrived, whatever they said to each other seemed to be the wrong thing. The person sitting beside her felt like a total stranger to her. And yet, she knew every intimate part of him. She knew his eyes as he undressed her, his erection that she kissed with intense pleasure. She knew his knees scarred from childhood games, his large, square hands that in the bedroom were unpredictably tender, loving, rough. It upset her to think of stopping everything once and for all. Forever. How would she go on without him? Would she go around the rest of her life looking for Joanasi in somebody else? She didn't have a vocabulary for what would come afterwards if they ended it.

He showed no sign of remorse, eyes darting from her to the window and back to her again. Outside, the light had dimmed. He swallowed hard and leaned forward, chin in his hands, elbows propped on his knees. He sat rubbing his temples with his fingers. She thought she saw tears welling up in his eyes, but she was wrong.

Everything happened fast, too fast, his fist out of nowhere slamming into the glove compartment. The veins of his forehead were popping out. "Fuck you, lady! FUCK YOU!" She was sure he would slap her, but he didn't. He jerked the keys out of the ignition and stuffed them into his pocket.

Whatever apology, whatever gentle words had been forming in her mind dissolved on her tongue. Instantly. This isn't happening, she repeated to herself. They were barely a block from the hotel, steps away from making everything right again. Everything was set and waiting for them, the cooled champagne, the strawberries, the silk sheets. She waited for him to calm down.

Her instinct was right. He spoke remotely, haltingly. "Why are you doing this to me, Aippaq?"

Me doing to this you, she wanted to say. She bit her tongue. She thought of the day at the Co-op when he dragged her by her elbow and said he would follow her everywhere for the rest of time the way Sedna's evil husband did; that he would never trust her enough to leave her alone, not ever. And what had she done about it? Nothing. She accepted his apology and they fucked and life went on as though nothing had happened. She could have been leashed to him like a dog and still she would have taken it. Not just tolerated it, she would have accepted it. She would have continued making excuses for his behaviour, the way a battered woman stays with her man because a small, faulty part of her still loves him. Because somewhere inside she is deeply damaged.

She was desperate to reach him. She needed to prove to herself that she was normal and that this was just a terrible misunderstanding between two people who loved each other. She had to before it was too late. "Hey, what's wrong with you?" She lowered her voice to a whisper. "Aippaq, suviit?" She combed her fingers through his hair, noticing how she towered over him the way she towered over her students.

She made a move to kiss him but his body tensed up and he backed away. It was only the second time in their relationship he had treated her as though she were invisible. His arm reached around to the back seat, to the floor of the car where he had dropped his bag. She heard a zzzzip and some rummaging around as he searched for the vodka. In her silkiest voice she said, "Think about it, you don't want to do this," but he did it anyway, without regard for her, he pushed the bottle into his mouth and pulled on it like a baby on its mother's tit, drawing every drop, working to exhaustion to drain it. She hated to see him under its spell again. She hated how little respect he had for himself and for her. She thought of how hard she had worked all her life to stay grounded, to stay level-headed, even when the temptation to let go was great.

He checked how much of the alcohol was left and capped the bottle and tossed it on the floor by his feet. A river of drool slid down his chin. He wiped it away with his sleeve, staring at her through the great hollows of his eyes. "I should of never—"

"Maybe you'll be happier without me." She realized only after she said it that it had the ring of goodbye. It felt as though everything they had shared together all these months could fit into a small valise.

He lit a cigarette and aimed the smoke into her face. "I was thinking," he said.

"About?"

"Would you care if I died?"

"What kind of question is that?" she said. "Of course I would." She thought of their cloistered night in the igloo when they made love like the very first humans on earth, the time he forced himself into her so hard she thought he had torn something inside her. She recalled the bliss she had felt afterwards in the rise and fall of their breathing.

He shrugged and looked away.

Her frustration mounted. "Did you hear anything I said? Or am I just a pair of moving lips to you with the volume on mute?"

He was dead still.

"Listen, if you want me, if you really want me, you can't be drinking or smoking dope or yanking me around wherever you go." She gently touched his arm.

He snapped it away as though it had been shocked with electricity. An ember of his cigarette landed on her wrist.

She flicked it off. "Because, Joanasi, you're killing us. You're really killing us."

He bared his teeth and punched his chest with his fist, as though nothing she was saying made any impact. "Answer me. Did you meet someone else?"

"Don't," she said. "Not again."

"I think I smell that fucking asshole on you. I'm warning you, if I find out …". He ground his cigarette into the dash and jerked down the zipper of his pants.

The panic rose in her. She fumbled for the automatic window button, keeping him in her line of vision. It seemed safe to assume that if she pressed it and the window slid down while people were walking by, he would immediately have to stop his nonsense. Then she remembered. He had snatched the key and the motor was turned off. His eyes swivelled and he lunged at her and all that flashed through her mind was why hadn't she flagged down the cop while she had had the chance? He forced her legs apart and rammed his fish-stink tongue into the back of her throat.

Butted up against the door handle, she sputtered and gagged but she found the strength to shove him off. "Pull yourself together!"

"It's that fucking teacher, isn't it? I knew it. I leave you two alone for a couple of weeks and …"

"You're being ludicrous, the booze has got you totally paranoid, now give me back my key before I …!"

"Before you what?" She felt the weight of him on top of her again. He pulled her dress up over her waist and groped her as though his hand were a fork. "I'll hurt you if you're not careful." When she tried to slap him away he slapped her even harder, across the face, and said "You do what I tell you or else."

She clubbed him with her fists and screamed until she was hoarse. "I said give me the goddam car key!" Her body went limp and he bashed her against the seat as though he were totally disgusted with her. She rubbed her cheek where his hand had struck.

Just then, a young father strolled past on the sidewalk with his child, a curly-blond girl dipping her wand into a pink flask of soap solution. She blew out a big, shiny, quivering bubble and watched it float sideways into the air and flatten out, briefly, before bursting into nothing. She wept and her father scooped her up to comfort her as they continued on their way. The sky was edging on dusk.

It was just that, Yasmeen would recall afterwards: a fleeting moment of inattention. Still trembling from their altercation, she was unaware of Joanasi's explosive rage collecting into a single point of energy. The outcome filled her ears, his piercing cry, his foot pressed against the windshield like a boot on ice, the fissure, a forked vein along the surface, widening until a deafening CRAAAACK shattered the silence.

And then, for what seemed an eternity, no sound at all. Slumped in the passenger seat, Joanasi gawked in disbelief at the damage he had caused, the way a dazed killer stares at his victim, thinking he had nothing to do with it. The torn strap of her sundress was in his hand.

"Give me my FUCKING key and get out of this car, right now!" she shouted. "NOW!"

He looked at her through stuperous eyes, refusing to budge.

"It's over. We're done! And this time it's for good!"

He shrugged.

"I said OUT!"

He stared through her, speaking robotically. "Go ahead, call the police. I don't care."

Her eyes darted into the street, empty of people and cars, no one around to save her if she tried to make a run for it and he retaliated. If he dredged up the last of his strength and decided to end her. He could have. He could have done it handily. She closed her eyes and waited for it.

She didn't know how much time had passed when she opened them again. The hotel was still waiting on the next block. Her windshield still had a giant gash in it.

Joanasi licked away a tear. He dug into his pocket and pulled out a fistful of money, large bills, mainly fifties. He said, "Take my money, take all of it, buy a new windshield, buy a new car, I won't be needing it anymore." He flung it like confetti into the air.

Neither made a move.

He dangled the key in front of her eyes before tossing it like a sword into her lap. Shaking, she started the car. He reached for his bottle and took his duffel bag from the back seat. She stared straight ahead, refusing to look at him. The sound of her finger pressing the unlock button in the handle startled them both. There was a scuffle at the door as he prepared to leave. She felt the weight of him lift up off the seat as he stepped out into the cooling air, the door slapping firmly behind him.

She closed her eyes. When she opened them again, the light was strange. She gasped when she remembered that she might be pregnant.

Through the flaked windshield, she watched their grand finale play out, this wreck of a night like a bad movie, Joanasi disoriented, stumbling along the sidewalk swilling down the last of the vodka. At the intersection he crossed against the red light toward Ste-Catherine Street. Yasmeen watched his faltering silhouette until it merged with the night air and disappeared.

In her flustered state, staring into the blizzard of broken glass, she thought of the polar ice and the young hunter, Adamie, his rifle aimed squarely at the horizon. Squinting, she saw his grandfather and great-grandfather trudging along behind him, all their ancestors going back to the first tribes who followed the antlered herds of the North. In a blink she saw them all. And then they were gone.

TWENTY-SIX

August 24, 1984
My Aippaq,

Yesterday it was too upsetting for me to stay here so I went camping with Tommy and Adamie. I didn't do any fishing 'cause I went up just to get away and get stoned. The feeling I have is very bad. And today it got worse 'cause the teachers are coming back. This is the day I've been waiting for all summer but it seems it's not the day that I've been waiting for. Knowing that you're not coming.

My hands are useless when you're not around. They only do what I don't enjoy, like work all day. I wish they could do what they like to do and that's touching you and doing things for you.

I'm in bed now with your picture right here beside me, I wish that you were here like this, the way you are in this picture. Reminds me of the things we used to doooo ......

Aippaq, I'M SORRY. Please come back, please my love please. If you're worried about the past please don't worry about it.

Your Joanasi

September 3, 1984
Aippaq,

Tutigumallipaa. I really miss touching you. When I think about the things we always did it makes tears run down my face. I wish that you were here. Remember after the long walk we took one day, we had a bath and decided to make love on the floor of the bathroom with that song by The Cars playing in the background? We had such a good time and I have never in my whole life had a good time like we had together.

One day on the air I said I need some hash and people called in and said they want some too. Nobody called to say don't talk about this stuff on the radio. People only called to say go for it. Anyway, I don't talk much like I used to on the air. I've been too down to talk. All I do is play music. Sometimes I say nothing all morning or afternoon. At night I just watch TV and play video games. I really never get you out of my head.

Oh god, what can I do? I'm feeling very alone and helpless. Why don't you come back? Please, I want you to try before I make a move.

Your Aippaq,
with lots of love and kisses

October 4, 1984
Dear Aippaq,

It's the weekend again, just another lonely and boring weekend. Sitting around and doing nothing but thinking a lot about you. You never write to me, why?

Every day when I wake up and go to bed at night, I see you. I look at you for a long time but you never seem to move because I only see you in a picture. And I always wish that I was looking at the real you.

Come over here so I can touch you again. Qaigit. My arms are open and waiting for you. Yasmeenaapik, I wish we could make a fresh start. Please TRY to find a way to come back here, please my love please. I know you can make it.

Hi again. I didn't finish this letter two days ago. I fell asleep. I ran a bingo game on the FM last night and my uncle came over so I had some drink with him after the bingo, just a little bit, 10 oz. I had the rest with Tommy, he had some hash so I went to his place and we smoked and it was fun feeling high for a change, but not too high in other ways, thinking of you, missing you. Paingupagit.

Your Aippaq

October 15, 1984
Dear Aippaq,

I have your picture right here as I write this letter, wondering if you have changed. You know I never really forgot you after all this time. I'll never forget the very first time you asked to kiss me on the cheek, it was fun that time, but now I wish that I could be the one to ask to kiss you on the cheek.

It's been a busy month for me trying to decide what I should do or what I want to do but I think I made up my mind. I decided to take a TV journalism course. I'm going to give it a shot and see how it turns out. I could end up with a job at CBC or maybe even IBC.

For a few days I thought that I was going to be a cop since the money sounded so good, but I changed my mind. My friend Aloupa who is a cop in Salluit was saying that it is a good job but it's not so fun when there's too much trouble going on. I don't think I would want to interfere with family problems all the time (well, not all the time) and I don't think I want to be stuck in town seven days a week since I like to hunt once in a while.

With my new job we could really make a new start. PLEASE SAY YES! Aippaq, I know you can.

With a big heart full of love for you …

oxox

October 20, 1984
Joanasi,

Everything is grey and wet. The leaves are gone. The rain is back. Winter will be here before we know it. It will be nice to see the snow again.

The other day, I remembered reading an old article. Something about how everything up north—mammal, bird, fish—flourishes quickly against all odds and then dies as suddenly.

Eight months. Do you know that's all the time we had together? I gave myself to you, but it wasn't enough. You always wanted more. I don't know what more I could have given, but I'm glad I didn't. Luckily, I never got pregnant. It would have been terrible. I know it will hurt you to hear it, but you have to. Probably deep down anyway, you know. You were always so afraid to lose me that you lost me. You destroyed what we had. I can't forgive you.

I'm pretty sure that eventually you'll find another woman who will mean a lot to you. As for me, I don't know anymore. You spoiled me. One day I woke up completely happy, happier than I have ever been in my life. You were there. I was there. It lasted a moment. The light was infinite.

Today I hiked to the top of Mount Royal and looked down at all the cars and buildings. It's strange how you can fit the city in the palm of your hand from up there. The North never fit into my hand like that. That was what I loved about it. But then I didn't love it anymore, partly because of you.

Maybe we only get one chance at pure happiness. Once it's gone, we have to figure out how to make everything that comes afterward mean enough to carry us through the rest of our lives. We have to let go of the ideal thing, that beautiful moment which is impossible to sustain. The best we can do is put the memory away somewhere safe knowing that at least we had that. You and I, we had it. That was our time, Joanasi. But it's over now.

You always said I was too much in my head. Maybe you're right. Anyway, it might surprise you (or not) to hear that I'm not teaching this year. I decided that it's really not for me. A teacher should be more certain about things than I am. Sometimes it feels like I was the student in Saqijuvik, and you and everyone else were my teachers. I don't know what I'll do now, but one thing is sure. I won't be back, so please stop asking. Don't expect any more letters from me. This is it. *Atsunai.* Goodbye.

Yasmeen

THE MAN ON THE PARK BENCH PRODUCES A PINK LIGHTER AND LIGHTS HIMSELF A CIGARETTE. He breathes in deeply and exhales a dense jet of smoke through his nostrils. "We used to be nomads," he says.

"Yeah," says Yasmeen. "I know."

"I'm hungry."

She is too, but not for food. That's been her problem all along, she thinks.

"I have money," he tells her.

"I know that."

A convoy of fire trucks tears down the street, lights flashing, sirens blaring.

"Must be a big one," he says.

She nods.

"People get hurt in fires."

She nods again. For the first time, she notices the T-shirt he has on underneath his open jacket. It seems a little snug across the chest, like it doesn't belong to him. Like it maybe comes from the Army Surplus Store or a church basement rummage sale. The writing on it says, My Next Husband Will Be Normal. It makes her smile.

"What?" he says.

"Nothing. It's nothing important."

A woman dragging a gigantic trash bag stops at their bench and yammers at him like they're friends but not good friends. She has ratty hair and her bag is bursting at the seams with old clothes and shoes. He reaches into his pocket for a cigarette and snaps her a flame with the pink lighter. She leans into it, almost catching her hair on fire, then jumps backward, snarling at him, something Yasmeen can only guess at, "Shithead" or "Thanks for nothing," and goes back to hauling her bag.

The snow has stopped. He leans down and stares pensively at the ground. Yasmeen looks over to where he is looking but doesn't see anything out of the ordinary. "Do you want to get something to eat?" he says.

She untangles herself from the strap of her shoulder bag and lays it down on the bench between them. "Not really. But you go ahead. I'm not quite ready to leave yet."

"You should," he says. "Nice girl like you." He squashes his cigarette out on the bottom of his boot and flicks it at the base of an old tree. "This isn't a place to be. Especially at night." Like something her mother would say before she stopped with her nagging. Her father, on the other hand, he would have just said, "Be cautious but don't let it spoil everything."

"Yeah, okay." She takes back her purse.

"You never know what can happen. There are a lot of people here you wouldn't want to meet."

"You're right." She stands and goes to shake hands goodbye. His palm is cold. He holds her hand in his for a long time, longer than he should. That's how she knows it's so cold. She almost doesn't want him to let go. But he does and so does she. They both let go at the same time.

"See you around," he calls over his shoulder, shuffling toward the street with his brown paper bag.

"Maybe," she says. "Probably not."

ACKNOWLEDGMENTS

Thank you to my publisher, Robin Philpot, for his generosity and commitment to this book. And to Elise Moser, editor extraordinaire, for her insights, attention to detail, and encouragement.

Thank you to Peter Burpee, who first introduced me to the North.

I am grateful for financial support from the Conseil des arts et des lettres du Québec and the Banff Centre, which allowed me to get a first draft on paper.

Janine Cheeseman and Endre Farkas read earlier, underdeveloped versions and offered editorial suggestions that strengthened the manuscript. I owe them a lot.

Without knowing the details of the story, a helpful team of Nunavimmiut assisted me with the Hudson dialect of Inuktitut and answered a multitude of questions: Dorina Anowak, Jeannie Calvin, Sarah Idlout, and Lizzie Tukai. Vicky Simigak and Nancianne Grey provided the names of the fictional Inuit communities. *Nakurmiimarialuk.*

Thanks to my parents and family for their boundless love and support; and to my son, Alex, for the homemade Mother's Day card of long ago that insisted I was "one hip Mama" who should keep on doing what I love "no matter what anyone says." It's faded but it's still on my fridge. Thank you to Endre for being a constant in my life—for stilling the turbulent waters and always reminding me to breathe. There's no one else I'd rather stay up late with, talking about sentences.

This novel grew out of an earlier short story I wrote called "Men of Stone," which appeared in *The New Quarterly* in 1991. I wish to thank Tomson Highway who read that piece in the course of his tenure as Writer-in-Residence at Concordia University and provided valuable feedback, which I incorporated into this novel. More recently he proposed the book's title, for which I am deeply grateful.

Finally, I would like to acknowledge the many authors whose works I consulted in the writing of this novel: Hugh Brody, Ingo Hessel, Lisa Qiluqqi Koperqualuk, Dorothy Mesher, Ulli Steltzer, Stephen Guion Williams, and editors Neil Christopher, Noel McDermott and Louise Flaherty.

BIBLIOGRAPHY

The People's Land: Whites and the Eastern Arctic by Hugh Brody, New York: Penguin, 1977.

Unikkaaqtuat: An Introduction to Traditional Inuit Myths and Legends, eds. Neil Christopher, Noel McDermott and Louise Flaherty, Toronto: Inhabit Media Inc., 2011.

Arctic Spirit: Inuit Art from the Albrecht Collection at the Heard Museum by Ingo Hessel, Vancouver: Douglas & McIntyre Ltd., 2006.

Puvirniturmiut Religious and Political Dynamics by Lisa Qiluqqi Koperqualuk, M.A. Thesis: Université Laval, 2011.

Traditions Relating to Customary Law in Nunavik by Lisa Qiluqqi Koperqualuk, Westmount: Nunavik Publications, 2015.

Kuujjuaq—Memories and Musings by Dorothy Mesher (with Ray Woollam), Duncan: Unica Publishing Co. Ltd., 1995.

Inuit: The North in Transition by Ulli Steltzer, Vancouver: Douglas & McIntyre Ltd., 1982.

In the Middle: The Inuit Today by Stephen Guion Williams, Toronto: Fitzhenry & Whiteside, 1983.